ABOUT THE AUTHOR

Josepha Madigan is the Family Law Partner at Madigans Solicitors in Dublin, Ireland. She is also an accredited Mediator and Collaborative Practitioner. Josepha is passionate about keeping families out of court during separation and divorce if at all possible. Her training as a Reiki Master inspires her work. She is married to Finbarr and has two young sons. This is her first novel. She is currently working on a law book.

ISBN-10: 1463519508
ISBN-13: 978-1463519506

Josepha Madigan © 2011

All rights reserved. No part of this publication may be reproduced, stored in a retrieval system or transmitted, in any form or by any means without the prior written permission of the author, nor be otherwise circulated in any form of binding or cover other than that in which it is published and without a similar condition being imposed on the purchaser.

All characters in this publication are fictitious and any resemblance to persons living or dead is purely coincidental.

JOSEPHA MADIGAN

NEGLIGENT BEHAVIOUR

A Novel

4 NEGLIGENT BEHAVIOUR

"The most difficult but the most essential thing is to love life, to love it even when one suffers – because life is all."

--Tolstoy

6 NEGLIGENT BEHAVIOUR

PROLOGUE

Ice chips. Endless thirst. Need more energy tablets to chew. Evian facial mist is being sprayed sporadically onto my red blotchy face. It feels like diving into the sweetest cool water in a volcanic desert. Midwives in Blue. The Heat. Dark outside the window. Lord above when will this be over?

I am lying propped up in the Delivery room. Someone somewhere says, "Well done, you are 10 centimetres dilated." Fifteen hours of torture. I have seen the colour outside the window go from dark to bright to dark. I have lost all sense of time and place. I am incredibly fatigued and inappropriately starving. Jesus the smell of faeces. God bless the midwives. It must be the most thankless job in the world. The first two left after twelve hours. Fiona and Angela. I can't remember the new ones names, even after three hours.

Not much pain anymore. The Epidural was manna from heaven even if my legs feel like lead. I feel numb all over. Numb from exertion and weariness.

How did I get myself into this mess? My belly heaves in and out like an Elephant's girth being squashed by a measuring tape. In and out. In and out.

Someone somewhere says, "Push, Push, good girl, you are doing great." I feel like slapping whoever said that across the face. Bet they never had a baby themselves. This is no joke. OmiGod I am going to burst every blood vessel in my face. Fucking hell. Dan gawping at me with a stressed- out- of- his- head expression. I don't have the energy to tell him to take his bloody hand off my arm. The weight of his hand is an extra pressure that I don't need, loaded in meaning. I am weighed down even more by the enormity of my predicament. I see my Consultant Obstetrician now. Mr. Dunne. He makes me feel better and I try not to feel embarrassed with my legs in stirrups. Or by the smell. My fanny on show for all the world to see. The sweat stuck to my head, the odd bead trickling into my mouth. I am panting like a St. Bernard and dribbling like one too. There are more people in the room now but don't ask me who they are. Everyone seems to be shouting at me. I hear only segments of orders: "....nearly there now..." and " good girl, keep it going." I am exhausted. I can't do anymore. I see surgical pincers, forceps. I know that prior to this the ventouse had been used. I somehow saw and felt it through the fog. It reminds me of a toilet plunger except ours has a brown plastic top and this one is pink. I wonder is that a sign it's a girl. They seem to try the forceps twice but the head won't budge. I get the impression the baby's head is in full view of all but me. It's a stubborn baby, just like its mother. I hear a discussion around me but I can't tell who is participating.

"She'll be in tatters," Mr. Dunne says. "We'll bring her up?" and he nods at Dan in a rhetorical fashion. Bring me up where? "We'll garb you up for Theatre." And again he nods at Dan. Before I know it I am manhandled onto a gurney which to all intents and purposes might as well be a shopping trolley for the comfort it affords me. Shooting pain in my lower back. A black dude wheeling me out onto the corridor and roughly with it.

We jerk into an elevator which resembles a steel solitary confinement cell. I lose all control and shout and scream obscenities to all and sundry. Fuck the dignity. Sixteen hours of decorum is enough. I've had enough. The pain is all encompassing and I am ashamed by my failure. My perceived lack of perfection at having a normal delivery. I know where this is leading. I am going to be C-sectioned. Ugh. Every fibre in my body wanted to push that baby out. I gave it everything I had and it wouldn't budge.

"Don't worry Helene." I turn my head and see Mr. Dunne beside me in the Theatre. "Your baby will be here very soon."

"I don't give a fuck about my baby," I scream at him. "Take this fucking pain away." And I bawl and yelp like there is no tomorrow. I feel like I'm in a straightjacket in a lunatic asylum. I'm ranting and raving and splaying my arms and head like a turtle on speed.

Out of the blue I feel an enveloping sense of peace and calm.

I'm floating in a narcotic haze. I ask the anaesthetist what he gave me and he tells me "a cocktail". I think to myself how terribly dishy he is, then reproach myself for using an old fashioned word. What a ride I think and unceremoniously laugh out loud. I laugh and laugh. I discuss primary and secondary schools with Mr. Dunne and my dishy ride. I am looking at Dan when I glimpse a flash of steel behind the green half curtain covering my lower body. I feel the cut but it doesn't hurt at all. I feel tugging and pulling but am as cool as a cucumber. I'm in the chill zone.

"My word he's a big one," says Mr. Dunne.

Right in front of my nose I see a squirming purplish baby boy with the biggest pair of balls I have ever seen. He kicks his legs like a frog. He lets a roar like a baby lion. I already want to call him Goliath. My eyes follow his every move. Dan rushes over to where the midwife has brought him. I hear him oohing and aahing while the baby is being cleaned. I am being stitched up and feel like I am watching someone else's movie. A bystander in the stalls. A witness on the corner.

Someone wheels me to the recovery room. Dan sits with me while we ring our parents and text our friends. I'm on autopilot. We decide to call him Orson. We don't care if no one else likes the name. He's our baby. I shed a tear when Dan says this but I can't tell him why. He thinks I am being emotional and kisses me on the forehead after wiping my brow.

"I am so proud of you Helene," he says tenderly. "You were fantastic."

I tell him that I don't feel fantastic. He tells me that I will feel better after a good night's sleep.

Someone wheels our baby in to join us. Orson Hugh. We learn he is 9lbs and 3 ozs. We learn he is 55 centimetres long. He has dark hair and blue eyes. Most importantly he is perfect. I am drained emotionally and physically. I resolutely refuse to breastfeed. I am too weary. After Dan has left and Orson is in the night nursery I sob into my pillow uncontrollably. Only one man is in my mind. I seem him every time I close my eyes. He wasn't with me today and he won't be with me tomorrow.

10   Negligent Behaviour

PART I

CHAPTER 1

"We should have sought discovery of the off shore accounts," says Murdoch Pierce. "There is absolutely no way of knowing the full financial profile of the Respondent if we don't have this information."

He glances at me quickly and in full view of my client. I sense that Murdoch is deliberately attempting to undermine my professionalism by this comment. I look at my client Dan Goodings. He stares at me in return waiting for a reasonable explanation as to why this was not done.

"That may well be, Murdoch, and I accept your advices in that regard. I would, however, like to point out that we cannot seek discovery of documents of accounts that we cannot even prove exist. Dan has informed me that his wife has off shore accounts in both Barbados and in Zurich but, and Dan you will agree with me here, we have no evidence to support this claim."

Murdoch was not going to let it go. "Well, could you not perhaps have hired a PI to investigate?"

"To investigate what?" I say with a blank expression.

"Surely Helene you have sufficient evidence by now to enable a competent PI to carry out the necessary checks?" Murdoch suggests in I'm-talking-to-a-3-year-old-tone. My client is just sitting there seemingly amused by the conversation. It could also be seemingly frustrated.

"Dan, if you'll excuse us for a minute. I just want to have a quick word with my Counsel in the Law room. We'll be back in a minute," and I give Murdoch a look that says get-out-of-this-consultation room now.

We walk out and over to the far end of the corridor. I am on the verge of boiling over with rage.

"What the hell is going on?" I spit out. "What do you think you are playing at in there?"

Murdoch looks at me for a second, leans over and whispers in my ear, "You look beautiful when you are angry."

"Why are you doing this to me?" I say exasperated. "We are at a High Court Divorce settlement meeting. This is not the time or place."

"Name the time or place then," Murdoch says and looks me straight in the eye.

"You only want me because you can't have me," I reply.

"I'd want you all the time if I had you," he sighs. "You just don't trust me."

"You're married for crying out loud!" I practically shout at him. "Grow up. The only reason I am still retaining you as Senior Counsel in this bloody case is because you are the best there is and my client thinks you're God or something. Plus his wife is a conniving wagon and Dan is such a dote. She didn't deserve him."

"Dan is such a dote!" he mocks. "He has his eye on you too you know... But I can tell you one thing for nothing he'll bore the pants of you. He'll treat you right but you'll be dreaming of me," and he flashes me a wide grin of the best white veneers money can buy.

"One of these days you'll give in. I know I turn you on."

"Jesus you are so cocky Murdoch," I say.

"You're right there," he laughs.

I think in my mind that this must be what sexual harassment in the work place feels like.

By the time we get back to the consultation room my client has being totting up the assets on his iPhone. Dan didn't want to spend the money on a forensic accountant unless the case was going to proceed to hearing.

"The way I see it," he states to neither of us in particular, "there is a pool of €9.3 million give or take. I am happy to take €4 million and she can have €5.3 million which should do her nicely. Those off shore accounts she got from her first divorce settlement and with all due respect to Helene, Murdoch, I don't think we do actually have enough information to seek discovery, as you put it, of those accounts. Quite frankly I'm not bothered anyway. I just want my divorce. I have had to wait four years as it is because of this country's ridiculous notion that couples might reconcile if they have to wait four years between getting separated and getting divorced. Sure she went off with that Martha one after six months of marriage. She says she's bi-sexual. She's clearly a lesbian but swung out her fishing rod to hook in a rich husband or two in the process. She's a good looking woman, I'll give her that much. Herself and her girlfriend can go off where they want now for all I care. Let her have the extra €1.3. She has the house in Parkview as well so they can have a nice little life for themselves." Dan is beseeching us to get this show on the road and let him get on with his life.

"In my view Dan," opines Murdoch, "you would really be selling yourself short and–"

"Those are my instructions," interrupts Dan. "I do appreciate genuinely all of the advices I have received from both you and Helene," he smiles, "but this is what I want to do. Give her what she wants, please. I don't want to have this set down for hearing. I do not want to go ahead with my Nullity application. I want it done and dusted today. Yes, she has screwed me over after the most ridiculous marriage in history but frankly I don't give a damn."

"That's absolutely fine Dan if those are your instructions," I say. "I will, however, have to get you to sign a disclaimer saying that you're not accepting our advices in this regard. You understand I have to protect myself here as your solicitor. You know we are of the view that she would only get a quarter of that in court but it's your decision and we respect your wishes."

Murdoch nods in agreement.

We leave the room to go to the Law room and get our renegade Junior Counsel to draft the agreement for both clients to sign. I draft the disclaimer and Dan signs it. I sit in the consultation room alone with him.

"Its not easy," I say to him sympathetically.

"It's been a nightmare to be honest," and he smiles. I notice how handsome he looks when he smiles. I check myself then and remind myself not to mix business with pleasure.

"It's 6pm already," he says scrutinising his watch. "Are you hungry?"

"I'm about to pass out from hunger," I laugh. Simultaneously it dawns on me that he is asking me out.

We wait until his wife signs the agreement which takes her all of five minutes. Surprise, surprise. She knows a good deal when she gets one.

There is torrential rain when we reach the pavement. Neither Dan nor I have an umbrella so we shelter under the annex of the Aras Ui Dhalaigh building to wait it out.

"I might as well have a cigarette while we're waiting," I say, trying not to look like I needed one.

"Sure I might as well too," he replies cheerily.

I'm glad he does, I feel less addicted sharing the guilty dirty pleasure as we drag on our respective Silk Cut Ultras.

Dan eventually hails down a taxi and we retire to a cosy little Italian wine bar. The food is comforting and delicious, not to mention the tasty prosecco. Thankfully it's a Thursday so I don't feel too bad drinking so much of it. The conversation is light, serious and pleasant all at once. We are getting on very well for an unexpected and impromptu date.

Although I have got to know Dan quite well over the last few years acting as his solicitor, I can't say that I know the inner workings of his mind. He always struck me though, even after our initial meeting, as an extremely genuine man. I felt sorry for him too but not in a condescending way. Simply that he had clearly married his wife on a whim. He went with his heart and not his head, but what else is a person supposed to do? It was obvious to all that she had married him with her head. Sometimes women are more "marriage savvy" than men. I knew I wasn't as I had avoided it like the plague for such a long time. I was hurt beyond hurt a lifetime ago but it was enough to keep intimacy at bay. No man was ever going to hurt me again. I had put a nice healthy barrier around my feelings. As far as I was concerned I was untouchable.

"So what's the next step?" he asks me much later on, looking a little worse for wear.

I totally get the double entendre but don't let on.

"Well, now the case is settled we just have to apply for a ruling date. Probably in a few weeks hopefully. The terms of your divorce agreement will be read out to the Judge and he will rule it and you will be divorced as of from then. It'll take a couple of weeks for the registrar to write up the actual decree, which obviously I'll bespeak for you, but you will be free as a bird from that date!" I said laughing. "Oh and you should get a new Will drafted as well," I continued. "I can help you with that as well if you like."

"Not just a pretty face," Dan says and smiles at me.

I must be exuding I'm-feeling-uncomfortable vibes as he suddenly says, "Look I'm sorry, it's been a long day and I'm a bit out of practice to be honest. Forgive me for being so gauche."

"Don't worry about it," I say as he clocks the waiter and asks for the bill.

I try and insist on paying for my half but he is having none of it. Dan orders a taxi and drops me off in Ballsbridge. He continues on to Ranelagh. He looks quite forlorn, I ponder, or is that my imagination?

The following day I am greeted by the wonderful sight of my boss, Mr. Andrew Peterson, the Managing Partner of Peterson & Co., sitting quite comfortably on the chair in my office. It is seven forty five in the morning. He's probably been in the office since dawn: he's a complete workaholic. I find it hard to believe though that someone can actually work more hours in the day than me.

"Oh there you are Helene," says Andrew smugly. "Nice leisurely breakfast again this morning, had we? Well, good for you. Keeps the old brain ticking over until lunchtime, isn't that right?" Just to make sure hes hit home, adding, "and as we all know, some brains need it more than others!" before he breaks into an irritating belly laugh. If he only knew how patheticlly he comes across, not to mind blatantly disrespectful.

"They say breakfast is the most important meal of the day," I counter with a deliberate smile. He'll never witness me crumble in front of him.

"Is that so?" he smirks. "Well then I might just have the perfect breakfast for you!" he adds with obvious satisfaction.

I feel that bleak sensation in the pit of my stomach. It suddenly occurs to me that I might have just fallen for the bait. Invariably this happens with Andrew. He is nearly impossible to outsmart. Quick on his feet, fast with his words. Throwing out his hook and reeling you unwittingly in. I should have known better.

"The International Legal and Commerce Association hold a breakfast meeting every Friday morning in the Mansion House," he continues. "Peterson & Co. was cordially invited through our contact in Luxembourg Mssr. Beauville. There is only one representative i.e., one member from each profession allowed attend. In short, the aim of the weekly meeting is to refer business on a reciprocal basis to other members. A sort of you pat my back and I'll pat yours, you know. I attended this morning to suss it all out and I must say I am impressed. Eighty five per cent of the members have quadrupled their business turnover in twelve months. Impressive, eh? There are only ten members which may sound tight but trust me, these guys are the crème de la crème. Top of their game. Every other week you will be required to give the group a fifteen minute presentation on the latest update in your area of expertise, so in your case, family law and civil litigation. And before you ask, yes, they can give a referral to our Firm that has nothing to do with your area, like a commercial conveyance or whatever. There are some real high profile contacts we could do with in there Helene, and since you enjoy your breakfast so much, and trust me they do provide an exceptional breakfast, I think you're the woman for the job! What do you say?" he beams at me.

"That's fine Andrew. Sure as I said, breakfast is the most important meal of the day." I beam right back at him, playing his game. Naturally I am kicking myself for opening my big mouth in the first place. I've never been good at zipping it unfortunately.

"Look, Helene. Someone has got to do the dirty work. You are a family law and civil litigation lawyer. You come in here with a referral from a client who is minted and whose marriage has gone to pot. Happy days! Or else you get a client who has suffered horrific injuries in a car accident and it's the other driver's fault. Happier days!" he announces gleefully as if he is talking casually about the weather. Andrew stands up and straightens his tie. He wipes the tiny white flecks gathering on his shoulders off his ostentatious suit and departs without another word.

After he leaves I spend not an insignificant amount of time staring into space contemplating what Andrew has just said. I never thought I would be a person that would make money on the back of someone else's misfortune. It really doesn't sit right with me. His veiled *shadenfreude* makes me feel sick. Perhaps he has unwittingly drawn my attention to what may be glaringly obvious to another person. I like to think that I help clients clean up the backsplash of murky residue left behind. There are no winners or losers. Certainly not in family law. Certainly not in a road traffic accident when no amount of compensation can ever turn back the clock.

I've been quite content. Right ok sometimes a bit lonely but I do have the odd date here and there. I'm also having sex, of course, on a not infrequent basis. Thankfully men do find me attractive because as shallow as it sounds, I don't know if I could live with myself if no one found me attractive. We all want to be fancied and flirted with, don't we?

I am just thirty five. I am single. Perhaps I should re-phrase that, I am in-between relationships. It sounds less desperate even though I am not. I live in my own mews. Really it is an apartment I bought three years ago but it's on the ground floor with its own front door so it has the feel of a mews. I have an octogenarian on one side of me and a newly married couple on the other. We keep ourselves to ourselves. I love where I live, apart from the car alarms that start at midnight and go on incessantly all night. I have only lately invested in a pair of ear plugs, as well as my usual night mask, to assist my sleep.

My friends drop by rarely, usually on the way home from shopping in town or after work if I am actually at home. My MWK (married with kids) friends hardly ever drop in as my home is not exactly what you would call child friendly. It doesn't really bother me though as kids and I don't really get on too well. I never know what to say or do with them. I'm an only child. Maybe this is the reason for my lack of charisma around them. I don't know. Or as I mentioned earlier, maybe I am just a teeny weeny bit afraid when I witness copious amounts of children left bereft from the inevitable emotional fallout of a broken relationship. We just seem to tolerate each other at the best of times. A mutual tolerance. I do not appear to have any biological clock at all. I adore little puppies and would buy one in a heartbeat only for the sad fact that there would be no one there all day to look after it. I wouldn't do that to a puppy, least of all a real live baby.

I meet Dan five weeks later when we rule his divorce. Other than a quick telephone call from me to tell him the date for the ruling, I hadn't heard from him at all. This intrigues me. I figure he might think he was a bit inappropriate at our last tete-a-tete. I didn't tell him that despite myself I had been thinking about him a bit too much for my own comfort zone.

"Will we grab some lunch?" he says after we come out of the ruling.

"Sure," I reply "just let me gather up my things."

We stroll over to the courts services coffee shop. I eat a sandwich and he orders soup, a sandwich and a plate of chips.

"You must be hungry!" I remark.

"Yep," he says. "I am just incredibly relieved, you know Helene...to be finally, finally away from that woman. My life is going to start again from this very moment. I know that sounds a tad dramatic but it sure as hell feels great! Thank God we had no kids. What a nightmare it would have been if we did. No doubt herself and Martha would have fought for custody. That would really have killed me. I'm not homophobic, honestly, it's just that I know she would be a shit mother. She is far too selfish. Come to think of it maybe she wouldn't have looked for custody because of the fact that she *is* so selfish. That means that I would have had sole custody but if it was a girl and she looked like her...Jesus, that would be hard. Anyway, sorry, I know I'm rambling on...it's difficult not to..." Dan laughed.

"Don't be silly. It's funny though..." and I trail off.

"What's funny?" he asks.

"Well, it's just that some clients have said to me the opposite. That the only good thing that came out of their marriage is the fact that they did have children. That at least they had their kids to be grateful for if nothing else...different views I guess."

"That's interesting," Dan remarks "I never looked at it that way. And what do you think Helene? Do you want kids? Would you think it was worth it?"

I notice he is scrutinising me intently. "Well, uh, em...yeah maybe...I don't know," I stutter.

"Sorry Helene. I'm being too personal again," he apologises.

"I have to say this though. You're a tough woman to get to know. You don't really let your guard down at all. I know you are being professional so I apologise for asking but what is it that makes you tick? I have known you for what over four years now and I don't know the slightest thing about you. I would really like to know more. I didn't foresee this coming, believe me, but you just seem to have this effect on me."

I can tell the forlorn look again. It melts my heart. I know deep down that Dan was beginning to grow on me. I love his honesty, his big heart, his beautiful eyes...

"Let's have dinner tonight," I surprise myself by stating, quite matter-of-factly.

He smiles.

"Even better," he answers, quite cheekily, "let's continue our lunch somewhere else..."

We hail down a cab and retire to the Shelbourne bar for a liquid afternoon. An afternoon of bubbly champagne for me, an afternoon of sparkling wit and contagious laughter from my accomplice. Time was flying by. I was learning a lot about Dan in the process. He wasn't just a handsome face either. Not alone was he running his own IT business employing fifty staff, he had jogged the last two Dublin City Marathons for charity and liked to cook in his spare time. What more could a woman ask for? I knew that I could search the earth and never find such desirable characteristics in a man as an intelligent mind, a sense of humour, a fit body (good in bed?!), a generous heart and creative cooking skills.

I am desperately trying not to think about the fact that he is freshly divorced. Well almost. A salient fact that my Mother and Father would not appreciate. Theirs was not a myopic Catholic view, rather a view formed by tradition and cemented with a fear of the unknown. I knew they would only want the best for their only daughter and only child. The institution of marriage does not hold the same attraction for me as it did and does for my parents. I have heard it said that Love is an irrational inexplicable phenomenon. I would certainly concede that is true. As for marriage being enough for me, well, I just don't think so. Apart from anything else, I bore easily. Drawing from my own experience I can tell you that no matter how in love you believe yourself to be with someone, that feeling can never last longer than the honeymoon period. In my view it's just not possible.

I don't really believe that there is such a concept as a "soul mate" or anam cara. For years my friends and I have been talking about finding "the one". I don't believe that any of them have found that. Nor have they found their soul mate in the truest sense of its meaning. Without sounding too introspective, I believe that true peace comes from within. Yes, I appreciate this is a laboured point for many. A laboured point that the average psychologist dishes out as advice no doubt. However, I *do* believe that you can find absolute contentment with someone else. But please don't be so naïve as to expect to find your soul mate. You are your own soulmate. Hmmm…is this me trying to avoid intimacy with someone else again? Do I really want to do this romance thing again? I am banishing similar quickfire thoughts away from my mind at the rate of knots. I wish I could just let myself go, not play it cool, stop playing nonchalant and go for it once and for all. It's not as if I haven't had plenty of offers. Just too scared. Pain isn't necessarily like shame in that you only feel it once. I don't believe that. I have done too well for too long protecting my wounded little patchwork quilt of a heart. There is no need to add another stitch. For once I fall, I really fall. That, my dear, is my Achilles heel, the point of no return. I think I should just stick with U2's mantra that a woman needs a man like a fish needs a bicycle. Yeah. That's right.

I am mulling all of this over in my head while simultaneously holding down a full-blown conversation with Dan. I guess this is what women call multi-tasking. It is really quite remarkable how we can sip a snipe of champagne, seem engrossed in dialogue and be thinking about something completely unrelated at the same time. Still, I am at this point pretty engrossed in Dan, pretty attracted to Dan at that. I excuse myself to powder my nose and when I return I see Dan standing at the revolving glass doors looking ultra smug with himself.

"What's up?" I say or at least I think I say. Maybe I slur slightly there and say, "Whassup?" instead. It really is of no consequence anyway as the two of us are as merry as Christmas. He hands me my coat and before I know it we are in a horse drawn carriage. We trot around St. Stephen's Green. It is an idyllic late autumn evening. A perfect early evening to cosy up under a tartan rug. He takes my face in his hands somewhere between the Fitzwilliam Hotel and University church and kisses me softly. A long softly stolen kiss. Then a longer softly gently mesmerising kiss. If truth be known it feels like the best kiss I have ever had the fortune to receive. It is a kiss whose journey began many years ago but took this long to reach its destination. We are both lost in the sheer magic of the feel and touch and love of this kiss. It is brimming with passion, joy, love and hope.

It reminds me of a kiss I had with a boy called Gary Clear twenty years ago. I was fourteen or fifteen. It was my fourth time at the local parish disco. I fancied him from word go and I couldn't believe my luck when he asked me to dance. Gary told me that I didn't know how to French kiss and that he would have to teach me. He was particularly confident in a cheeky, cute way for a fourteen/fifteen year old. He wasn't gangly or pimply. He didn't have a horrible Adam's apple or have any other knobbly hard things down there sticking into you at the slow set. I distinctly remember him telling me, "You see Helene, I have to teach you.

You see it's not how deep you fish, it's how you wiggle your worm." I don't think either of us knew the real sexual connotation of this phrase at that time. Suffice to say he spent four hours that evening teaching me how to kiss. I recall him being exceptionally pleased with his student's enthusiastic progress. Although we arranged to meet at the same disco in two weeks time we somehow missed each other. Sadly I never saw him again.

Dan and I can hardly get the key in the door of his house we are laughing so much. We are thoroughly exhilarated, both from the sobering effect of the fresh air as much as our giddy excitement at the moment. There is of course an underlying knowing of what is going to happen next. It is not said out loud. It is breathed and sensed. Voltaire said that it's not enough to conquer, one must know how to seduce. We discover that we are both well matched in that department. I admit I wasn't taking in any of my surroundings. I breathe in his scent as he skilfully undresses me. He kisses me delicately all over, making me feel like the most precious jewel on the planet. I feel adored and revered. I haven't felt like that in the longest time. My body tingles with anticipation. We embrace lustfully. We caress tenderly. We are lost in each other and in the moment. His strong hands guide my body to the blissful heights of ecstasy. I am in heaven. Dan is a formidable lover for sure. I eventually fall asleep with his arm around me, safe and snug and satisfied.

The next morning I wake, forgetting temporarily where I am. It takes less than a few seconds for my foggy brain to adjust. Just as I am about to do my usual oh-my-God-get-me-out-of-here walk of shame, I hear someone humming in the shower. I turn around to my left and spot Dan enjoying the delights of warm suds and water. The door to the ensuite is ajar and it's impossible not to gawp at him. He turns off the water, opens the shower door, grabs a big grey fluffy bathrobe, rubs his face dry and squints at me. I quickly turn back and pretend to be asleep.

"Would you like a coffee?" Dan enquires, clearly sensing that I am wide awake.

"Em, that would be great. Thanks," I reply. "What time is it anyway?"

"It's 8.00am already. Time sure flies when you are having fun," he adds cheerily.

I wonder how he can possess such a sunny disposition with a

hangover at this hour of the morning. We certainly didn't get much sleep last night, that's for sure. I am hoping that he will just leave the room and make the coffee. At least then I can get up without feeling completely self-conscious. He leaves. Thank God. I am saved the indignity of scouting for my crumpled, smelly clothes around the room with nothing on but my birthday suit.

There is nothing worse than wearing yesterday's clothes as today's clothes. I decide to shower at home because I need to get to work quickly. I am tempted to use his toothbrush as my mouth feels like someone has just left a decomposing corpse in it. I resist.

I remember that I have an important personal injury (PI) settlement meeting at lunchtime at the Law Library. I know that I still need to work on the updated special damages. I really have to get out of here now.

"Dan, I'm sorry but I really need to go," I announce as I arrive into the kitchen. It is cosy and warm, or maybe that's the alcohol in my blood. "I have to work on a case for today."

Dan seems a bit disappointed I think to myself. Then again I don't think I am really in the right frame of mind to be judging anyone's feelings this morning.

"That's grand," he states, "but I am insisting on driving you back to Ballsbridge. It'll take me all of two minutes to throw on my clothes. Just knock back some coffee and I'll be back in a second." He makes a quick exit and is back before I have had my third sip of coffee.

"So," he glances at me, "when can I see you again?"

I fasten my seatbelt. "As my client or my lover?!" I proffer teasingly.

"Hmmmm...can't I be both?" He laughs.

"Actually, I don't think there is any rule against it in Ireland. Perhaps in the States but we are not yet that sophisticated here," I joke.

"Well, that's that then. I'm off to London for a couple of days but I'll give you a buzz when I get back, if that's okay with you? I don't see how you can say no anyway since you are my solicitor!?" he adds cheekily.

He pulls up outside my apartment cum mews. Despite the fact that I must reek of God-knows-what, he puts his arm around me and draws me in for another of those kisses.Wow, he must really like me if he can bear to do that to stinky little me.

Chapter 2

"We need to raise our profile and start netting some major players out there..." continues Mr. Andrew Peterson, in our weekly Partners' meeting.

"We are way behind target for this quarter. However, I myself can take full credit for ensuring the business of our esteemed new client Magret Holdings Ltd. who, as you all know, are prolific players in the building world..." and on he goes. I listen to the drone and try to concentrate. It can be acutely painful to listen to his grating voice for any length of time. It is five o'clock and Dan is picking me up at six. For once I want to leave my desk early and go and have some fun. I haven't seen Dan in two weeks and it seems like an eternity. I have become used to having sex on a regular basis. I think I'll burst if I don't see him this evening. I even have my brazilian freshly attended to. Nothing nicer than to sacrifice your sandwich at lunchtime for the indignity of a brazilian. Still, it'll be worth the wait I'm sure.

"Helene, wouldn't you agree?" and I realise Andrew is talking to me. I come out of my reverie and glance at Conor across the boardroom table for some clue as to what he just said.

"Wouldn't you agree?" he says urgently one more time. I desperately look for inspiration. I am literally saved by the bell when Andrew's P.A. interrupts over the intercom.

"Sorry Mr. Peterson for disturbing you but the gentleman...Mr. Walsh from the Law Society is in reception for you. He says he won't leave until he has an appointment for an inspection."

"Tell him I am busy! I will call him later with an appointment. He has no right whatsoever to come barging in here like this. I will bring an official complaint about this matter. It's an absolute disgrace!" he booms across the intercom. I smile to myself knowing that there is no doubt that Mr. Walsh would have heard that for himself, loud and clear. We all look at one another, the five of us left in the room. We are used to these outbursts. I don't know what has happened to Andrew lately. He is running such a tight ship but he never seems to be happy these days. I guess the stress of this business isn't easy. I can get terribly strung out myself at times but at least I'm not the Managing Partner. That's a whole other ball game. Despite his terrible tantrums and undesirable characteristics he is a damn fine solicitor. Secretly I have huge respect for him in a career context. As a human being, not remotely. He'd eat you alive.

"Yes, Mr. Peterson. I'll pass on the message," cowers the PA. Elaine isn't long in the Firm. God love her working with Andrew that closely. It's like he has permanent P.M.T.

Andrew regains his composure. I do note, however, a bead of sweat trickling down his neck onto the top of his robin starched shirt.

If Andrew's hair wasn't thinning so much, he wouldn't be a bad looking man. The middle aged paunch doesn't do him any favours either. Nor do his geeky spectacles. He's always a sharp dresser though. I'll give him that.

"As I was saying Helene, it is your responsibility as the Family Law and Civil Litigation partner of this Firm to ensure that new business....and I mean, big business with that, is attracted to our offices. I realise that you are a woman, and I am by no means being disrespectful about that, I am simply saying that it can be more difficult as a woman to be aggressive with regard to marketing. We men have the natural hunter instinct, the drive, the ambition. We are not afraid to sell our souls to get these people in the door." He belly laughs as he studies the four other men in the room, satisfied he has them sitting quite nicely in his lap.

Conor darts a sneaky look at me. He rolls his eyes surreptitiously. I am too angry to stifle a smile.

"Andrew," I begin and this time it is me who has to keep my composure. "I am quite confident in securing new business over the next quarter. You may note that I have had two high profile P.I. cases since January and this has, as you put it, attracted quite a steady stream of new business through the door. The figures speak for themselves. I take my role as a fee earner seriously. You may remain confident in my services to this Firm at all times."

"I accept that Helene. You are an asset to this Firm, without question, but none of us can afford to get complacent, especially now with this recession about to hit, or hitting, as we speak. Times are changing. Anyway, enough said for today. I am bringing Peter Magret to dinner this evening in that divine establishment, the Periwinkle, if any of you care to join us, although I am sure you all have work to concentrate on. Dinner is at 8pm in any event."

Andrew leaves as ceremoniously as he arrived. We all give a deep sigh of relief.

"He really is a sexist pig Helene," Conor says to me.

"I know Conor, but he is dealing with the wrong woman," I say challengingly.

"Oh there is no doubt about that Helene. No better woman," he encourages.

I run to meet Dan downstairs.

He is waiting patiently across the road in the second love of his life, his shiny new Mercedes. I slag him that he is too young to be driving an old man's car but secretly it makes me feel special being ferried around in style. I couldn't care less about cars myself, in fact I haven't even got around to buying one yet. There is really no point since I live a stone's throw from where I work. Other than that I grab a cab or take a lift from a friend. I never venture too far. Certainly not enough to justify spending thousands of euros on a mode of transport that would gather dust in the car park.

"Hi sexy. You look as gorgeous as ever," Dan embraces me as I sidle in to the front passenger seat.

He looks equally ravishing.

"Well, it would be an understatement to say I didn't need to hear that, Mr. Charming. I have had a day from hell. Andrew is as insufferable as ever and my time recording sheets are gathering dust!" I gasp.

"Thank God I have never met him or he would see the other side of Mr. Charming I can tell you," says Dan indignantly.

"You're my hero," I smile at him and ruffle his hair affectionately. "Where are we going anyway?"

Dan likes being in charge of what we do but not in a controlling way. More in a traditional way. I enjoy letting him make the inconsequential decisions. I have enough responsibility at work. It's a relief not to have to be the boss in the relationship department as well as the work department. I like the spontaneous adventure of it all.

"We're going to meet my parents," he announces as if we are going to the shops.

I instantly feel my hands go clammy.

"You're joking," I hope to second guess him.

"Nope. Sure they only live up the road. It'll be fun. They are real young souls. Mum is a bit of a spiritual buff but she has a heart of gold. Dad's your typical old lad. He loves a pint of the black stuff and a rugby match," he says nonchalantly.

"I know, you told me," I remark curtly. I feel acute pressure.

"Right, Helene. I was just letting you know." He looks offended.

"Sorry Dan, it...well, it just seems a bit soon, you know. I mean your divorce only came through two weeks ago...and I don't know if I'm, if I'm, you know, ready for that..." I stutter.

"What, ready for commitment?" I note the sarcastic tone.

"I thought we agreed we were going to move in together." His tone is wounded now. I am not so emotionally unintelligent that I can't pick that up.

"Yes Dan. I did agree to that. I'm unequivocally happy about moving in with you. Seriously. Please don't be hurt. I'm just nervous I guess. You know how I am about these things. I just don't want to rush what we have together." I try to explain. It occurs to me then all of a sudden that I am not even dressed for the occasion.

"Jesus, apart from anything else you could have warned me. Look at the state of me! I look like I've just come out of a funeral parlour!" I exclaim. I'm just shattered after the day and the thought of having to make small talk is not appealing, putting it mildly.

"You know how much this means to me Helene. And you look fabulous. Believe me I'd tell you and they are going to love you anyway. They have seen how happy I have been for the last three months–"

"Yes, Dan, it is *only* three months," I interrupt. "For all I know they might think you are on the rebound and I'm on the look out to nab you as my husband like your ex-wife!"

"I know your views on that subject Helene. And if you think I am on the rebound then you are very much mistaken. I had left, rather my wife, had left our marriage long before it was technically over, as you well know," Dan says in barely audible tones.

There is a long moment of silence and I know that this time I need to be there for him. This is my way of proving to him that I do love him. I realise that this can't be easy for him either.

"Pull over," I demand.

"Where am I supposed to do that?" he scowls. Then he pulls up on the kerb just before the lights on Baggott Street.

I take his face in my hands and I tell him that I am sorry and that I love him. I tell him that I am tired and emotional. I tell him that he got me at a bad moment but that I would love to meet his parents. He says sorry for not giving me enough notice. I put my hand on his thigh reassuringly as we listen to Amy Winehouse en route to his parents. He puts his hand over mine. It feels safe.

After all we are just two lost people in the world, doing our best to give love and be loved, never perfectly but always genuinely. We are blessed to have found each other. I sure as hell don't want to mess it up. I don't want to be lonely again. Neither does he. I think of Jung's theory of synchronicity. He said that people who are destined to meet will do so, apparently by chance but at precisely the right moment. I think maybe Jung has it in a nutshell. Life is good. I had forgotten how sweet love can be.

"That went well, didn't it?" Dan casts a furtive glance in my direction.

We are on our way to my place after leaving his parent's house. I want him to stay over with me tonight. I'm not in the mood for accommodating anyone else's needs this evening. I just want to be in my own space, with my own things around me. I am a bit of a creature of habit.

"Yeah. I think it did actually. Your Mum is really sweet. I can't believe she gave me a St. Therese relic, to as she put it 'keep all those awful monstrous lawyers at bay'! She most definitely has a sense of humour and she didn't grill me too much either, thank God. I don't exactly go to mass every day of the week, not to mind every Sunday. Actually, it's usually someone's wedding or funeral when I get to mass. Terrible really." I do feel bad about that momentarily.

"Mum has a good heart. I told you that. I thought Dad was a bit quiet until he mentioned quite indiscreetly, in my view, that the Munster/Leinster match was about to kick-off on the box!" Dan recalls with affection.

"To be honest, really honest, it was a good thing. I simply would not have been capable of eating another flapjack, delicious as they were! She must think I need fattening up or something..." I joke.

"You are perfectly proportioned to me, my delicious muffin..." Dan teases.

"Stop Dan. You're embarrassing me."

"Yeah right. You love it. I can't wait to get a bite of my little tasty muffin later..."

"Seriously Dan, stop. We've just left your parents for God's sake and I've St. Therese's relic in my hand. It's blasphemous!" I say with true Catholic guilt.

"Oooh. I love it when you talk dirty!" Dan mocks.

"Stop that Dan. Enough" I chastise him.

"Alright. Alright. I'm only messing with you. Don't get your knickers in a twist..."

"What knickers?" I slyly murmur under my breath.

We run three red lights back to my apartment.

CHAPTER 3

Hugh is standing in front of my desk with his head hung low. He doesn't even have the courage to look up at me.

"Hugh. Seriously. Tell me you are having me on! You couldn't possibly be for real! The Martin case is on for hearing the day after tomorrow and you haven't even followed the Advice on Proofs. What the hell do you think that means? Advice. On. Proofs. In other words advice on the proofs that we need for the hearing of a case! You don't need a rocket scientist to know that. How simple can it be?!" I roar at him.

I know I am losing the plot completely with Hugh, my favourite newly qualified solicitor, but this is not funny. We are running a High Court action in two days. My client has lost both legs in an occupational injury and liability is fully at issue. The other side is putting on a full fight and we are at serious risk of losing the case.

"The reality of the situation, Hugh, is that if our client loses the case it is out of our hands. He is aware of the risk. He is also aware that costs could be awarded against him if he loses, but, and it's a big BUT, if we have not done our homework properly and have not properly prepared for the case, then we are going to be the ones in the firing line. I have always tried to tell you that clients are our enemies! It's the first rule of law! No matter how much you think they like you, they'll sue your ass in the morning if you fuck up. And this is a fuck up! We have no loss of earnings quantified by an Actuary. Did it not even register in your head that he has been out of work for four years since the accident happened!? We have no rehabilitation expert report, we have no certificate from social welfare, no Notice to Produce has been served, we only have two updated medical reports and absolutely no idea of the costings of the prosthetic limbs that he needs into the future...Jesus, Hugh. You have really landed me in it here. More the fool me for trusting you. Do I have to keep an eye on every bloody file in this office. How am I supposed to attract business to this Firm if I will have to keep watch over my clearly incompetent staff at all times. Fuck it anyway!"

I bang my spectacles case on the desk so hard that my secretary Yvonne looks scared for the first time ever. I know I am angry, in fact I am boiling over. The perfectionist side to me is seething that I could have been so stupid not to check on the file myself. I am more annoyed with myself than I am with Hugh. I put my head in my hands and try to take a few deep breaths.

"Would we...would we, maybe, like, be able like, to get an adjournment?" this meek male voice says tentatively.

"Jesus Hugh. Do you honestly think that the other side are going to consent to an adjournment at this late stage? Huh? For starters they will have all their expert witnesses, doctors, consultants, engineers etc on stand-by to give evidence. Most of them require a minimum of 48 hours cancellation notice, otherwise they will insist on their full stand-by fees which could run into thousands in the High Court. How many expert witnesses do they have? Huh?"

I receive a blank look in response.

"Did you look at the disclosure notice at all? That will tell you how many they have. Do you even know what a bloody disclosure notice is??!" I scream at him. "Look, just leave Hugh. It's a disaster but as usual the buck stops with me. I'll have to sort it out. I should have dealt with it myself. Just don't come near me till I have calmed down because I'm afraid of what else I'll say or do."

Hugh leaves trembling. I feel terribly bad but I can't help it. I am berating myself for taking my eye off the ball, for maybe being too distracted with my happy love life to be as vigilant as I normally am. Damn it anyway. This day was not turning out very well so far. And just as I think it can't get any worse I see Andrew Peterson coming into my office and closing the door behind him. I am surprised to register the fact that he looks as bad as I feel. The last thing I want now is have to tell the Managing Partner about this absolute fuck-up. He seems stressed enough these days without my ineptness adding to his worries. "Listen, Helene. Just a quick word. The Law Society, in the guise of Mr. Walsh, will be investigating, well, that's what they call it anyway, our Firm, commencing from next Monday. Just make sure you have your files in order. I know you keep your Invoice file and your Section 68 file but, you know, just make sure it's a tight ship. You know what I mean. Any of those cash files you do, well I don't want to know, so just keep it kosher. Understand?"

"I don't do that Andrew," I say, quite taken aback by his directness.

"Yeah, sure, whatever Helene. I'm just saying...look, it's only routine but just give them the right information. Capiche?"

He totally makes my skin crawl with his pseudo macho lingo.

"Of course," I say sanguinely. "Nothing to worry about from my end, Andrew."

"Good," he says and is gone again without closing the door behind him.

I am beginning to wonder if bad things really do come in threes and hoping they don't when Yvonne buzzes me to tell me Dan is on line four. I am temporarily relieved.

"Hi hon," I say, almost on the verge of tears. "I wish you could give me one of your bear hugs. I'm having just the worst day so far."

"Oh. Sorry babe. I hate to make it even worse but I'm just ringing to say that we are nearly there with this deal and I'm going to have to stay here in London until the deed is done. It's going to be Friday I think to be frank..."

"Feic it, Dan. I really could have done with seeing you tonight. It's only Monday," I sigh.

"I know, I know. Look I'll make it up to you when I get back. We'll get a nice bottle of red and a good DVD and a snuggle on a couch made for two with our names on it. Okie dokie. Listen I gotta go. Love you babes." Dan dashes off into the London air.

"Love you too. Bye."

Great, bad things do come in threes. The good thing is that the three things have happened or at least theyre known, I think. What a start to a week!, Ok, I've got through worse and I'll get through this. I know, Jesus, of course I know! All this headshrinking pressure comes with the territory. No one ever said it would be a walk in the park. Anyway, I know I can salvage something with the

Martin case. That's what I'm paid for after all. Ok, I know most of the litigation expert witnesses by first name, even those on Harley Street. Oh god, I know that I'm attempting to convince myself here...but I'm determined to get us back in the saddle with a fighting case straight away. I have no choice, anyway, just get on with it...I'll be the laughing stock of the day down in the Round Hall if I don't. The two Senior Counsel, not to mind the Junior Counsel, must be wondering where their bloody briefs are at this stage. How the hell did I allow this horrific situation to arise? I resign myself to working through the night and the night afterMy reputation is on the line and in my business it's vital that it stays intact. Peterson and the precious Law Society will have to wait. I have to attend to more crucial matters first.

Reluctantly I tell Yvonne not to put through any calls for the moment, unless it's to do with the Martin case. I pray for guidance and on cue it occurs to me that I should contact Murdoch Pierce. It kills me that I have to even consider ringing him. He is the only one, however, that can get me out of this rut. M. J. Pierce is an eminent SC and an expert litigator. He only accepts briefs in Family Law matters on behalf of clients that he knows. Believe it or not he has acted for quite a few of his friends' marriages that have fallen apart. I always wonder how he does that. How he can actually represent a friend of his in a Divorce or Judicial Separation when he was also a good friend to his friend's wife. Business is business he always says. Thankfully I have never yet been put in that position. It has been hinted on occasion but either I mention my difficulty with the ethics of it or I politely decline. I do have some principles. In any event I decide to ring Murdoch.

"Hello Murdoch? It's Helene McBain here," I say nonchalantly.

"What a pleasant surprise Helene! Just a moment and I'll talk to you properly..."

I can gather that he is clearly in the middle of a restaurant with all the noise in the background. No doubt a few pre-Christmas libations being downed in the process.

"Well hello there, Helene. Sorry about that. What can I do for you, my darling?" he says jovially.

My skin crawls with his casual intimacies. Nevertheless I am at the serious damage limitation stage. Far be it for me to be ruffled by his inappropriateness.

"I'm in serious difficulty with a case that's on for hearing in the

High Court on Wednesday. I really need your assistance at this late stage. There are two Seniors that are already briefed, or should I say, about to be briefed in the matter but that's another story, Anyway a)I don't want to trouble them b) I feel they might want to apply for an adjournment which I don't want and c) they do not have the inroads you have in this particular area. You may recall that I did attempt to brief you in the Martin case but you were unavailable? The Plaintiff lost both his legs in an industrial accident."

I continue with my incessant chatter for a while and am somewhat astonished at my own honesty. It occurs to me that it's probably not exactly a prudent move. How can one even attempt to be professional when one's emotions are all over the bloody shop. Not to mind that most solicitors wouldn't dream of letting themselves down by calling on such an eminent senior counsel as Murdoch Pierce. There goes me trying to look like I'm on top of things. No more head up, shoulders back down in the Law Library. There goes pride and respect and strength. There I go, a sucker for punishment. But I just have to go and rub salt in the wound with big fat saline tears, losing all shred of dignity in the process. Wonderful.

"Oh yes, the Martin case," Murdoch interrupts.

He has probably being trying to get a word in since hello. I am seriously embarrassed now and wondering what on earth possessed me to ring him at all. I should have counted to ten before doing anything. I could have gone for a walk, had a brandy, smoked a cigarette or whatever. Damn.

"I do recall that matter. It's unfortunate I was not available but I've been in hearing since Monday and it's going to go on another week at least. It is certainly not my intention to upset you any further Helene but how on earth did this cock up, excuse my french, come about then?" Murdoch enquires delicately.

His kindness takes me by surprise but it only serves to compound my feeling of sheer panic. I explain the situation to him in between sobs. I explain that ultimately this is my fault in that I had relied on a newly qualified solicitor with little or no experience to prep a P.I. case in the High Court. I tell him that I *have* to rectify matters, like yesterday. I tell him that it just isn't an option, even at this late stage, not to run the case on Wednesday. I tell him, against my better judgment, that I am under serious pressure from the

Managing Partner with regard to my profit margins for the Firm. I explain that I categorically require a miracle. Loaves and fishes stuff. I tell him that although I'm a partner the recession is practically upon us and I don't want to be in the firing line. I wonder immediately why I am being ridiculously dramatic. I suspect I simply want a sounding board. I realise there is little he can do to help me out of this cock up, as he puts it. I'm annoyed with myself for not ringing a friend. Then again I don't get to see them that much since I'm either in the office or with Dan. I couldn't just ring a friend out of the blue needing help, could I? Moreover, none of my friends are lawyers, the lucky ducks.

"I see," he replies. "Who is counsel on the other side?"

"Jack Barrington and Stewart Carey." I can't recall the name of the Junior Counsel off the top of my head. This proves to me that I am really not thinking straight.

"Ok. Leave it with me. I'll come back to you on it," and he was gone.

"Murdoch?" I question, even though I know there was no one on the other line.

What in God's name does that mean? I ask myself. When is he going to come back to me on it? I sit there for what feels like an eternity going over the conversation again and again in my head. I am still none the wiser. All I do know for certain is that I can only rely on myself to rectify the situation. Firstly, I have to pull myself together and fast track my brain to stellar standard. I take out another tissue from the box on my desk. I take out my compact mirror and check my face for running mascara. I put on some powder and lip gloss. Next my socks and runners. Then I leave. I need to get out of my office and clear my head. I tell Yvonne I'll be back in half an hour, deliberately leaving my Blackberry on my desk. I just want to be incommunicado for a while. I am ashamed at myself for letting my emotions get the better of me. I instantly regret having rang Murdoch. What was I thinking of? I should have rung Dan but I didn't want to be annoying him when he is up to his eyes himself. The whirlwinds in my mind are on overdrive. I can't think straight.

It's only when I am in the elevator alone that I hear my stomach gurgling. I realise I haven't eaten lunch. I decide to walk by the Canal onto Stephen's Green and eat a sandwich on a random bench. It's freezing outside yet I welcome the cold, crisp air. It blows away the cobwebs. I start thinking of Christmas which is only a few weeks away and how special it will be this year. My first Christmas with Dan. This time last year I was all alone. I am grateful to have him in my life. I can't wait to see him on Friday. I hear another voice say, *yeah, if you last that long*. Great. I'm even talking to myself now. Stress can make people do the strangest of things. I don't finish my sandwich but decide to keep walking.

By the time I come back to the office it's dark. Judging from the amount of emails and messages in my in-tray, I must have been gone a few hours. I feel somewhat refreshed following my expedition. I needed some head space to motivate my brain back into focus. I am still aware, however, that I am not operating with all cylinders on full blast. I start sifting through my messages. Yvonne pops her head around the door,

"I just thought you should know that Lacey & Mortimer solicitors were on twice while you were out. They said it was urgent." Yvonne looks at me in a quizzical fashion. She probably suspects I was out doing some Christmas shopping on Grafton Street on the sly. I wish that was the truth. Yvonne should know by now that I hardly have time to buy my own underwear not to mind presents for other people.

My family knows me as lastminute.com since all birthday/Christmas and any other occasion presents are bought at the eleventh hour. So be it. I've enough on my plate without having to worry what my nosy secretary thinks I've been up to.

I somehow manage to ask Yvonne to call back Malcolm Lacey in Lacey & Mortimer. Why I am even bothering to call is beyond me since it can only be bad news. His Firm represent the Defendant in the Martin case. They haven't even received our disclosure notice outlining what medical reports we will be relying upon, what expert witnesses we will be calling on to give evidence *und so weiter*. I usually start thinking in German when no other words in my vocabulary resonate with quite the same gravitas.

Yvonne buzzes my office. "Malcolm Lacey is holding on Line three."

"Thank you Yvonne," I reply.

"Hi Malcolm. Sorry for the delay in coming back to you on this. I do need to speak to you anyway with regard to the Martin case on Wednesday because…"

"Helene. I'll stop you there." Malcolm cuts me off short. "I was hoping to catch you before the close of business today. In fact I was just about to send you over a fax. I have a strictly without prejudice offer for you with regard to the hearing on Wednesday. I am instructed to offer your client the sum of €3,500.000 to include special damages plus High Court costs in full and final settlement of your client's claim. This, as you know, beats the tender offer by €1,250.000 so you are obviously covered in respect of costs. Off the record I take issue with the many procedural flaws in the Plaintiff's claim. Notwithstanding that fact, as I said, the offer is on the table. The sole contingency is that the offer is only open for a further two hours ergo I will obviously need to take my medical people off stand-by should the offer be accepted by your client. I'll take the liberty of faxing it over to you now in writing since I have it ready and so we are clear on the terms. I'll let you take instructions and I'd be obliged if you would come back to me on it by five thirty today. Thanks Helene."

"Thanks Malcolm," says Ms. Tiny.

I'm rendered mute. I am utterly flabbergasted. Forget the loaves and fishes, this is Lazarus stuff! This is unheard of. Did I actually pray to God when I went out for my walk? I don't remember, but someone is looking down on me. No client in their right mind could refuse this offer, legless or not. It is more than reasonable under the circumstances. Not alone is liability strongly disputed, we have not built the Plaintiff's claim into what it should be. We are not armed with a dozen expert witnesses. The pleadings are a mess. Wow. Maybe they don't want the media to report the case? There are always newspaper hounds hanging around the Four Courts, sniffing out the latest juicy bone. The Defendant is one of the largest construction company's in Ireland. That's probably it alright.

Hmm. It just seems incredibly coincidental. Out of the blue I have a lightbulb moment. Murdoch Pierce. There's something. But how? It would be impossible for him to pull that one out of the bag, now wouldn't it? Or would it? It's not a secret that the inner circle of the Law Library has its own set of rules. But surely not. One Senior Counsel to another Senior Counsel. I'll scratch your back, you'll scratch mine. It is true that often they don't even want their own solicitor listening in on their negotiations. The old boy network at its peak. I feel like a penny has just dropped. I dial Murdoch's mobile number and it goes straight to his voicemail. *Leave it with me,* he said, *I'll come back to you on it.* How serendipitous then that I get this call from Malcolm a few hours later.

I really don't know whether to laugh or to cry. Prior to doing either I ring Mr. Sebastian Martin to tell him the good news. He is overcome to such an extent that he has to hand the phone to his wife. I half listen as she tells me how stressed they have been lately. Both of them are on sleeping tablets to assist their sleep. The thought of the imminent trial has been keeping them up all night every night. Mrs. Janet Martin thanks me profusely to the point of me having to shush her. She tells me that no money will ever compensate her husband for his loss but the monies will help for his care into the future. I half listen because it is only registering with me how this telephone conversation could have been terribly different. I feel undeserving of her gratitude. Yet I am grateful to be the bearer of gifts, good tidings of comfort and joy and all that.

I call Malcolm and confirm the settlement. He assures me that Mr. Martin will have the monies before Christmas. I fax over a confirmation letter outlining my client's acceptance of the Defendant's offer. I also email it to be on the safe side. I'll contact all other parties in the morning. I do not fully understand how this came about but right now I don't care. Between our solicitor/client fee and party and party costs I have just made close to a million euro for my Firm in fees. It is time to celebrate and I know exactly with whom. I buzz Hugh.

"Hugh," I say, getting up from my desk to walk over to him. He looks scared. "Don't worry," I laugh. "Believe it or not I have just settled the Martin case. 3.5 mill. Seriously. I'm not winding you up! Grab your coat. It's time for some champers!"

Hugh and I hug each other with sheer relief, joy and excitement all at once. I sense he is about to burst into tears. I order him up to turn off his PC and meet me in the lobby. We sit in the snug of the Four Seasons bar, feeling as if the world is our oyster. Hugh is visibly drunk after only a glass of champagne and I'm not far behind him. "I just can't believe we got away with it, Helene. It's just a complete stroke of luck!" Hugh says, animatedly. "You must have friends in high places!" he jokes. If only he knew!

"You must be more savvy than I give you credit for, Hugh, but let's just leave it at that. The less said the better."

Chapter 4

Almost as soon as the dust has settled on the Martin file, it's time to brush the cobwebs off some other forgotten files. These are the files targeted by Mr. Walsh on his hit list. All partners and solicitors are furnished with a list of their own individual files which Mr. Walsh wants to inspect at random. All of us in the Firm find this highly amusing. Poor unsuspecting Mr. Walsh has already been nicknamed Mr. Bean. Not an entirely inaccurate description I must add but cruel nonetheless. We joke about how he we should park him in the coldest room at the top of the building and put an OUT OF ORDER sign on the elevator door. Thirty flights of steps would certainly keep him fit and out of the way. We all just want Mr. Walsh and what he represents in and out. This extra hassle is the last thing we need. Our time recording sheets are enough to keep us tied to our desks not to mind an unwarranted intrusion like this.

"Excuse me Ms. McBain," says a whispering voice somewhere in the near vicinity. "I wonder would you have a minute?"

Mr. Walsh finally comes into focus in front of my desk. No one else would dare enter my room and stand in front of my desk without firstly passing Yvonne's strict code of entry. The Law Society, however, is the equivalent of Big-Brother-Watching-You. There is a slight fear element and one wishes to be seen as cooperative as possible. No way was Peterson & Co about to have any blot on its otherwise pure and untarnished copybook. For this reason alone Mr. Walsh has free rein to snake and ladder the corridors of our Firm.

"Oh, hello Mr. Walsh. Sorry I didn't see you there. Yes, of course I have a minute." I really didn't see the need for not addressing each other by our first names. No need, however, to irk God's representative unnecessarily. I therefore keep my mouth firmly shut.

"I won't take up too much of your time," Mr. Walsh says apologetically, "but as you can appreciate this is my only my second day here at Peterson & Co. and I have quite a substantial amount of files to get through during the requisite time span allotted to me."

"Not at all, Mr. Walsh." I gesture for him to sit down in the chair positioned directly opposite my own. I try to maintain some degree of composure yet I am mindful of my own heavy caseload. There are simply not enough hours in the day. I always think that my work is like housework in that it never seems to end. "What can I do for you?" I enquire politely, my smile a mask for more pressing matters.

"Firstly, thank you for your swift delivery of all the files I had requested from you. Some of your own colleagues haven't been as swift I might add," says Mr. Walsh with not a trace of humour. "In any event there are two files in particular where there would appear to be a Section 68 non-compliance issue, in other words, I don't see any letter on file, nor in keyhouse, where the client was advised with regard to the costs of their case in advance. Perhaps you can check these out for me and let me know. I have written down the case code numbers for ease of reference." Mr. Walsh leans over and hands me a handwritten note.

"Certainly, I'll look into that for you," I tell him, somewhat taken aback that there could be any hint of imperfection on my part.

"And also," he queries, his voice having reached a higher decibel now, his words finding momentum, "I wonder have you been keeping a separate Section 68 file with all your Section 68 letters together? Obviously a separate Invoice file for your Fee Notes would also be most helpful. This is more of a recommendation than an actual regulation but it makes my job a whole lot easier as you can imagine. From a superficial inspection, and I stress only a superficial inspection, there are also a couple, if even a couple I might add, of client balances that I need to address and figure out what's happening. I am slightly confused as to how the final client balance originated. I have written these out for you also on the bit of paper I gave you there. Perhaps you might be able to shed some light on these for me. Lastly, it would be most beneficial if I were to have delivery of all of this information by lunchtime tomorrow. I am usually in Room 301 for most of the day. In this way I can strike you off my roll so-to-speak"– he enjoys his little pun and has a quiet snort to himself – "and get on with the rest of my duties here in Peterson & Co. As you can appreciate I have an extraordinary amount to get through. My assistant will also be available for any questions you may have. We would just like to make some headway before we break up for Christmas."

"It will be done Mr. Walsh," I assure his turned back as he leaves my office. His crepuscular bald head leaves a trail of flaky skin behind him. I notice the tiny white specks on my royal blue carpet, like a line of tiny lice eggs. I suspect he realises he does not need to even wait for a reply. Mr. Walsh simply cannot be disobeyed one way or the other. Unless, of course, one wishes to incur the sanctimonious wrath of his big brother. Despite my never ending supply of emergency, "very urgent "and "urgent" work, I make his requests a priority. To do otherwise would have been foolish.

I call Yvonne into my office. I hand her Mr. Walsh's handwritten note and ask her to retrieve the particular files for me from Mr. Walsh's assistant. I salvage my Section 68 and Invoice files from under a pile of as yet unread legal *Gazettes*. I am relieved to find that they are mostly up-to-date. I simply need to insert my most recent Invoices, including the Martin file Invoice. I must additionally double check that I have inserted copies of all Section 68 letters. I am confident that Yvonne will be able to assist me in finding the elusive few that have escaped somewhere in the mountain of paper at Peterson & Co. I know they'll turn up. I pride myself on my organisational skills and my conscientiousness.

Luckily, my mother had always told me that pride comes before a fall. Right on cue Andrew is sitting in the chair opposite me, the seat still warm from Mr. Walsh's large bottom, no doubt. Andrew doesn't appear to notice, however, and crosses his left pinstriped ankle over his right pinstriped knee.

"So Helene. What did Mr. Law Society want then?" he asks, looking me directly in the eye. For some reason Andrew makes me feel guilty about something. My head knows it's silly as I have never been guilty of any type of impropriety or illegal behaviour in my life. I would never jeopardise my career in that fashion. His eyes are steadfast and his aggressive gaze makes me squirm. I feel my cheeks flush despite my mind's constant reassurance. As usual there is a time delay between my head's thoughts and my body's actions.

"Oh you know," I answer as blasé as I can, in wonderment why I can't just answer normally, "just the routine type questions re Section 68 letters, my Invoices and a couple of queries re client balances..."

"Which client balances?" he rudely interrupts before I am even finished my sentence.

"I can't quite remember Andrew. I gave Yvonne the slip of paper he gave me. You can ask her. I can assure you there is nothing to worry about." I am already feeling definitively guilty, like I'm already shackled in the dock. I know I am probably coming across extremely defensive to Andrew. It's hard not to be when the Managing Partner is sitting opposite you with a suspicious disdainful look on his face.

"Indeed Helene. Indeed," replies Andrew and leaves abruptly. I hear him query Yvonne at her desk. I hear her fumbling for the piece of paper I gave her.

I can't really take in what just occurred. Am I under suspicion for something? Does Andrew think I have been up to something that he doesn't want the Law Society to know about? I am at a loss to explain why he would waste his precious sweet time, as he always labels it, quizzing me over such a trivial matter. A trivial matter in the grand scheme of things in his work day anyway. This was completely perplexing. How he even knew that Mr. Walsh had just been into my office was in itself fairly remarkable. It's a big Firm with seven partners and eighty solicitors, not to mind all the support staff: Trainees, legal executives, legal secretaries, law clerks and receptionists. It is a 35,000 square foot building with many corridors and stairways. Mr. Walsh could have been anywhere and with anyone. Yvonne didn't even see him come in as she was on her extended lunch break. Andrew must surely have the eyes and ears of a bloodhound. I had attempted to talk to him about the recent Martin case on his way out of the office. I didn't stand a chance as he was gone in search of Mr. Walsh's treasure trail instead. Andrew is usually on top of every case on every day in every court, even if his own actual expertise is in the area of commercial and residential conveyancing. It was conspicuously inconspicuous of him not to mention the Martin case.

It was bad enough having Mr. Walsh interrupt my day seeking explanations on such tedious matters as Section 68 letters and client balances than having the Managing Partner watching my every move. I buzz Conor's extension.

"Hi Conor. It's Helene. What's going on with Andrew? He is being really hands on with this Law Society guy," I confide in a low voice. "I feel like he is suspicious of me or something but I've nothing to hide. He was in here like a man on a mission after Mr. Walsh left. I cannot for the life of me fathom how he even knew he had just been in my office!"

"Beats me, Helene. He was only in with me about an hour ago," Conor replies conspiratorially. "Mr. Walsh had asked me a couple of straightforward enough questions. I was just about to take a conference call and had to put them on hold while his Majesty held court right in front of my nose. I got the third degree on my entire verbal exchange with Mr. Walsh. I felt like I was in kindergarten again! I mean, who does he think he is, just waltzing in like that whenever he feels like it? We are partners of this Firm too, you know. Just because he is Managing Partner doesn't give him the Godforsaken right to be breathing down my neck all the time. I've enough on my plate, like I'm sure you do too. Andrew's always got on my wick but he is really pushing it these days Helene. The way he schmoozes around this office like he owns everything in it, including us and all the other staff. He better be careful, we are too bloody iconoclastic for that!"

"I know Conor, I know. It's just unusual for Andrew to be this transparent. If I were to ponder it seriously I would be of the view that he must be worried about this Law Society inspection. He even called it an investigation which strictly speaking it isn't. It's all very strange. Anyway, look I won't delay you anymore. We'll grab a coffee early next week and see how the land lies at that stage," I say sounding as pragmatic as always.

"Perfect. Talk to you later." Conor rushes off the phone.

At least another partner is feeling the same way as I am. Andrew seems to be oscillating between extremes of over enthusiasm in one subject and abject disinterest in another. It doesn't make sense to me at all.

I manage to achieve some of my work targets on Friday afternoon. This always puts me in a good mood for the weekend, except, of course when I have to come back in on Saturday or

Sunday to prepare for a case. Often I can manage wherever I am though as I always have my blackberry and laptop with me. They are my only constant companions. I am terribly excited about seeing Dan. It has been such a stressful week that I really can do with some tender loving care from my significant other. That's what Dan calls himself sometimes to wind me up. He knows I hate the word *partner* and he doesn't like to be called my *boyfriend* since he maintains he is not eighteen anymore and it is, in his view, an age appropriate word. I find the term *significant other* just a little bit too PC for my liking. Nevertheless I'm happy to call him any thing he wants at this particular time on this particular day.

I arrive home to my apartment, just after seven in the evening and laden down with shopping bags from Marks and Spencer's Food Hall. I dash into the shower before I even unpack the groceries. My feet are throbbing from the high heels that I inflict upon them on a daily basis. I want to feel fresh and relaxed. I exfoliate my body with a gorgeous apricot body scrub and lather up soft, citrusy suds with my lemon oil bodywash. There is nothing nicer at the end of the day, save an actual bath if one had more time. A luxurious Chanel body cream seals the deal. I feel like Marilyn Monroe in my white bathrobe.

Dan is coming over for dinner at eight fifteen. I have time to lay the table, light some mood-enhancing candles and uncork the red wine to allow it breathe a little.

I only like to cook a dinner when I have a whole day in front of me and lots of time to prepare and execute its delivery. The perfectionist streak in me cannot tolerate a rushed performance. I become too stressed and agitated. I have learnt, therefore, that the ready made home made option is the best solution on a Friday evening.

What is the point of making a glorious meal for my *beloved* when I have had no time to enhance my own female ingredients? That would only be half the package. For surely the desert is as important as the starter and main course? I know exactly what I want for dessert and exactly how to go about getting it. I probably spend as long attending to myself as I do the dinner preparations. But isn't that the point? We both know the ultimate desired outcome of this seduction. Isn't everything else superfluous? My desire for Dan is instinctive. The thought of making love to him intoxicates me, the hot-blooded female within me becoming alive. I feel sensual and sexy when I am in his company. Denying this inner harlot is denying me to myself.

CHAPTER 5

Once I have all the dinner preparations attended to, the heavy handed gin and tonic I have fixed for myself glides me into my bedroom and helps me into my dress. A little black dress that I feel sexy wearing. I leave off my shoes and make a mental note to put them on when I hear the knock on the door. I play an emotive Jacques Brel CD and put the finishing touches to my make up and hair. A faint spray of Eau de Parfum and dessert is ready. I lie on my onyx coloured chaise longue, close my eyes and enjoy the moment.

A short lived moment when I hear Dan's voice "Did you not hear me knocking on the door?" he quips as he struggles through the entrance with his suit carrier, overnight bag and bulky briefcase.

I jump up and run to him, forgetting all about putting my shoes on in the process. I throw my arms around him and kiss him passionately. Poor Dan hasn't even a chance to protest as his hands and face are both otherwise engaged.

"You can knock on my door anytime," I beam at him and we both laugh at my cheesy line. It breaks the ice.

"Well, if you continue to leave your door open there'll be no need for me to knock, now will there?" he remarks sarcastically. Dan is terribly protective of me, he hates when I put my own personal security at risk.

It can take a little time for us to acclimatise to each other again, even after only a week apart. When you live with another person every day it may be true that familiarity breeds contempt but the converse is equally true. In such an environment a pregnant pause doesn't exist. There is no such thing as an uncomfortable silence.

You are used to the other person's habits, foibles and idiosyncrasies. One can glean the simplest respite in that alone. Perhaps this is why some couples can stay married for what seems like forever. They don't even notice each other growing old. They spend such an inordinate amount of time together that they morph into each other, they are intertwined.

"What's for dinner? I'm absolutely ravenous," Dan asks hopefully. I can tell he is tired after his flight.

"Would you believe Mr. Marks and Mr. Spencer spent all day at my stove cooking up a storm, especially for you...isn't that a treat? Not alone that, they even threw in a beautiful bottle of Bordeaux since they know it's your favourite," I reply with a glint in my eye.

"My, they have been exceedingly thoughtful alright. Truly surpassed themselves this time!" Dan remarks with an exaggerated tone. He plumps up the cushion on the chaise longue, removes his scarf and coat whilst kicking off his shoes.

I pour Dan a large glass of wine and fix another gin and tonic for myself. Dan lies on the chaise longue with his eyes closed. I can't tell if he is listening to the lyrics of Jacques Brel or in such a state of somnolence that he might just nod off. I decide to ignore this. I sit down on my yellow armchair.

"Anyway, in reply to your question. To start, we will be having pan fried scallops in a petis pois and shallot sauce. For our main course, we will be having steak au poivre with dauphinoise potatoes and green beans with roasted almonds. The dessert, of course, is optional but comes highly recommended. In fact, very highly recommended," I say smartly.

I expect to receive a response to this flirty offering. And indeed I do. Dan opens his eyes as if he has temporarily forgotten where he is.

"Come here," Dan says as he extends his left hand in my direction. He pulls me towards him gently. Before I know it we are kissing again passionately and lustfully. God it feels amazing. I am lying on top of him now. He is warm and smells of a man. A real man who knows exactly what he is doing. A man who has perfected the art of love and the process of being in love.

"Let's have dessert now", Dan whispers to me inbetween his loving kisses. He leads me into the bedroom but we are both too impatient to make it that far. We fall trance like onto my soft

Moroccan rug by the fireplace. I love the feel of his skin on mine. A week's worth of pent up desire leaves me hungry for his touch, his body. Dan confidently but tenderly opens the buttons on my dress one by one. I do not resist. I cannot resist as every fibre in my body aches for him.

"I've been dreaming all week of this moment," he says softly. I want him badly. I am not capable of uttering a single syllable, he's just magnetic. He caresses me, kissing me all the time. My lingerie is discarded and we momentarily find ourselves transported to another place. A place where time stands still, our only immediate concern is our mutual pleasure. How can this not be heaven on earth?

I help him undress. Our tender kisses belie the urgency of our movements. I am not embarrassed being naked with him. He is too assured a lover, too sensitive a man to make me feel like that. We lose ourselves in our own voluptuous world. I cannot get enough of him nor him of I. We have urgent, intense sex and I would give anything to stay this way for eternity.

Why is there a tear coming down my cheek? It catches me off guard. I am in love with this man! The penny drops. All of a sudden I am scared at how vulnerable I feel. It has been a long time since I have felt like this. Why does my mind always say one thing and my body the other? I know only too well that the body never lies. I cannot deny my feelings for Dan anymore. We have just made love! It wasn't just sex. I am sure he feels it too.

We hold each other afterwards, both of us breathless, both of us satiated. Dan pushes the hair off my forehead and smiles at me. I know that he is about to say something quite significant. I will really die if he says he loves me; I'm not ready for that yet! It's bad enough that I realise I have fallen in love with him. I don't know if I can go down this route again. Oh please don't let him say I love you. What on earth will I say back? I don't want to have to fake it. Before I know it he'll be proposing to me! What on earth was I thinking? He's done it before, no reason why he won't ask me this time. I'm just not good at this intimacy lark. After all our sexual exertion and lack of food, I feel as if I am about to faint.

"I have a present for you," Dan says. Oh Lord, he really is going to propose! "You just stay there while I go and get it and don't be staring at my sexy butt! I'm watching you!" he jests.

Slowly but surely I am becoming aware of the fact that I am

buck naked on the rug. Buck naked with carpet burns to add to the humiliation. I feel cold but my skin is hot and covered with a thin film of perspiration. Maybe if I go and have a bath he might think the moment is gone and forget about proposing altogether? I make a run for it when his back is turned and sprint into the bathroom. I'm only there a split second when I hear him calling my name and opening the door of the bathroom which I foolishly left ajar.

"I'm just going to run a bath," I holler as I frantically dash to turn on the hot and cold taps. I'm too late though and I see Dan standing in front of me with a small blue turquoise box held strategically in front of his manhood.

"Yes, I can see that," I half mutter under my breath. I resign myself to sit on the side of the bath. Dan sits beside me. Our white bodies in the reflection in the bathroom mirror would surely make me laugh out loud if my predicament wasn't so serious.

What a way to propose! Dan should know better. He knows I don't believe in marriage per se. Why does he have to put me through this torture?

"I love you Helene," Dan says and puts his hand over mine. There he's saying it! What am I supposed to do now? "I don't expect you to say it in return. I know that even though you are hot stuff" – he smiles teasingly – "I also know that you can be a bit of an ice queen sometimes so I don't expect you to say the same to me...not yet anyway!" and he laughs in his usual endearing and self-deprecating way. I sense a speech coming on now, why does he have to ruin everything? Aren't we fine the way we are? We are moving in together officially next weekend but that doesn't mean I want to marry him!

"...and because I love you, I wanted to give you something special."

Dan hands me the box. I take it with my right hand. It feels like a ton of bricks.

"Open it," he encourages. Oh God, here we go. My hands tremble as I struggle with the ribbon. I lift the lid and there sits a shiny silver key.

"What the...?" I stammer.

"I just thought that since you are going to be officially my housemate, that I would get you your own snazzy, special key for Banville Road, Look, your name is engraved on it too. It's solid sterling silver. A specially commissioned bespoke piece for a special woman," Dan explains. He is clearly delighted with himself.

I am in shock and feel such a sense of relief that I burst into tears.

"Aw bless Helene! I'm so glad you like it," he says gently. "I just wanted you to know that I am truly looking forward to you moving in with me. I wanted you to know how much you mean to me. Banville Road will be your home as much as mine. It's a present from both of us!" He laughs and hugs me tightly. "It's from Tiffany & Co.," he adds.

Oh wow, I couldn't care less where it's from as long as its not an engagement ring. Dan is terribly thoughtful and sweet. I couldn't hurt him like that. But what a relief! How silly I was to think it was going to be something else entirely! I start to laugh uncontrollably. I am that delighted with my new gift!

"Dan, this must be the most thoughtful gift I have ever received," I say quietly, with a mixture of excitement and relief.

"It's my pleasure," Dan says as he kisses me all over again.

"Be careful!" I laugh. "We're on the verge of toppling over!"

"So what?" he murmurs as we fall on the floor, kissing and giggling. "Well, at least the floor is heated," Dan quips, as I lie on the cosy bathroom rug.

"A pillow wouldn't go amiss!" I say bossily as I pull Dan closer to me.

"Your wish is my command, darling," he replies, fluffing a quickly-grabbed pillow under my head. We take our time and make love slowly. It feels heavenly. "More champagne, babes?" Dan says, topping up my glass without even waiting for a reply.

"I think there is more champagne in the bath than in our glasses!" I say, laughing.

"Yep, more champagne bubbles than bath salts bubbles if you ask me!" Dan says as he piles the suds high on top of my head.

"My sexy Cleopatra!" he teases, kissing me.

"My sexy Julius Caesar" I tease back.

"As long as it stays that way," he says softly, "I don't want a Mark Anthony coming along and whisking you off into the sunset."

"Never" I say affectionately. And I mean it. This is pure unadulterated bliss.

Dan and I spend the rest of the weekend in pretty much the same fashion. It is such a treat for both of us not to have to rush into work. We lay in bed in the mornings, our arms wrapped around each other, our thoughts only on what delicious brunch we might enjoy. In the afternoons we stroll up Grafton Street buying our respective family Christmas presents. In a few days Dan and I will be happily ensconced in Banville Road, officially a living together couple. We will enjoy our Christmas dinner with all the trimmings in the company of his parents and his gay brother Walter. My own Mum and Dad are staying in my aunt and uncle's house in Devon. It's a big change for my Mum who takes great pride in her Christmas cooking. I'm delighted she will be having a well earned break from domesticity.

"We should throw together a little drinks party over Christmas," Dan announces when we discuss that Christmas Eve would be an opportune time for me to move in my belongings. I plan to rent out my apartment after Christmas. No point having it sitting there idle, although the thought of complete strangers using my kitchen and bathroom, not to mention the bedroom, freaks me out altogether.

"You're the freak!" Dan teases me when I tell him my fears. "There is no need to worry about that. I'll vet any prospective tenants. Don't you worry about that," and he puts on a mock superhero voice. I can't help but laugh even though part of me squirms at being mollycoddled. I like to be independent yet I accept that in embarking on a serious relationship an element of that becomes lost. I am just adamant that this time I will retain my uniqueness, not lose my sparkle. I cannot allow that to happen again. I hug Dan, sensing his love, and vow to make this relationship work, albeit on my terms this time.

CHAPTER 6

I have to tear myself out of bed on Monday morning. At 7am I rise later than usual. Dan has already departed for work. Two much sloth over the weekend has set my body clock out of sync. I splash cold water on my face and my eyes gradually become accustomed to the bright lights in my bathroom. It is still dark outside but I can hear the near hum of traffic, meandering its way already through Dublin's busy streets.

It is only as I enter Peterson & Co, skinny latte and croissant in hand, when that familiar uncomfortable vibe at being back in the office hits me. Something has changed over the last while. I can't quite put my finger on it but my intuition knows I am right.

I turn on my PC and check my email, which I have miraculously not checked over the weekend. The first email I read is, of course, the most recently sent email. It's Andrew Peterson. He wonders if I can let him know when I am in my office. He sends this email at 6.05am this morning. Another similar type email is sent at 6.30am and another at 7.04am .What the hell is this about? I look at the clock above my door. It reads 7.40a.m.

Ok, I accept that I am later into work than normal but at least allow me my caffeine and sugar fix first. I cannot function properly in the morning without them. My head remains too fuzzy until the drugs kick in clearing the fog in the process. Well, you know, he can just bloody well wait. The cheek of him. What is up with him at the moment? His behaviour is incongruous and erratic. The worst part is that I don't know if it is me or him. I have never been much of a mind reader anyway but with Andrew you could be a NASA scientist and still not second guess him.

I hear Andrew's deflated voice somewhere nearby. "You're looking a tad peeved."

I look up and attempt to say "good morning to you too" except that my mouth is full of croissant flakes. Andrew looks downright shocking. Have I ever seen him as dishevelled looking in his life?! If he tells me that he has spent the weekend sleeping under his desk, I wouldn't be remotely surprised. I take a large gulp of my latte, nearly burning my throat off in the process. The caffeine hit is worth it though.

"You are certainly eager to see me this morning, Andrew," I say as lightheartedly as possible, "Is everything okay? You look a bit…well, a bit stressed, to be honest?!"

Andrew closes the door and makes his way to the chair opposite my desk. I observe the dark circles under his eyes, the visible red veins on his cheeks, the stubble spattered with clumps of grey. Were they always there? Maybe I never noticed before?

"I need to talk to someone Helene. I believe you are the only one I can trust. I know we are breaking up for Christmas in three days but I need to get this off my chest before we break up…" and he trails off. Andrew's eyes are downcast. I can visibly see he is struggling with imparting whatever knowledge it is he wishes to impart. I somehow get the feeling that I might not want to be part of this confidence. Sadly, my insatiable curiosity overrides my need to protect my self from gossip. We are all human, after all.

"What is it?" I say gently, half of me wanting to know, the other half terrified of what I might hear.

"Peterson & Co may be in trouble," he states, matter- of- factly. "We could all be in trouble. I can't really tell you the ins and outs but suffice to say that there has been impropriety on my part with regard to clients' monies. There is quite a substantial deficit in the Firm's client account. I don't think that I can reimburse any of it. I can't even offer you an explanation for my actions at this stage…."

Andrew glances up at me to double check he still holds my unwavering attention. He needn't worry. I am that shocked that I can't even open my mouth. I nearly spill my coffee all over my desk. What in God's name is he talking about? Is this a joke? He can't be serious.

"What are you saying, Andrew?" I stammer. "There must be some mistake. What do you mean there is money missing from the client account?" I say, not really believing the words are coming out of my mouth. "I don't understand what you mean," I say, imploring him for a reasonable explanation for what he has just said. This can't be true! Andrew just sighs and shrugs his shoulders.

"It's obvious to me that Mr. Walsh from the Law Society is about to stumble upon these errors, if he hasn't already done so. No doubt we will have a reprieve over Christmas but I am under no illusions that there will be repercussions in the New Year..." Andrew glances furtively at me again. I feel as if all the blood has drained out of me. I stare vacantly at some distant spot on the wall behind his head.

"You're probably wondering why I am telling you this Helene. I have no one else to talk to ...." Andrew's voice hesitates. I think he might be about to break down at any moment. I'm not far behind him but am too tongue-tied to offer any compassion. Not that he deserves any. I can't see why he can't unburden himself on his wife. Why me? I don't want to be embroiled in this shambolic saga.

"I just thought you deserve to know what's going on so that you can sort something out over the holidays...or at least plan an alternative future." He stresses the last few words.

What the hell is he talking about? He's the one in trouble here. I have committed no wrongdoing myself.

"I would appreciate your discretion in this matter, Helene." Andrew makes a hesitant move to exit.

"This is your mess Andrew," my voice manages to say quietly.

"Yes, Helene, but you are a partner in this Firm too." His red-rimmed eyes penetrate my own. I understand the implications of what he is saying but I don't want to register that fact. His grave tones leave me under no illusion as to their meaning.

Andrew leaves me sitting motionless at my desk. I feel numb. I am too stunned to feel any emotion This is a nightmare! What the hell is going on? I can't cope with this. That lovely cosy weekend feeling has evaporated. My entire body is starting to shake and it's not from the caffeine. I need to get out of here. I want to call Dan but I'm not sure if I can. How do I explain what has just happened? I'm a partner too. What a loaded statement? Jesus, I am too. Does that mean I am going to suffer for his sins? God, I can't cope with this. I feel nauseous. Is this my reality? Everything I have worked for to fall apart in front of my eyes? Surely I'll wake up from this catastrophic illusion. This can't be happening. This doesn't happen to me, it mustn't happen to me.

I hear Yvonne coming into the office with her usual chirpy chat. I can't bear her to see me like this. I don't know what to think!I have an incredible amount of work in progress to attend to. Clients to meet, cases to prepare, briefs to compile. I can't stomach it all today though. What's the point anyway? Will I ring Conor? Our suspicions of what we didn't know are now known. Who wants to be the messenger of bad news? The whistleblower? It feels like Armageddon to me.

"Would you like a cup of tea?" Yvonne peers behind my door. "I've just put the kettle on." She smiles. I wish I could be part of that smile, get lost in it and never come back.

"No. I'm okay, Yvonne, thanks," I reply meekly. OmiGod, I think I am going to be sick!

"Are you sure? You look a little pale, if you don't mind me saying so. It must have been a good weekend!" Yvonne starts to laugh yet stops abruptly when she can see that I am in no mood for pleasantries.

"I'm just going out for a bit," I tell her as she sashays down the corridor to make her tea. I need to get to a bathroom fast!

"Okie dokie," Yvonne replies breezily. I wish I could swap places with her. I can't even speak now in case I puke everywhere!

I notice that my hand shakes when I press the button for the elevator. My mouth is dry and my head is thumping. I stumble into the ladies and vomit uncontrollably into the toilet. My throat stings as I bend over the toilet bowl, my eyes filling with tears from the exertion. I'm desperate to regain some sort of composure. I can't believe this was going on right under my nose! I had no idea what Andrew was up to! Why didn't I notice anything was amiss? I sit on the toilet seat, wiping my mouth with toilet paper. I've got to get myself together. I need to act fast on this! I freshen up at the sink, cupping mouthfuls of water into my parched mouth. Thank God there is no one else in here.

This is serious. I walk on autopilot. I don't really know where I am going but I suddenly find myself in the Firm's library. I need to check out my status as "partner" in this Firm. I need to know what the legislation states. I have a fair idea but I must see it in black and white to know how serious this is for me.

"Hi Lynette. Can you give me any books you have in stock on partnerships and liability? In this jurisdiction obviously. I'm just doing a little reseach." I smile sweetly at our resident librarian.

"Of course Helene," and off she goes. This is Lynette in her element. She likes to have a purpose. She derives enormous pleasure from obtaining the exact statute or directive or regulation tailor-made for your specific query.

I know that Lowe's book on Commercial Law is approximately thirty years old but as far as I am aware the same provisions apply. I have no doubt that will be amongst the litany of literature Lynette will return with. I wait patiently at the reception desk. My hands are clammy, my underarms perspiring. I am stressed beyond belief yet desperately trying to keep my composure. What a mess this is! What a disaster! Please God let me be wrong in what I think I might find out. Please please.

"I believe this to be the authority on partnerships and liability. There is no updated edition," says Lynette, offering me Lowe's bulky book in her outstretched hand.

"Ok Lynette, that's great. Thanks a million. I won't need it for long." I smile sweetly once more. I think to myself that I can be a wonderful actress at times.

I sit down at one of the private reading booths. My hands are trembling. I find it hard to focus on the index. I come across Section 5 of the Partnership Act, 1890. I read the following:

"Every partner is an agent of the firm and his other partners for the purpose of the business of the partnership; and the acts of every partner who does any act for carrying on in the usual way business of the kind carried on by the firm of which he is a member bind the firm and his partners, unless the partner so acting has in fact no authority to act for the firm in the particular matter, and the person with whom he is dealing either knows that he has no authority or does not know or believe him to be a partner."

I read it once. I read it twice. I read it three times. I can feel a hot flush creeping up my neck, crawling up my cheeks. The word "bind" is pertinent in this context. It's like a beacon yo-yoing off the page straight at me. Then, alarmingly, the words start to mix themselves up in front of my eyes. I cannot seem to focus on what I am reading anymore. I hear a voice in my head telling me to get out, to get out now. I have to leave! My mouth is dry. Incessant, hot tears are building up behind my eyes. The dam will break at any moment, the pressure is intense. I have to get out of here now! This is simply too much for me to bear. I need to find a solution to this and I can't do it here.

I find myself outside Peterson & Co on the grey pavement. It's bitterly cold yet the festive excitement of the passing pedestrians is palpable. I feel weak and as if I am going to faint. Then all is black. The next thing I remember is sitting in the airy reception of Peterson & Co being attended on by all and sundry. I beg them with my eyes to for God's sake leave me alone. For crying out loud, can't you see I want to be on my own!

"She looks very pale," says Dean, the security man.

"Maybe we should call that ambulance to be on the safe side," he says to all the other assembled voyeurs. That is what the worried faces look like to me at the moment, car-crash witnesses. They want to be in on the activity, a break from *la vie quotidienne*. The daily grind. They have no idea what I am feeling. My body and my mind are in abject shockI strain to utter the word "no" in reply to Dean's desire to err on the side of caution. Yet no sound passes my lips. I can say it in my mind but not in a way that's recognisable to the human ear. I have a sense of déjà vu. All my senses have shut down. I can't even articulate the simplest of commands. I am screaming inside but no one is listening I catch my boyfriend in bed, having sex with my best friend. I cry out in agony. I am lost somewhere in time and space. The pain is acute, my mind overloading with information. I must be in hell.

"Listen love, I don't want to be snooping, like, into a young lady's handbag but would you mind telling me where you put your keys, like, so I can give them to the taxi lady who is going to be bringing you home?" Dean asks me politely. I note the crowd of helpers have disappeared, happy to have something to talk about, no doubt. Someone worse off.

"Don't be so cynical, love," Dean says softly but firmly. "They were only trying to help." It occurred to me then that I had been speaking out loud. What else had I said?!

Dean tells me that he will inform reception who in turn will inform Yvonne that I am not well and will not be in work for the rest of the day. I crawl into my bed. My head is pounding, the Nurofen not having reached my brain cells yet. I pray for sleep. I desperately need some respite from the thoughts in my head.

Despite the turmoil in my mind, I still manage to conk out for a few hours. It's only the persistent ring of my Blackberry that eventually wakes me up. There are eighteen missed calls. It is not even in silent mode. I get up, go to the bathroom, get back into bed and call Dan.

"Hi honey bun…what's up?" he enquires cheerily.

I consider telling him the truth but think better of it. "I had to come home as I wasn't feeling too well, to be honest."

"Oh you poor thing. I must have worn you out at the weekend!" he laughs heartily. "Seriously though, are you alright?" I can hear the genuine concern in his voice.

"I think my mobile is about to go," I mumble quickly. "I'll call you later," I say as casually as I can. Damage limitation! I really need to get off the phone as I am on the verge of tears all over again. I rest my eyes and start to pray to God if He is up there somewhere. I need guidance on this one. I have absolutely no idea what to do next! God, what's going to happen to me?

CHAPTER 7

I work on automatic pilot in Peterson & Co. over the next three days. This is despite being on the receiving end of pitying glances from Dean in reception. I am terribly self-conscious every time I enter or leave the building as I feel Dean's eyes boring into my very marrow. He means well, of course, but I want to be chameleon- like in my movements. I don't want any attention at this time. Six o'clock on Thursday is my finishing line. I need to pace myself in the interim. It is in my nature to act before I think and to be impulsive in what I say. I struggle with holding my tongue and am afraid I'll start blurting everything out to Dean by way of explanation for my recent fainting spell.

These three days in work are busy in and of themselves, not to mind the added strain of Andrew's cataclysmic revelation. I'm going out of my mind with worry! The minute I come up with one scenario, another takes its place. Keeping it is a secret is excruciating. I am at a complete loss at what to do. This is not usual for me. Goddamn it! My emotions fluctuating like the Irish weather. The only decision I make is to make no decision. I will contemplate this most horrible of circumstances over the Christmas break and come up with a plan. What more can I do? There is no one I can trust with such sensitive information.

I try and concentrate on my files as best I can but I'm fooling myself if I think I am making any progress. Every time I open a file I think it might be the last time I'm looking at it. Every time I meet a client I think it might be the last time I'm meeting him or her. What am I supposed to think? My working world has been turned upside down!

Andrew has been noticeably absent from work. I am recalcitrant in my desire to contact him. It is as if I don't want to know any more than I already do. Perhaps by sweeping *that* conversation under the carpet I can act as if nothing has changed. Does anyone else in the Firm know what's going on? Has Andrew confided in anyone else?? Am I really the only one who knows?

"You look like something the cat's dragged in!" an alarmed voice booms in my ear. I hadn't even noticed Conor sauntering into my office.

"Are you on for a drink after work? I can see a refreshing glass of bubbly with your name on it! You look like you need it, if you don't mind me saying so. What's up?" Conor remarks in a puzzled tone.

It is one of those moments when the floodgates could open. That situation when you are desperately hanging onto a life raft and someone says a kind word to you. You lose your grip and fall rapidly into the swirling waters. I cling on tightly. I cannot afford to let go.

"Ah, you know yourself. Just trying to tie up a few loose ends before the break. I don't want to be fire-fighting these files as usual in January! I guess I'm just psychologically tired, it being the end of the working year and all that. Have you sourced all your Santa presents yet?" I throw in a curveball question which I hope will redirect his unwanted attention. It seems to work.

"Don't remind me. The missus is on my back every minute of the day about Santa's presents. She is bit hormonal putting it mildly but I guess she is up the duff with number four and..."

"Jesus Conor. I hate that phrase. It's so crass. Can you not just say she is pregnant like everyone else!" I exclaim.

"Hey, steady on there Helene. Sorry. Jeepers, I didn't think you were so PC! Maybe you're up the duff yourself!!" he remarks laughing defensively.

I'm beginning to unravel. I half resent his presence as I am bursting to tell him what Andrew has told me but I muster the strength to hold back.

"Sorry Conor... *Mea culpa*. Let me just finish up here and we'll head off in an hour or two if that suits? What about the Cellar bar at the Merrion for a change? It's got a real cosy festive feeling at this time. I'll ring and reserve a booth by the fire and ask them to uncork a couple of bottles of Chateauneuf for us...why not? It is Christmas and we're worth it! I'll leave it to you to round up the troops!" I banter nonchalantly.

"Brill! See ya later," Conor beams from ear to ear.

He leaves me recovering from a near miss. I wouldn't mind but I hadn't even had any alcohol to loosen my tongue. How in God's name will I hold it in later after a few glasses? It is perched at the fore of my mind. I know it'll come out as the evening progresses. I feel as if I am the holder of the secret of Fatima or something. I breathe a sigh of relief but not for long. I know I can't go on like this. A familiar name comes into my head. Murdoch Pierce. Can I trust him? I think I can. At least I need to think I can. I really need some good sound advice before this two week break. What would I advise my own client to do? I'd advise them to get the best possible legal advice available. Eureka! I unconsciously dial Murdoch's number.

"Murdoch Pierece. Helene McBain here. May I wish you all the compliments of the season!" I say in an exaggerated formal manner.

"You certainly may Ms. McBain," Murdoch replies, equally salutary. "How may I be of service to her Majesty?"

"I need some advice Murdoch. Quite urgently in fact. I don't want to talk on the phone but could we meet somewhere? I am actually available at the moment. Are you at the Law Library? I could meet you half way?" I enquire in a breathless rushed manner. I chide myself for not being as good an actress as I think I am. Oh what's the point anyway, he'll understand when I tell him! There is nothing to gain by putting on my usual professional persona. Following a brief pause Murdoch arranges to meet me at four o'clock in the pit bar of the Four Courts.

I would rather meet on more neutral territory which would lessen the risk of bumping into half the law library, not to mind potential eavesdroppers. I then recall that the end of Michaelmas term has been and gone and the Four Courts is officially closed. Of course, I remember! Arthur, the barman who runs the pit bar is a close buddy of Murdoch's. He is married to his niece and will gladly serve Murdoch behind closed doors so-to-speak. I text Conor en route and arrange to meet him at six o'clock at the Cellar bar. He texts back to say he is already there. And already half cut I think to myself. Its no harm as if I am delayed he may not take much heed of my absence.

I ring Murdoch for the security code for the Four Courts. I type it into no less than five key padssecurity. I arrive and find my way seamlessly down to the pit. I feel like a character in a Dan Brown novel on a secret mission.

"Her Majesty!" Murdoch feigns a mock bow when I arrive. Arthur winks and pours me a large Gin and Tonic without me even asking. "To what do I owe this honour?" Murdoch jests.

I nod my head to the right indicating that I want some privacy. We can sit and talk in the corner at ease without a mole like Arthur lapping up our every word. I can't take the chance of this getting out into the public arena. The press would have a field day. Luckily Arthur seems to get the hint. He utters some excuse about having to do a stock take and heads off behind a doorway at the rear of the bar.

"You seem serious Helene," Murdoch says suddenly. His jovial mood giving way to his intuition. I start to talk and I can't stop. I tell him everything from the Law Society's inspection under the guise of Mr. Walsh, Andrew's erratic behaviour and finally his potentially catastrophic admission. He listens intently and only interrupts occasionally to probe further. I clarify various parts of the story for him as I'm aware I'm relaying it haphazardly. I see his eyes darken as I tell him about my last conversation with Andrew.

"*Corruptio optimi pessima*" he states quietly.

"In English please, Murdoch" I plead.

"The corruption of the best is the worst," Murdoch says plainly. "Andrew possesses one of the finest legal minds in the Republic. Such a waste. He defines arrogance and avarice. A cautionary tale indeed," he says more to himself than to me.

"Murdoch, I really need to know what to do," I say, concerned. "That's why I've come to see you. I'm going out of my mind!" I say, sipping my drink. "If Andrew has taken clients' monies, and it looks as if he has, then where does that leave me? Does that mean that as a partner in the Firm I'm in trouble too?" I ask, resisting the urge to fire more questions at him. "I just really need to know where I stand in all this... that's the bottom line," I say, resolving to shut up and let him answer me.

We sit in silence for a while, Murdoch is deep in thought, I don't know whether to disturb him or not. I decide to let his genius legal brain work out the bigger picture. I cant bear the silence and feel like offering a few more "and another things" but I hold my tongue. I knock back the rest of my Gin and Tonic and go up to the bar. I ring the bell for Arthur.

"Hey," he says as he glances sideways at Murdoch, "another G and T for the lady." Arthur's transparent quick fire looks from Murdoch to me and back to Murdoch make me uneasy. It's clear he knows something is up but over my dead body will he find out. Arthur pours another pint for Murdoch and thankfully disappears once more. It crosses my mind that the pit could be bugged. God, I really am getting paranoid here! This cloak and dagger scenario just doesn't sit right with me. I have no choice. I need to know what I am facing in the future.

"It's grim, Helene." Murdoch looks at me softly. He takes a large gulp of his pint and savours the flavour. I nearly expect him to say "That's bass!" and sigh. He doesn't.

"Obviously I only have the details you have given me and I don't know what allegations will be in Mr. Walsh's report but from a cursory look at it, it would be fair to say that you are in deep shit here. Particularly after Andrew's half-hearted confession. There is no point me beating around the bush Helene. Partnership law is pretty damn watertight. It's just bloody unlucky you were made a partner at all. His sins are your sins. It doesn't make a whit bit of difference if you are blemish free. At the same time, there might be a glimmer of hope if we can prove that your hands are clean."

The tears start to roll like big bouncing boulders down my face. I can see that Murdoch is struggling to find the right words to advise me or even comfort me. Oh Jesus! I think to myself. What on earth am I going to do? I'd laugh if it wasn't so bloody serious.

"Listen. All I'd suggest you do at the moment is get a good rest over the holidays. There isn't much you can do in the meantime. I'll have a look at the legislation again and see if I can find any loopholes. The Law Society may have you stand censured and admonished. They may not actually have you struck off the roll of solicitors, unless they appeal a ruling of the Disciplinary committee to the High Court. The High Court takes a stricter view on these matters. That would be the worst case scenario. Andrew will get a jail term of course but I'd bloody well fight that you don't. Try not to worry Helene. We'll battle this out together," Murdoch says compassionately.

When Murdoch tunes into this side of himself he can be the nicest man in the world. I feel his empathy is genuine. I desperately need his help. This is no laughing matter!

"Does that mean that you'll represent me?" I ask faintly. I have no energy to beg. "For the going rate, of course," I hasten to add.

"It would be my pleasure, your Majesty!" he says light heartedly.

Amidst the tears and snot and manky tissues I conjur up a smile.

"That's more like it," Murdoch announces. "One for the road Arthur!" he bellows to an empty bar. Arthur appears in a flash and magician- like two more drinks appear at our table.

We continue to chat on a superficial level. We reminisce about the magic of Santa when we were small, how we are going to spend this Christmas day and our plans for the New Year. I am aware that Murdoch's gaze lingers a little too long sometimes. I choose to ignore it. I can bear the odd linger or nuance. I need him on my side. I know in my heart and in my head that he is the only person that can rescue me from this black hole to nowhere.

"Happy Christmas!" he says cheerfully as we leave. "Talk to you in January."

"Happy Christmas," I reply. I flag down a taxi to the Merrion Hotel.

"Merry Christmas!" says the taxi driver.

"Merry Christmas," I reply.

Chapter 8

Moving in to Dan's house on Banville road distracts me temporarily. I am gobsmacked at how much I have accumulated over the years. I find throwing out the inevitable rubbish I come across quite cathartic putting it mildly. I am sure a Feng Shui expert would have something agreeable to say on the subject. In anycase, Im so preoccupied with all of my baggage, I manage to avoid having a heart to heart with Dan. I am reluctant to tell him anything until I know for certain where I stand. Dan will only worry and plague me with well-intentioned pearls of wisdom and guidance I convince myself that this isn't deceit, its just that there is nothing to gain by telling him. I mean, why should he have to suffer over his holidays too? This isn't his problem, its mine Hasn't he enough stress with his own work? I know men tend to try and find solutions to a problem. I know he d only drive himself around the twist trying to find a solution, despite the fact that there isn't any.

"So what's Santa bringing you this year?" Dan raises his eyebrows theatrically.

We are surrounded by boxes packed by the removal company. It is late. We perch exhausted on the only available space left in the living room, a rolled up dusty Moroccan rug.

"I think I've been a really good girl so Santa should be bringing me something really special this year," I say confidently.

Dan gives me a plaintive look. "Well, I think you are going to get a lump of coal," Dan remarks casually.

"Excuse me, Dan Goodings. I have behaved impeccably all year!" I retort with derision.

"That may well be but you are just about to be a really *naughty* girl! The naughtiest you have ever been in fact..." Dan, the schoolmaster, lifts me up over his shoulder like a bag of potatoes and takes the stairs in his stride two steps at a time.

"Now close your eyes, you naughty girl!" the schoolmaster orders as he eases me lightly to the ground. I do as I am told. I hear a door click open. I am led inside and the scent of incense fills up my senses. Dan takes off my shoes. I feel a soft plush carpet under my feet. He takes me by the hand and sits me down. I fall into the fluffiness of cotton puffed with down feather.

"Open your eyes," the schoolmaster dictates. My eyes take a split second to adjust. I think I see tiny lights everywhere. Then I realise they are little red tea light candles. They are everywhere! There are pink and red and white rose petals strewn all over the room.! This is truly the most romantic setting I have ever seen.

"Oh wow, Dan!" I exclaim, quite overcome. "It looks just like a fairytale! You are too good. What did I do to deserve this? You really spoil me sometimes!" I say emotionally.

Dan sits beside me on the beautiful four poster bed. He cups my face in his hands, then he kisses my forehead.

"I wanted to welcome you to Banville Road in the style you deserve. I think you've had a lot on your mind recently and I know I've been away on business a good bit... I guess I just wanted to show you how much you mean to me. I want us to have a really special first Christmas together Helene. You make me so happy." Dan sounds emotional himself.

I take his face in my hands and kiss him and kiss him. I never want to stop. I have never met a man like Dan Goodings before. I feel incredibly blessed and grateful to know him. God knows what he sees in me but I don't care. At this moment in time I just want to make love to him all night every night. Dan's soft light tickle tight love is a welcome respite.

It's the 25th December. The Four Patrons Church in Rathgar is full to the brim. We decide to go to the children's 10 o'clock mass, purely to fit it around the turkey.

We are both slightly tipsy after our glass of Buck's fizz for breakfast. Dan spoils me, yet again, with smoked salmon and scrambled eggs with chives on a crisp white linen tray.

"Hot toast with lashings of Kerrygold butter and Earl Grey tea, especially for you, my darling," Dan says, pampering me as usual.

"A breakfast fit for a queen," I say, lapping up this luxury.

"Don't be too long, Helene. We don't want to miss 'Away in the Manger'!" Dan teases as he leaves the tray.

I feel as stuffed as our turkey as we quickly walk up the steps into the Church. I practically knock down Andrew Peterson in the process.

"Happy Christmas Helene! My, you two are *brave* to come to this mass with all these mad little urchins running around! You'll be worn out after this mass, I can tell you!" Andrew's wife laughs heartily. Tanya Peterson is the epitome of elegance. If she were a song she would be Lionel Richie's "Three Times a lady". I think what an amazing wife she would be to an Ambassador. The effusive diplomat's wife with a photographic memory for names and faces. Tanya has only ever met me once. How does she do it? Five children under six and still looking a million dollars. I decide that she is either the Bionic Woman in disguise or a Prozac fiend. When I say this to Dan later, he insists that it's because the Peterson family probably have about eighteen nannies, thirteen housekeepers and ten cleaners. Yes, he might have a point there. Anyway, I'm not going to ruin Christmas day by pouring my heart out to Dan about Andrew! I wouldn't inflict *that* on him!

"Happy Christmas," Andrew mutters mutedly, his eyes downcast. I can't quite bring myself to reply. He's the last person I want to see today... He appears relieved he has his children as armour, they shield him from any social interaction. My heart stops briefly, the post- adrenalin rush only starting to subside half way through "Little Donkey".

"Helene, I think we are going to have to bring up the gifts!" Dan whispers to me half-panicking, half-laughing.

"No way! " I protest. "It's the children's mass. They'll be doing that themselves,"I say assuredly. How wrong I am! It seems all the children are busy playing Joseph or Mary or being a star or something. Before we know it, Dan and I are balancing the water and wine in our shaky hands, delivering them to the bemused priest, before we collapse back in our pew, stifling our giggles.

I can see the outline of Andrew's head a few pews up from me. He looks like a pillar of the community. He's a fraud! I feel like shouting out in the middle of the church. It's impossible not to think of this sorry mess on Christmas day when he is right there in front of me! It's the fallout that bothers me. Poor unsuspecting Tanya and their innocent children. How on earth is she going to cope with the inevitable bombshell? How will I cope? I hum along to "Silent Night" and a silent tear trickles along my cheek. Dan grabs my hand and glances at me quizzically. I smile at him as if to say it's just the beauty of the lyrics of this hymn that have sent me off, not the awful burden of knowing, that the wheels are about to come off my oh so controlled perfect life.

"Good tidings!" Walter announces, bouncing into the hallway of Banville Road like a kangaroo on red bull. Even just looking at him makes me feel tired. Walter is laden down with flowers, chocolates, wine and meticulously gift-wrapped presents for all. He is probably one of the most magnanimous men I have ever had the occasion to encounter, "dispensing largesse with exuberant fervour" as he would say himself. Walter is a human cocktail of charm and colour. Younger than Dan by only two years, he appears and acts a decade less.

"That dinner smells perfectly delicious! I'm absolutely ravenous....what time are we sitting down? Oh dear, there I go again, forgetting my manners! Manners maketh the man, don't you know! Not that *you-know-who* took any cognisance of that!" Walter's intonation goes up an octave towards the end of the sentence. Dan swiftly hands Walter a snipe of pink champagne, more of a ruse to shut him up prior to being subjected to the inevitable soliloquy on his catastrophic love life. "Oh Laurent Perrier Rose! Undeniably my favourite! Back in a dash, my darlings, must powder my nose!" and off he sways in a flurry of blue velvet and highlighted hair.

"Well, he is certainly a character!" I laugh.

Dan rolls his eyes. "Wally is fine in small doses. He has a big heart but his mood is dictated by the amount of attention he gets. One minute he can be the life and soul of the party, the next as petulant as The Grinch at Christmas! Believe me you'll have had enough of him by the end of the day," Dan grimaces affectionately.

Walter returns and I urge Dan to retire to the drawing room with him while I get on with the domestics. I owe it to Dan to plate up an unparalleled feast for his family. It's the least I can do.

I take the turkey out of the oven to rest for the requisite half an hour. I cover it with tinfoil and a teacloth. The scent of roasting turkey indulges my senses, reminding me of childhood years in Devon. Sitting up at the table with my mother, pushing the black thread and big darning needle in and out of the turkey, sealing in the stuffing. I am in a daydream as I butter the Brussels sprouts, arrange the roast potatoes and mash the carrot and parsnip. The smell of homemade gravy wraps itself comfortingly around me. I feel an unexpected pang of nostalgia for my own parents and make a quick mental note to call them in Devon before we sit down to eat. I am putting the Christmas pudding in a pot to boil and dusting the mince pies with flour when the doorbellrings.

"I'll get it!" I holler into Dan and Walter. I don't bother taking off my "I'm Santa's little helper" apron before I answer the door. My face and hair sprayed with stray flour . As a result I am greeted with an unedited roar of laughter from Dan's father and a speedy reprimand from his wife. Anne Goodings pulls me into her bosom for a sincere if slightly suffocating hug. She stoops to place two big presents under the Christmas tree. Her husband, David, pats me fondly on the shoulder and shuffles past me to a royal welcome from his two chalk and cheese sons.

"Let me give you a hand in the kitchen, love," Anne offers courteously, "and I won't be taking no for an answer. It's our territory for now, they can do the wash up later. I hope you have a spare pair of rubber gloves for our Walter, God forbid he has to put those precious hands of his in dirty water. He's worse than a woman you know!" she chuckles. I have to surrender and let her help me. Anne would be insulted if I refused her assistance. "'Tis many a meal I've cooked here for your boyfriend," she confides in me. "He had his dark days after that ex-wife of his left him high and dry. Thank God he's found a good one in you," she says peering at me from under her fringe. Anne is warm and honest. I feel like unburdening everything on her strong solid shoulders but I keep my mouth shut.

"You're a good mum," I say openly.

"Thank you, Helene. You'll be a good mum yourself one day. Now get a move on with those crab claws," she teases, "at least if we can get the starter into them they mightn't get too drunk too quickly. I'd like Dan to say grace when they can still get the significance of the prayer."

We eat until our stomachs ache and drink until our livers give out. David has us in hysterics at charades with his dire attempts at explaining "The Snapper" to his amused audience. The common consensus is that he is a crab with an unusually large belly. Walter does indeed morph into The Grinch since no one is listening any longer to his latest tale of unrequited love, even if the telling of it is highly entertaining. Dan is in his element surrounded by those who love him. I am warm inside from the memory of ringing my parents and hearing the contentedness in their voices. That niggling thought of the New Year and what it holds creeps into my mind occasionally. I distract myself as best I can by concentrating on the moment. Anne amuses me with countless stories of Dan's childhood, not least his penchant for 99's with strawberry ripple sauce on their trips to the funfair in Tramore. Walter becomes maudlin on gin and whinges that he never got as much attention growing up as golden boy Dan. Anne placates him by regaling numerous funny anecdotes of his childhood in turn. Walter laps this up like a toddler on his return from the naughty step.

All the family is staying over in Banville Road. Anne has probably only had two glasses of white wine all day but she would rather stay as that was the original plan. Their car will still be there in the morning to transport herself and David to their usual ten o'clock mass. Anne and David bid goodnight at midnight and retreat to the guest room. By the time we succeed in manoeuvring Walter upstairs it is nearly three o'clock in the morning. This is, of course, after Dan and I endure successive outbursts of tears, then apologies, then tears again. Dan's earlier warning is spot on. Walter, an acclaimed artist, seems to swing between periods of productive elation and abject melancholy. He appears a tortured soul to me. Either that or we can blame it on the gin! Dan and I are asleep as soon as our heads hit the pillow.

CHAPTER 9

"Isn't this the life?" Dan sighs. We are ensconced snugly in front of the TV, watching another black and white classic movie.

"It sure is!" I respond as I sneak another Leonidas chocolate into my mouth. I'm sure Marlene Dietrich could resist the temptation but not I. The post-Christmas days are rolling into one big lounge fest. We wake at our leisure, partake in a hearty brunch then set off on a long walk to wherever takes our fancy. After blowing out the cobwebs all we feel like doing for the rest of the day is to kick off our shoes and warm our cold fingers and toes. Such a simple existence I haven't known for some time. It seems indulgent yet I know I need to recharge my batteries for the year ahead.

Every now and then an unwelcome uninvited thought pops up into my head but Im getting good at pretending that everything is rosy. I consider ringing Murdoch on numerous occasions, particularly after a few glasses of wine. I'm finding it hard to keep schtum to Dan about the impending Peterson & Co fiasco. There is a black cloud hanging around my shoulder, and despite appearances to the contrary, it can darken my mood in an instant. Dan comments on more than one occasion that I seem lost in my own reverie at times. I tend to change the subject or make light of it. Once I know what is contained in Mr. Walsh's report, then I'll be able to weigh up my future as a solicitor. I think I am hoping beyond hope that the whole scenario is just an illusion. That I'll wake up in the morning and the conversation with Andrew will seem like a mirage, that it has all just been a figment of my imagination.

"Your mobile is ringing, again!" says Dan in mock

exasperation, "you better answer it Helene, it's been beeping non-stop since we came home!" he exclaims as he tosses a cushion at me.

I'd begun to doze off on the couch. "Okay, okay!" I surrender. "I'll answer it!" I walk zombie-like into the kitchen. I just miss the call but before I can even check my voicemail it rings again. "Hello?" I say inquisitively.

"Helene, it's Caroline. I'm *so* sorry for disturbing you at this time of the year. I didn't know where else to turn. Everything is such a mess! James has ...." and she breaks off into floods of tears for a few moments. Caroline regains her composure and tries again "James has been having an affair with that woman Leanne O'Toole. She's on the parents' association for Scoil Thomas. Oh the humiliation of it all... what a fucking bitch! Sweet Jesus. What the hell am I supposed to do for crying out loud?! I haven't said anything to James yet. I swear to God, I'd be afraid of what I could do with a kitchen knife, God forgive me! I just can't get my head around this. Oh God, Helene, I don't know what to do?" Caroline wails down the line so badly I hear the phone drop. I can picture her in a ball on the floor, her black mascara leaving a trail of ink along her cheeks, her eyes bloodshot and wild. Shame on you James Murphy.

Although I haven't seen Caroline in a few months, she is a good friend. I can count my close friends on less than one hand. We don't keep a checklist on who calls who last or take umbrage if the other hasn't been in contact recently *but,* and it's a big but, we are always there for one another. Caroline nursed me back to health when The ex-who-shall-remain-nameless left me for my best friend. The ex-best friend-who-shall-remain-nameless was also Caroline's best friend. We helped each other through a difficult time. Now, here we are again. As the first duty of love it to listen, that's exactly what I do.

By the end of the telephone conversation I find myself still listening to her on my mobile as I arrive at her home beside the sea in Monkstown. Luckily James is out for the evening at a Golf Club dinner in some hotel in Wicklow. Caroline and I will have the evening to ourselves. Darryl and Dervila, the twins, are innocently sleeping upstairs, oblivious to the drama unfolding in their family life.

"Thank you so much Helene. I was nearly about to ring The Samaritans before I rang you. I really appreciate you being here,"

Caroline sobs as she embraces me gratefully. I can smell the cigarette smoke the second I walk into the house. "Please don't give out to me for smoking again. I'm not too bothered about my physical health right now, more my bloody mental health. Nearly four years without so much as a drag of nicotine and I've already a splitting headache from smoking this lot." She waves a hand at the overflowing ashtray. "Still, I could have hit the bottle. That would be worse!" she reasons.

"I admire your strength of spirit," I say. We both then laugh at my unintended pun.

"You never fail to cheer me up, hon," Caroline says quietly, "but what on earth am I going to do now?" she asks, exasperated. "I can't believe he has done this to me again."

"What do you mean *again*?" I ask, not knowing if I'll like the response.

"We've been here before," Caroline says, sighing.

"Oh," I say, having no idea what to say next. I had no idea James had ever been unfaithful.

"Yeah. A few years ago. Some wagon he met at the gym. '*It was just sex*' he said at the time. Like as if that was going to make me feel any better," Caroline says, stubbing out another cigarette. "I thought we had put a line under it. I knew we should have gone for counseling at the time but we didn't. And here he is off at it again! I don't know if I can cope this time. I think I've had enough!" she weeps hysterically. "I can just hear him saying the same words all over again, '*I'm sorry Caroline. It won't happen again. It's you I love.*' How am I supposed to believe him this time, Helene?" she says, as I hug her tightly.

"Does he love you?" I ask.

"I think he still does," she replies.

"Do you love him?" I ask in return.

"Of course I love him," she retorts. "Even if he is a cheater and a liar and the lowest form of life, it doesn't mean my feelings have changed. His mobile beeped this morning when he was in the shower. I never, and I mean ever, look at his texts but he had been banging on about this Architect's meeting the night before and seemed really stressed out about the whole thing. I just checked in case it was something urgent about that but lo and behold I read this text 'Hi sexy, so looking forward to the Golf Dinner later. What a great escape we have lined up! Room 69….don't laugh babes! Will have the champagne on ice...can't wait!' of course she signs if off then," Caroline continues, "with I don't know how many X's and O's after her name! The nerve of her! James must be drinking again. He hasn't had a drink in years, it makes him aggressive. I thought I caught a whiff of alcohol off him the other day but I presumed I was imagining things. He has been incredibly cranky recently and forever preening himself in front of the mirror like some overweight peacock! Bloody mid-life crisis, that's what this is!" Caroline barks, putting her head in her hands.

"That one Leanne seems to have been on more hotel pillows than a chocolate mint," I say deadpan. Caroline slowly digests this and erupts into a fit of laughter and tears. "Seriously though, she is the town bike, the monkstown bicycle. I've heard rumours about her before." I add. Caroline is in convulsions by now. "He'll get bored with her, wait till you see, she's all fur coat and no knickers," I state as a matter of fact. Caroline begs me to stop as she says she has a stitch in her side from laughing.

We sit and talk for hours. I urge Caroline not to do anything hasty. I try to be practical in my advice to her. A whole family's future is at stake here.

"Look, I think you have a few choices here," I tell her. "Firstly, you could say nothing to James and hope it'll blow over and you can be smart about that, like not giving him an available spare minute to meet Leanne or pretending you are sick on occasion so in that way you'll frustrate his efforts to meet up with her. Secondly, you tell him you know he is drinking again, set up a meeting with a drink counselor or something and get him back on the wagon, remember this could be a *huge* factor in why he has gone off side, or thirdly, you could also go to a marriage guidance counsellor together and sort our your respective issues. I know James loves you and you still love him. There is still a lot of love between you, I know you'll work it out. It'll just take time," I say as I hug Caroline tightly, in part to comfort her, in part to comfort myself if I'm honest. I'm just glad this is not me, that I am not married myself.

These situations always tend to confirm my support for the "no to marriage" camp. It seems to bring nothing but trouble. Every day at work I meet countless of normal human beings who have been destroyed by infidelity, addiction or just downright contempt in their marriages. I know I'm a cynic but I'd rather be realistic. It's the poor children who suffer the consequences.

"Thank you for everything Helene. I don't know what I would have done without you. I'll sleep on it and pray I do the right thing. I could hit him over the head with a brick if I started to think about it too much! Thanks for looking after me and for listening. You are such a rock of strength." Caroline thanks me profusely as I wave goodbye and head back to Banville Road. It amazes me how wonderful I can be at dishing out advice to someone else, yet totally inept when it comes to myself.

Dan is in bed by the time I get home. I collapse in beside him only to be woken at five o'clock in the morning by my mobile ringing angrily.

"It's that Godforsaken phone of yours again!" Dan groans half-asleep.

"Hullo?" I mumble.

"Thath shonofabitch Shames ishn't home yet. I'm going to ring thath hushband of hershs and tell him whaths going on!" Caroline slurs her words. I knew I shouldn't have left her on her own. What was I thinking? What will the kids do when they see her in this state? It's New Years Eve and there are fireworks at dawn.

"I'm coming straight over, Caroline," I say firmly. "Have a glass of water, I won't be long." I'm afraid to tell her to make a cup of coffee in case she scalds herself with boiling water. I explain everything to Dan hurriedly, throwing on some clothes in the process.

The front door is wide open. I find Caroline slumped in a heap by the kitchen island. The smell of booze is overpowering. I can see bruises on her right arm and leg. She must have fallen heavily on the stone tiles. Thankfully the girls still seem to be asleep upstairs. I try to wake Caroline but fail miserably. I find James's phone number on her mobile and ring him but it goes straight to his voicemail.

Just as I am standing there wondering what on earth I am going to do, James walks into the kitchen.

"What's going on here?" he looks completely taken aback. I can tell he is sober which is a small mercy in the scheme of things. "Caroline found out you are having an affair *again*. This is what you have done to her," I say, putting the blame squarely at his feet. There is no point hiding the truth, now she has drunk herself into a stupor. James looks in the other direction, making no obvious effort to assist his crumpled wife. "I don't want to get involved James but

I suggest that right now you help me get Caroline up to bed or at least into the settee in the living room. I'm sure you don't want Daryll or Dervila to see her in this condition," I say in a practical manner.

James remains silent.

We work together and succeed in covering Caroline with a blanket on the couch, drawing the curtains and leaving her to sleep it off.

"Sort it out James, "I tell him maternally. "You don't realise how much you stand to lose if you don't." James just stares blankly ahead. He knows I have enough experience in these matters. "Happy New Year!" I add sarcastically. I try not to be judgmental but I can't resist a jibe. I should know better. There are always two sides to every story with the truth somewhere in the middle. I get back into Dan's car, once again, and make my way home. I remind myself that it is always the darkest hour before the day. At least Caroline is having her dark hour now, mine is yet to come. God help me.

As optimistic as I am by nature, the wheels of fate are already in motion to career me right off track. I notice another unintended pun and smile to myself. I crawl back into bed with Dan. I can't sleep. All I can think of is poor, poor Caroline. Despite my allegiance to her, I know James must be hurting too. When did life become this complicated? Wasn't everything much simpler when we were younger or has nostalgia fogged my memory? For what does it profit a man to gain the whole world yet lose his soul?

CHAPTER 10

The frivolous and frenetic days of Christmas are over. That queasy feeling in the pit of my stomach is back with a vengeance. It never really went away, it just festered slowly over the holiday, culminating now into a mass of nauseating stress. I walk in the revolving doors of Peterson & Co. not knowing what to expect yet knowing enough to surmise that it won't be pleasant. When will the proverbial shit hit the fan? Will it happen today or tomorrow?

I want to call Murdoch who hasn't been far from my thoughts over the break but term doesn't recommence for another week. No doubt he is still across in Clifden making the most of family life. It seems to me that Barristers take the same holidays as teachers. Of course Barristers are at pains to tell you that it is during these periods of recess that they catch up on all their paperwork but I wonder. Or maybe as a lowly solicitor I'm just plain jealous.

I scan my diary for the week ahead. I am focusing intently on this simple task when Yvonne walks into my office.

"I have a referral for you, Sandra Mulhall. She says she got your name from Murdoch Pierce who is a friend of hers. She is splitting up from her husband and they are looking for a family law Mediator. The only thing is that it's pretty urgent by the sounds of things. Her husband has apparently left the family home already but they can't agree at all on access to their kids. If she is the same Sandra Mulhall I'm thinking of she is the one off that TV3 programme? You know your one who does the celebrity clothes show? Basically they show you, like, all the latest trends the stars are wearing and then..." Yvonne is on a roll. If I don't interrupt her yarn she'll go on forever. I've learnt from experience to stop her mid-flight otherwise we never hit the runway.

"I'll meet herself and her husband at four this afternoon. Please courier over the Mediation Information Form and a copy of the Mediation Agreement to both of them this morning. Ask them to courier back the MIF to me before two this afternoon and they can sign the Mediation Agreement in our first session," I tell Yvonne who appears slightly deflated that I haven't indulged her forensic programme analogy. I am not inclined towards small talk.

I am beginning to wonder why on earth I agreed to take on a mediation at all today. Truly you need to be in a Zen frame of mind to undertake the role of Family Law Mediator. The mediation process can be emotionally fraught for the participants. For this reason the Mediator needs to be centred. I am rethinking my decision when my desk phone buzzes in that high-pitched tone I have come to despise.

"Helene McBain," I say languidly.

"It's Andrew," says the voice on the other end of the line. "Happy New Year, Helene. Can you make yourself available at half two this afternoon for a partner's meeting? Boardroom 8."

Andrew does not wait for a reply. A picture board of scenarios clogs up my already foggy brain. I ask Yvonne to cancel the freshly made consultation with Sandra Mulhall and her husband. I don't give an explanation but just ask her to rearrange the appointment for a time later in the week. I know it is urgent but I am in no state to help anyone. I cannot see straight not to mind mediate. In fact I think I need to self- medicate. If I had a valium I'd swallow one in a heartbeat.

I miss Dan already. Have I created a distance between us by withholding how I am really feeling? Can I confide in him, should I confide in him? I am innately mistrustful of people but I know deep down that Dan would support me. What is stopping me? I think I am afraid that if I tell him then it becomes my reality. If I say nothing it might just go away. Just disappear. I am pretending everything is the same when I know deep down that everything isn't. That everything is about to radically change. I feel like I am on death row waiting patiently yet anxiously for the bell to sound, the whistle to blow for my last meal before my execution. I am weary with worry.

At twelve I navigate myself through a tense meeting with a disgruntled client, Sean Tynan. I suffer the wrath of this irate husband arguing over our legal fees. Consciously he is disputing the fees, unconsciously he is arguing with the fact that he has to give his wife any money at all. He just wants someone to blame and I happen to be the scapegoat. Lucky me. It takes all of my wherewithal to hold my tongue. I sit there imagining a smorgasbord of castration options. I have held Sean's hand through a contentious and laborious divorce, going beyond the normal call of duty.

"You did well out of your divorce Sean," I tell him confidently. "If the case had run in front of Judge Delaney you would not have faired so well. And that's an understatement. I know his form and he would not have taken kindly to your blatant disregard for the discovery process. Your wife's settlement was a lot kinder to you than it was to her. She may have retained the family home but you have held on to all your investment properties, not to mention joint custody of your children and the other matters which we won't mention." I look at him squarely when I say this. Sean knows I suspect he accepts an extensive amount of cash in hand. He is too shrewd and I can't prove it (apart from the fact that I don't want to know as I have a duty under the money laundering regulations to report anything of this nature). In other words he has done better out of this settlement than he is actually letting on.

"We sent you a section 68 letter with regard to our fees at the outset of this case. I am not prepared to reduce our fees any further. You must bear in mind the sheer number of billing hours and work that has gone into your file over the last two years. We have given you the most expert advice. In our view you have emerged from this divorce with the best possible outcome." I see Sean grimacing at this as if he was being given a poison chalice.

"The law is what it is," I continue. "We had to negotiate for you within the backdrop of the High Court and in anticipation of what Judge Delaney might have ruled. I will expect full payment of our Invoice within the normal twenty eight day period. If this is not forthcoming I will have no option but to issue proceedings for the recovery of this debt. We can also refer the matter to taxation if you so desire. I should warn you though that this is at your peril as the taxing master will, in my view, allow for a much more substantial figure than we have billed. Nevertheless, I'll leave you to make up your mind on it."

I leave Sean sitting there, his eyes pointed at me as if I was

Goebbels himself. I am in no humour to pander to ungracious clients. As my mentor always told me, get your money as you get no thanks for not doing so. I have delivered a service and I expect payment as agreed. Yet it is on days like this that I feel like throwing in the towel. It hurts not to be appreciated when you give more than a hundred per cent commitment to your profession. You don't hear of people arguing over their Doctor's bill?

"Happy New Year!" I hear Conor say cheerily, "I'm dreading this meeting with Andrew now. No doubt he'll have new year resolutions coming out our asses by the end of it!" he complains.

"Conor, please!" I say, admonishing his turn of phrase. I like Conor but sometimes he is over zealous in his heart-in-the-right-place desire to have me treated as one of the guys. Sometimes I just want to be a lady, despite the fact that I might be a minx underneath.

"Is it half two already?" I panic, then realise I have enough time for a coffee and a wrap before the big partner's meeting.

Conor sits with me while Yvonne runs to fetch me a chicken caesar wrap and my skinny latte. "What's up, Helene? You seem elsewhere...are you still pining after Dan the man?" he teases.

"I'm just hungry" I mutter. How can I say anything to Conor? If Andrew has something to tell, surely this meeting is going to be about that? Conor chats amiably about his Christmas holidays, how Santa brought a puppy for the children and the finer details of his wife's delivery of their fourth child. I nearly choke on my wrap at his persistence in telling me midwifery details that I really don't want to know about. I gulp down the rest of my coffee while Conor trails behind me. He is rambling on about the agenda for the meeting but my thoughts have wandered off in a different direction. I am wondering what agenda Andrew himself has for the meeting. Will Andrew tell the rest of the partners what is going on? Do I have a duty to tell them if he doesn't?

There is an air of joviality in the room when Conor and I get there. This always happens when the male partners get together. All that male testosterone between them. There is lots of high- spirited banter as we sit around the boardroom and wait for Andrew. Elaine, his tolerant PA, tells us that he is on his way. I nod and smile at appropriate intervals yet I am still lost in my own reverie. I cannot switch off my thoughts and am dreading seeing Andrew walk in the door. Nietzche once said never to gaze into an abyss too long or the abyss will gaze back into you. Am I going to be proof of this?

"Good afternoon everyone!" Andrew booms as he marches into the boardroom. "I trust you all had a wonderful Christmas. Let's start then with the first matter on the agenda..." he proceeds authoritatively. I note that his confidence belies a deep apprehension. Andrew is doing his best to hide his nerves but the downcast eyes, transfixed on the Agenda are a give away. He is avoiding eye contact, especially with me. Does he wonder if I have said anything to the other partners? What information will he share with all of us today? I have raised no points on any of the first four items on the Agenda. I cannot concentrate at all on what anyone else is saying. I am single-mindedly focused on Any Other Business. Why is Andrew keeping up this charade? What is there to be gained by calmly discussing all other items on the Agenda as if nothing has happened? I am silently screaming inside. Suddenly I am aware that no one is speaking. I look up and watch Andrew remove his glasses, fold them neatly and place them on the Agenda sheet in front of him. I know from experience that this is when Andrew gets serious. His eyes remain on the sheet in front of him. He appears as if he could burst into tears at any given moment.

"Elaine, could you please bring in the copies of Mr. Walsh's report?" Andrew asks Elaine on speakerphone, uncharacteristically quietly, not to mind politely. Elaine appears on the double like a frightened rabbit. Little does she know that she needn't be frightened of him anymore. He looks like he just walked out of his suit and left it sitting by itself on his chair.

"Elaine is passing around the Law Society's investigating accountant's report to each one of you. I'd ask that you refrain from reading it until after this meeting as you will have a lot to digest. What I will tell you, however, is that there are–" Andrew breaks off, and swallows quickly. He takes a deep breath. "Breaches of the solicitors' regulations. It is with great regret that I have to confess that these breaches are as a result of my own wrongdoing. I am guilty of using client's monies for my own use and benefit. Although I would like to point out that I had every intention of replacing the monies taken, it was really just a loan and just for a short period but I suppose that's neither here nor there now," he says as if looking for sympathy. Where is this guy's ethics? Is he for real? "It is more my regret that you will all come under the same scrutiny but there is nothing now that I can do to rectify matters." Andrew continues as if it actually makes a difference what he says now. It would be like getting a half-hearted apology from your child's murderer. You can't turn back the clock!

There is utter silence in the boardroom of Peterson & Co. solicitors. I feel a jolt through my body. The hairs on Conor's arms are standing up in fright.

"I understand that the Law Society will apply on Monday for orders freezing the accounts of this Firm. They also want my practising certificate suspended. In this regard I would urge you all to seek legal advice in relation to your own exposure," he continues, finding his stride, and as if he is casually talking about the weather. I feel like vomiting. None of us can look at each other. No one utters a single word. We are united in shock. Jesus, this is happening. What in God's name are we going to do?

"I will be leaving Peterson & Co directly following this meeting. I simply wanted to impart this knowledge to you myself out of courtesy–"

"Well, that's fucking big of you Andrew," Conor interrupts him unexpectedly but hardly surprisingly.

Andrew goes instantly pale.

"You fucking bastard! And the fancy house in France and your villa in Spain and your fucking e-class Mercedes, not to mention your private helicopter. We must have been blind! What the fuck were you thinking?" Conor shouts loudly at him. "You better not bring me or anyone else here in this room down with you, Andrew Peterson, you sonofabitch motherfucker or I swear to God I'll cut off your balls and hang you out to dry!"

Andrew is speechless for once. He just sits there, bedraggled like the velveteen rabbit. Except that in this instance the rabbit is about to be hung, drawn and quartered.

Another partner, Stephen, has started to bawl crying which only serves to escalate the tension. We always call him sensitive Stephen and slag him off about it. This time I just feel an overwhelming sense of compassion for him. He is a good skin. None of us should be put in this predicament! We don't deserve it! All the years of unwavering dedication to Peterson & Co and this is how we are thanked in return! Truly a travesty!

I sense that Conor could punch Andrew at any given moment. Elaine, who has been hovering somewhere by the door, catches my eye and thankfully has the cop- on to call security. Andrew takes his leave, accompanied by a six foot tall and four foot wide security man on either side. He has no idea of the trail of destruction he has left behind him. Conor looks like he is going to have a heart attack, red-cheeked and breathless. The rest of us just sit in the boardroom wondering how on earth this came to be and why it had to happen to us. I take a quick glance at Mr. Walsh's report. I read that the regulation committee of the Law Society had met to discuss the report over Christmas. The chairman of the committee describes the investigating accountant's report as one of the most serious and damaging reports ever put before the committee. Great!

"Fuck Helene," Conor says to me.

"I know Conor, I know," I reply resignedly.

We sit in solidarity and contemplate the awfulness of our situation.

"Fuck Helene," Conor says again.

"I know Conor, I know," I repeat.

CHAPTER 11

I wake up feeling wretched the morning after Andrew's cataclysmic bombshell. I decide my stomach is just about brave enough to digest some toast and a cup of earl grey tea. The central heating must be on the blink. It's freezing in my bedroom. I start coughing uncontrollably all of a sudden and have a flashback to chain smoking all kinds of cigarettes in the wee hours of the morning. What was I drinking last night? I feel horrific. I cover my wounded body with Dan's dressing gown and put woolly socks on my feet. My legs are barely capable of supporting the rest of my body. I hobble out of our bedroom door and over to the staircase.

Who is that lying on our spare room bed? The door is ajar, a pair of black slip-on shoes nearby. I glimpse a blue-suited male with brown hair spread-eagled across the bed. My heart skips a beat. I know it's not Dan, he is away in Birmingham this week. He practically never wears a suit to work either. Gradually my memory returns and Conor's familiar form rescues me from a rising panic. Thank God for that!

I decide to leave him sleep while I make us some breakfast, not expecting to find sensitive Stephen on the couch in the drawing room and another partner of Peterson & Co, David, on the couch in the TV room. Memories of last night's raucous behaviour come back to haunt me. I remember blasting Michael Jackson's "Billy Jean" in the living room with the aid of Dan's precious Bang & Olufsen speakers. There is some vague memory of dancing too but I brush it to the back of my mind. Don't really want to torture myself altogether.

Apart from the fact that I'm not a sado masochist, I am under no illusion that my roommates will fill me in on the details. That is, of course, if they can remember themselves. It is extremely doubtful, judging by the *detruit* in Banville Road this morning that anyone was even vaguely sober last night.

From the kitchen I turn on the central heating and make preparations for a big fry-up for my errant housemates. Luckily my local supermarket delivers online and I ordered a full fridge for the week while Dan is away. My hands tremble as I take out the necessary cooking utensils and ingredients. Rashers, eggs, tomatoes, mushrooms, black pudding, sausages. I grab a can of beans as an afterthought as I figure that since Dan likes them maybe my sleeping beauties do too.

Who is that snoring? If Dan saw me buttering toast for a selection of male overnight guests I don't think he'd be too happy somehow. As if on cue. "Danny Boy" comes up on the display screen of my mobile.

"Good afternoon sleepy head! Did you sleep it out? I've rang you about three times this morning already," he says affectionately. A quick glance at the kitchen clock and I see that it's nearly one o'clock. I can't believe I slept in this late in the day.

"Hi honey, I must have," I say, definitely not lying. "I stayed up late watching some old movie on the TV and fell asleep on the couch," I add, definitely lying this time. "I feel much better today, thank God," I lie again. I have another one of those flashbacks reminding me that I had texted Dan last night letting him know I was sick and staying out of work today.

"So, what's it like being back to work?" Dan asks, "as busy as ever, no doubt? I got your text last night so as you asked I didn't call you. We were up to our eyes in negotiations all bloody night. I'll be home on Saturday morning on the red eye. Keep the bed warm for me and I am glad you are feeling better. It could have just been a bout of the January blues or an I'm–allergic-to-being-back-at-work virus!" he jokes. If only he knew.

"It could be, it could be," I play along with the joke. "Call me tomorrow if you can. I miss you." I add sincerely because I do miss him. I also know that I'll have to tell him everything when he gets home.

"Miss you too babes. Talk to you tomorrow." Dan hangs up while blowing me air kisses into the receiver.

I really don't deserve such a good man, I think to myself. Here I am, being duplicitous about everything, whilst wearing his dressing gown, in his kitchen and cooking up a fry for three men he has never met! Innocent as it may actually be I resolve to come clean in all departments upon his return. I'll buy a nice bottle of his favourite red wine and with the aid of the dictum *in vino veritas* I'll put matters to right once and for all. I owe it to him.

"Jaysus, Helene! What time is it?" Conor is standing at the kitchen door looking like a pale, creased version of himself.

"Time for brunch!" I say brightly, trying to make an effort to appear none the worse for wear. I pour Conor a long, tall glass of orange juice which he drinks in one swift gulp. I let him pour himself a second glass as I go to wake David and Stephen. They both look content in their sleep. Do I want to be responsible for waking them from the sanctuary of sleep back into their living nightmare? For a split second they won't recall yesterday's events, then slowly their minds will re-fresh their memories.. At least they will have some food in their bellies to help then face the day, albeit feeling hungover and looking like death warmed up.

"This is a fine bit of grub, Mom!" David chuckles as he tucks into his third slice of toast with his third fried egg and rasher. David's belly hardly fits between the chair and the table. Naturally he is subjected to the usual slagging match from the other two fine fit specimens who pride themselves on their honed physiques. Or at least that's what they perceive them to be. It is with great satisfaction I watch none of them hold back their appetites today. They eat with relish and appreciation. I begin to feel like a mother hen feeding her hungry brood. Even Stephen, who to my eyes, looks like he only ever eats lettuce and muesli, seems to be enjoying every morsel. That is, right up until he starts sobbing agitatedly, with his head in his hands, much to the alarm of the rest of us.

"Stephen, for God's sake, not again," Conor says bluntly. "We had enough of your tears last night. I thought we had talked this through at length," he lectures, as if to a child.

"That's news to me," David adds sheepishly. "I don't remember much from last night at all." It is certainly news to me too. I can't recollect any such conversation. "I *do* remember Helene though, giving us an ab fab rendition of a pole-dance with the sweeping brush!" David says, guffawing loudly. "That's definitely one for Youtube. Tina Turner's "Private Dancer" will never be the same again. I'll hold that vision in my head for years to come." David laughs his head off. Conor joins in and even Stephen can't help but chortle to himself.

"Very funny,"I say, simultaneously getting up to start clearing the table in an attempt to re-direct the slagging elsewhere. I start loading the dishwasher.

"Seriously though, Conor. What did we agree last night, if anything?" I hear David enquire. "I can't remember a bloody thing. It's not surprising the way my head is pounding at the moment. You don't happen to have any Nurofen or Solpadeine handy, Helene, do you? I'm in bits here. It's just hitting me now, I think," he whines.

I bring over a packet of Anadin which is all I can find in the medicine box. I continue to tidy up while Conor is left with the burden of having to explain once again what we apparently discussed last night.

"As you all know the Law Society will apply next Monday for orders freezing the accounts of Peterson & Co. as it is suspected of dishonesty. You might recall that I managed to find out through a barrister friend of mine that when the matter came before Mr. Justice John White on an *ex parte* basis, he ruled there was no basis for it to be heard in private." Stephen is on the cusp of tears again, until David gives him a don't-you-dare stare. "Having read the affidavit of Mr. Barnaby Walsh, no sniggers at the name again please, and after hearing submissions from counsel for the society, the judge said he was satisfied to allow the society apply on Monday for the various orders, including suspending Mr. Andrew Peterson's practising certificate along with all the other *partners'* practising certificates and freezing the Firm's accounts," Conor recounts, clearly recoiling at the last sentence.

"Jesus Christ," I say, instinctively.

"Jesus Christ is right," David says. Stephen's head is heavy again and back in his hands. "Mr. Justice White said he was satisfied the matter required the urgent attention of the High Court and he has listed it on Monday before the president of the High Court."

Conor continues, visibly not enjoying his role as messenger. "It seems the Regulation of Practice Committee of the Law Society has expressed concerns that Peterson & Co, well, we know it was that bastard Andrew Peterson, allegedly gave undertakings to various financial institutions to stamp and register deeds when not in funds to do so. Not alone that, the conniving prick, went one further and managed to borrow money from a substantial range of banks and building societies without furnishing proper security for the borrowings in the form of mortgages on his own properties. Andrew was building a substantial property portfolio using those borrowings. Separate to acting as a solicitor he was also receiving deposits from property investors who expected to buy developed properties from him in due course," Conor concludes, obviously deflated by the content of his speech.

"So basically the bastard has been raising and receiving finance in his own name but paying it into the client account! I could figure that much out myself from Barnaby Walsh or whatever his name is, in that report. The reality must be, then, that there is an absence of executed or registered mortgages on the properties on which the loans were advanced?" David poses an incredulous rhetorical question.

"Happy New Year," I say, feeling the way Stephen looks. "The Media are going to go wild on this one. They hate us solicitors as it is. Those journalists out for blood will be in their element. I can't believe it won't be heard *in camera*. It's bad enough having to go through all this without the world and its mother knowing every damn thing. We just need to get ourselves the best legal representation available," I add, solemnly. I don't mention my chat with Murdoch. What's the point? It's not as if it'll make a whit bit of difference at this stage.

"If we had just caught him *in flagrante delicto*, we might have been able to exonerate ourselves from all liability," Stephen says, forlornly.

"We will exonerate ourselves from all liability!" Conor retorts with derision. "There is no way I am being implicated in that asshole's corruption."

"Hear! Hear!" David remarks.

I don't bother mentioning Section 5 of the Partnership Act. They'll find out for themselves soon enough. I am certain they all know deep down what lies ahead. We all know the implications of becoming a partner in Peterson & Co. For far too long we were riding the crest of a wave, none of us could have foreseen this.

"Action must be proportionate to the aim being sought. If we are to try and come up with some sort of defence, we need to look forward, get proper legal advice and put up a united front," I advise my co-defendants for what its worth.

"What kind of conscience does Andrew have? He must be some kind of sociopath. I mean, he must have no feelings at all for anyone but himself. You'd never have known by looking at him what he was up to," Stephen comments, looking as perplexed as the rest of us. "Andrew obviously has no conscience; he doesn't seem to have any internal moral authority on important issues," he continues.

"Well, to quote Shakespeare, there's no art to find the mind's construction in the face," says Conor gloomily.

"Didn't think you were the literary type, Conor!" I remark, genuinely surprised that such an alpha male has a poet residing somewhere inside.

"I'm not. It's written on the table mat in front of me," he replies deadpan.

This causes us all to erupt in laughter and lightens the mood considerably. If we have ever needed a sense of humour its now. Gradually all my overnight guests make their way home to their respective houses. They will probably all have a lot to answer to when their wives see the state of them.

Perhaps though, on the second cup of tea, the wife's anger towards her husband might soften when she hears the truth. She will realise the true extent of Andrew's deceit. The shock reality of her plight will hit home in no uncertain terms. Will her husband convince her of his innocence? How will these wives react when their weekly extravagant budget is, dramatically reduced? Because theres nothing surer…that'll be the first to go. As my mother always says, it is one thing to go up in the world, it is another to go down.

I finish tidying up and return to the sanctuary of my bedroom for a nap. I am only just holding down my brunch, my hands are clammy and my head throbs. Sleep beckons as a tempting enticer. I fall asleep heavily as if dead to the world.

I awake with a start. Dazed and scared, I slowly come around from a cacophony of dream-like states, none pleasurable, all portentous. I find myself behind bars, naked and alone. A dirty bucket serves as my commode, my bed a straw and bug-infested mat. My bald head like a shorn sheep, I cower in the corner, shaking from the cold. I wipe real tears from my face as I jump out of bed, as if to shake off this veiled threat of subterfuge.

I know that I need to talk to Murdoch. He may still be in Clifden but I need some advice now on the best course of action. I shower enthusiastically, washing away the remnants of my fragmented dreams. I sit on the drawing room couch and call Murdoch's mobile number. It rings.

"Hi Murdoch. It's Helene. I hope I'm not disturbing you?" I ask, feeling self-conscious all of a sudden.

"Not at all Helene. I am just doing some research here on my PC. Frances is making the dinner as I speak so I can talk for a few minutes. How are things? I hope you had a lovely break at Christmas and were duly pampered. A good looking girl like you should be waited on hand and foot," Murdoch sleazes. The irony of it, I think, with his poor wife waiting on him hand and foot.

"Eh, yes, Murdoch. Anyway, I won't keep you long. I just want to make an appointment to see you next week if at all possible. There have been some serious developments as I anticipated with regard to Peterson & Co..." I tell Murdoch that my worst fears about Andrew have been realised. Murdoch interjects with "I see" or "hmmm" occasionally. Finally, when he thinks I've finished, he calmly says, "Res Ipsa Loquitur."

"The facts speak for themselves??" I translate. "That's quite an ambiguous thing to say, Murdoch! Is that it?"

"Oh, don't be jumping to any conclusions, Helene. Let's meet next Wednesday, as I said, and we'll have a proper consultation then. I must dash. Frances tells me the honeyed ham needs to be carved. Must attend to my manly duties!" Murdoch says, painting a picture of the honourable husband. Not that I am that gullible.

"Of course," I reply. "See you next week." I press the red button on my Blackberry.

I sit on my couch staring into space, not feeling any better. Where is this all going to lead? Murdoch isn't giving much away. Surely I'm not going to be implicated in this fraud as well? I haven't done anything wrong! I know Im innocent. I've got to fight my corner. I am not going to be the fall guy for another man's sins; no way.

96 NEGLIGENT BEHAVIOUR

CHAPTER 12

I am licking my wounds the next day, like a cat crawling out of a dog-fight when Andrew Peterson's mobile number comes up on my phone. Against my better judgement I answer it. How he thinks he can have anything worthwhile to say to me is beyond my comprehension. Much to my surprise it's his wife Tanya.

"Helene! Thank you for taking my call! You probably thought it was Andrew but he has left his mobile here on the kitchen island and I have no idea where he is. He has told me everything and I have to tell you I am beyond disgusted! I had no idea that this was going on. It's just a complete nightmare. He went out yesterday evening after we had a row and I can't track him down in his usual haunts. I found your number in his phone. I hope you don't mind me ringing you as I'm sure you are angry yourself but I didn't know who else to call. Have you seen him recently?" Tanya says and I hear her voice falter.

"No. I haven't seen him since the day before yesterday when he filled us in on the extent of his deceit. You do realise that his actions could result in all us other partners being implicated as well? This is really serious Tanya!" I exclaim loudly. I really don't believe Tanya had anything to do with her husband's skulduggery but I can't help being angry.

"Helene, you have to believe me when I tell you that I don't even understand half of what he said to me!" Tanya says pleadingly. I can hear the quiet desperation in her voice. "I just know that it's obviously illegal, whatever he did. He left after we had a row and I haven't seen him since. He could be dead for all I know. Maybe if you could explain to me what was going on maybe

I could help rectify all this? I couldn't get a proper explanation from Andrew at all, that's the reason he left! Can you please explain it to me, I'm begging you? Is it something to do with Peterson Holdings, his property company? I know he was spending a lot of time recently working on promoting its business in Spain. There was talk of his first major East-European project in Romania I think as well, or maybe it was Hungary. God, I don't know Helene. I ran the house, Andrew ran the business. Please tell me, I need to know! I'm at the end of my tether!" Tanya confides, her usual composure shook to the core.

How can I not help her? How can I not assist someone who is practically in the same boat as I am? At least I don't have four children in private schools, their good name tarnished forever. I struggle with what to say to her. I can hardly explain to myself what Andrew has done, not to mind his own wife!

"Andrew is a con-artist," I reply flatly, thinking at the same time it's the understatement of the year.

"What do you mean a con-artist?" Tanya says, puzzled.

"Well, to be honest, it would appear that he had a great scam on the go," I say, wondering how I am going to explain this to her.

"What kind of scam?" she asks, gravely. "I really need to know Helene."

"Right, well, look," I say, "I'll try and spell it out as best as I can. Basically when a property was bought by our Firm for a client, the client could apply for a loan to say, for example, the SBS building society, ok?"

"Yes" she says.

"If the Loan approval was, for say, €300,000, the SBS building society would pay that over on the strength of an undertaking from our Firm to lodge the deeds and mortgage with them in due course, ok?" I ask.

"Yes" Tanya says.

"In the meantime," I continue, "Andrew was taking out multiple mortgages on the *same* property at the *same* time from other Lending Institutions or Banks, none of which knew about each other as the deeds had not yet been registered in the Land Registry. Are you still with me?" I ask Tanya.

"Yes, I understand," she replies, her voice falterning

"So as well as the €300,000 SBS building society loan, he could have drawn down five or six other loans for €300,000 each on the same property. He was therefore pocketing the extra monies for his own use and he could have raised maybe 1.8 million on the strength of a single property. Do you follow me?" I ask Tanya.

"I, I think so," she replies quietly.

"All of the banks would have thought they were the only mortgagee on that property when in reality there were multiple mortgagees. The solicitor's undertaking was sufficient for them to release the funds. Do you follow?" I ask Tanya again, still checking she is following me.

"Yes, I think so." she sighs.

"In other words, Tanya, it would appear that your husband was using this money to fund the breakneck expansion of his property business as well as his own personal property empire," I say, gritting my teeth. It nearly kills me to say these words but I'm trying to keep it together.

"Oh. I see. Right, Heavens above," Tanya says.

Heavens above! Is that all she is going to say?

"So how much is missing?" Tanya continues before I have a chance to say something I might regret. "I mean, how much do we need to put back? Like I'm sure if we sell off a few of our properties or whatever we'll be able to pay the banks back most of their money anyway, wouldn't we?" she queries, naively.

"All 180 million of it?" I reply, without a trace of sarcasm.

"Oh. I see. God. Are you sure it's that much Helene? I mean, how could he have raised that much money?" Tanya says, baffled by her own question.

"I've been asking myself that every minute of every day Tanya!" I say, stifling a scream. "If you don't know that, how could I possibly know? Not that his motivation makes a whit bit of difference at this stage. What's done, is done," I say, trying to be philosophical before I lose it altogether. "Look, I know it's not your fault but I really don't think it's a good idea that we are talking about this at all. You can understand that I have my own immediate concerns right now. I'm sure Andrew will come home soon. I really should go now," I say, apologetically.

"I understand, Helene. I do appreciate you talking to me," she says, gratefully. "I just still can't really believe that Andrew would do such a thing. I'm not trying to be difficult here, but are you *sure* it's him that did this? I mean, he's just not like that! He's the most generous man you'd ever meet!" she says and I know that she is in denial. Maybe if she actually thinks about this she might realise why he is so generous!

"I know it's a shock Tanya," I say, in an attempt to normalise what she is feeling. "Sometimes people do things we have no control over," I say as I find myself thinking about my ex-boyfriend and my best friend. "Look, I have to go here," I say abruptly. "For what it's worth I wish you all the best," I say as she hangs up reluctantly.

I'm not sure who I feel sorriest for. Neither of us has fully grasped the sheer scale of destruction Tanya's husband has caused. His greed has catapulted us both into a state of confusion and insecurity. The whirlwind of desire corrupts a simple heart. Was Andrew's heart ever simple? Andrew must have known that such a scheme could be uncovered by a Law Society audit but, with this property boom showing only tiny signs of abating at the time, he probably thought he could easily make enough money to ensure nobody was left out of pocket. How arrogant of him!

Andrew was in pursuit of such tawdry trophies as status, wealth and success. This was his nirvana, the pinnacle of his search for enlightenment. His arrogance propelled him onwards in his addictive intoxication with all that glittered, none of which was gold. I'll be damned if he'll bring me down with him.

The pressures of keeping the scheme afloat were beginning to take their toll on him, particularly when Mr. Walsh, the face of the Law Society came knocking on his door. How long would he have kept up this charade? If the Law Society had not been regulating its members, would any of us partners ever have uncovered the truth? Ignorance of the law is no excuse. I have no defence to say I didn't know. None of us do. It doesn't matter. I have been duped by my own profession! The profession I have believed in since I was a young child. I remember debating in inter- school championships thinking how great it would be to be a real advocate, to promote justice in the world, to make a difference. Here I am now, bitten by the hand that fed me or have I fed the hand that bit me? Andrew Peterson will go down as an icon of unbridled greed. Greed, the mother of all sins.

I miss Dan. His smell, his touch, his face. I feel lonely without him. I consider ringing Caroline but think better of it. I am sure she has enough on her plate after all the Christmas drama. I ring Dan but his message goes straight to voicemail. I receive a text two minutes later telling me he is in a meeting and can't talk but he'll call me later. I turn on the radio, grab a book to read and try to relax. The Lithuanian cleaning lady, Sonja, tiptoes in as I am drinking a coffee and smoking a cigarette in the living room.

"I know, don't give out! I haven't quite managed to quit yet. I'm working on it. I've just too much going on at the moment..." I blurt out spontaneously. She is the first human being I have seen in two days, her familiarity a welcome reprieve from me, myself and I.

"Don't vorry about it," Sonja soothes. "I smoke myself sometimes. Specially when Im sad. You look a bit sad I tink," she remarks gently. Before I have any handle on my emotions, splashes of tears fall from my eyes, leaving big puddles on the pages of my favourite book. I needed a good cry. I need to release all the pent-up anger, frustration, upset and sheer trauma that has been inflicted upon me over the last few weeks. I cannot keep my guard up anymore. My vulnerability is to the fore. I feel lost and lonely. Everything I believe in has come crashing down around my ears. I need to take up my shovel and start re-building my strength, my confidence. Thank God I have Dan anyway. I know he will stand by me and support me.

"Good to cry. Good to cry," Sonja whispers. The poor girl just wanted to empty the wastepaper basket and embark on a bit of dusting, instead she got a self-pitying woman in her mid-thirties bawling like a hyena on the living room couch. God bless her. I am grateful to her for allowing me an opportunity to let it all out.. Above all I appreciate her lack of judgment and her discretion in not probing any further into the cause of this meltdown. I couldn't explain it to her as I can't even explain it to myself. I feel calmer afterwards and rest on the couch for a while, the silence only intermittently disturbed by the soft moan of Sonja and her Dyson hoover.

My secretary, Yvonne, has tried to call me a few times during the day. She is probably completely mystified as to what's going on. I will call her tomorrow. I need to tell my parents too. No doubt this will be next week's flamboyant headlines. I can already hear the blood-thirsty journalists braying at my door, itching for an angle, a photo worth a thousand words. Whatever about fame, infamy is certainly not a pill I wanted to swallow. I must harness any brain cells I have left to defend myself from the wrath of the Law Society which will, no doubt, follow

God, I really do miss Dan. I won't be able to cope with this battle ahead of me without him. He's a rock of sense and I'm not exactly thinking straight at the moment. My head is all over the place!

"Hi honey. I can't wait to see you tomorrow!" I chirp to Dan, who rings me just as I come around from my little nap.

"You're still at home then?" he questions. "I rang your office but the phone number rang out. Maybe I dialled the wrong number? I probably did, to be honest. I'm not thinking straight at the moment with the stress of this deal going down. Are you still not better? Poor baby. Well, do you want the good news or the bad news?" he says earnestly.

"The bad news," I reply. Better to get that out of the way first.

"I won't be home tomorrow. I'm sorry. It'll be next weekend. Too much going on here, I'm afraid. Now, before you say anything, ask me the good news?"

"What's the good news?" I ask feebly, totally gutted.

"To make up for this weekend I am whisking you off on a surprise weekend on the weekend I am home, to a five star destination that you are going to just *adore*! No expense spared. The best of, and I mean the best of style, luxury, opulence. You name it, you'll have it. Will you forgive me now?" Dan pleads.

"There was no need to do that Dan. I don't need grand gestures from you, but that's not to say I won't relish every minute! I'll look forward to it. I miss you though hon. I've been feeling really poorly over the last few days," I tell him, half hoping me might guess that there is more to my "illness" than a mere physical ailment. He doesn't.

"Lots of Lemsip and sleep. There is a great hot water bottle in the hot press. It has a really soft cover on it so bring that up to bed with you. You can pretend it's me keeping you warm.! You know I'd be home if I could. We are so close to nailing this deal, I just can't afford to uproot right now. Come here, I have to go! Matthew is looking for me. Love you loads babes. Talk to you later."

Dan's voice disappears. I hold the phone close to me, relishing his last words. They are manna from heaven to my hungry ears.

How I miss him! How did childless wives survive all those years ago when their husbands were out at work, or worse, working abroad? Too many hours in the day to occupy oneself. With no children, no cleaning, no pets, no project of any kind, I am at a complete loss as to what to do with myself. I need my job back! I have no intention of becoming the missus at home. I am not wife material, nor indeed mother material! It could be true that my identity has somewhat merged with my career, in that even I can find it hard to distinguish my real self from my lawyer self. Which is the true me? Have we all lost our true identities through our chosen careers? Do we define ourselves solely through the work we perform? Can they be mutually exclusive?

I contemplate all of this at my leisure as I put the kettle on the boil. I startle when I see a mature woman and a man looking in through the basement window at me. She looks familiar, he does too. It's my parents! I run to the kitchen door and embrace them warmly. I have missed them both too!

"Mum, Dad, come in. It's so good to see you both. I'm so sorry I haven't been in touch. Things have just been hectic really. Dan is away at the moment. You'll get to meet him one of these days, for sure. How was Devon? I know you filled me in on most of it on the phone but I want to hear all the details!" I tend to rant when met with the unexpected or when I'm excited. I really am pleased to see them both.

"I'll make the tea," Mum says, being her usual helpful self.

"I'll do it Mum. Please. You've made me enough cups of tea over the years! For God's sake, sit down. Dad, take off your coat," I order. I notice Mum isn't her usual curious self in someone else's home. She wouldn't have missed a trick in my apartment. A lover of interior decoration, she could spend hours discussing chintz or skirting boards or colour schemes. Normally she would be effusive in her words being in such a beautiful kitchen, the dresser, the red Aga. Even the polished bronze cooking pots, strategically placed to hang in front of the stove, don't seem to catch her eye.

"So how are you Dad? You seem quiet. Is everything okay?" I enquire, puzzled by my Father's obvious lack of joyfulness. He is usually the joker of the three of us, always smiling, forever charming.

"We know what's going on, Helene. Well, we have a fairly good idea anyway," Dad says bluntly, looking more serious than I have ever seen him. "We decided to surprise you in your office today, bring you to lunch or something if you were free. Anyway, your mum wanted to have a good look at the décor, since your Firm won that award last year for its elegant interior, fat lot of good that does it now! Anyway, the doors were locked and there was no one on the reception desk, as far as we could see…"

"We were just leaving," Mum continues the story, "when a lady beside us, Yvonne was her name, wasn't it Gerry?"

"Yes, that's it," Dad answers.

"She must have heard your Dad and I discussing you, well, she must have heard us mention your name or something, because she starts unloading this whole Andrew Peterson saga onto us. So much so that we ended up giving her a lift to her house out in Fairview, which is, of course, way out of our way, but sure we couldn't leave her there, sobbing her heart out. She was telling us about her little boy, I can't remember his name, and how was she going to afford a crèche now if she has no job to go to? I mean, she was terribly distraught altogether!" Mum adds, clearly moved by the whole event. "My heart went out to her. A terrible situation altogether."

"She said she has tried to call you a few times but you didn't answer," Dad takes over the mantle once more. "She said no one has told her anything and she doesn't know what's going on. There is some rumour about a Judge hearing the case next Monday? What in God's name is going on Helene? And why on earth didn't you tell us? We are hurt that you couldn't confide in us Helene. You are our only child. Our beloved daughter. You are the most important thing to us in the entire world. You know we would do anything for you!" Dad looks me in the eye.

I love him more at that moment than I have ever loved him. My mother too. The one and only true unconditional love, a parent to a child. Maybe I will never experience that love. Maybe the responsibility of that love is too overwhelming, too powerful for me. To be hopelessly in love with your child, to depend on them to love you back. What if they don't love you back? What if they don't grow up the way you want them to, love you back the way you want them to? I do not want to risk my heart again. It's like there is a shield around my heart now. Even though I love Dan, he will never have my whole heart. I gave that away once and once was enough. I have learnt from past blunders. It will not happen again. I will keep a safe control on my love. It is too precious to have it thrown back in my face.

I sit with my parents and we talk long into the night. For the first time in a while I feel safe and loved. I missed the company of family. I missed, in particular, being loved unconditionally. A no-matter-what-love. A come–what-may-love. The purest kind.

106   NEGLIGENT BEHAVIOUR

Chapter 13

I miss Dan terribly all weekend. Seeing my parents helps somewhat. At least there is some respite in my hermit induced existence. On Sunday I wake up with thoughts of Caroline in my mind. I really want to talk to her and see how she is. I need to tell her my career prospects are appearing as bleak as her marriage prospects. It might make her feel better to know that we all have a cross to bear, that none of us escape a burden of some type in life. Scratch under the surface of anyone's veneer and there will be a story, a tale of woe or an anecdote of survival; we're all human.

We arrange to meet at four in the afternoon for coffee. The Birches bistro seems quieter than usual. It's probably a mixture of the usual post-Christmas lull and the slight hint in the air of an impending recession. Either way, it's nice to have a safe haven where we can chat. We could have called into each other's houses but I am in no humour to make small talk with James and I am in desperate need of a sojourn from Banville Road.

I arrive first and sit in a cosy booth, ordering a cappuccino and a slice of homemade carrot cake. I watch Caroline from the bay window, parking her car and pulling her coat closer to her as she rushes in from the cold. Her bright eyes and welcoming smile suggest a woman who has made peace with her turmoil.

"How are you? It's good to see you," I say, giving her a kiss on her fresh, rosy cheek.

"I'm good. Great to see you too," she responds, ordering an Americano and a slice of carrot cake herself. "He's a cute waiter, isn't he? I love that tousled hair, rugged look. Nice butt too!" she adds.

"You're a gas ticket, Caroline," I say, laughing "and you're right, he is cute!"

"Well, I'm only window shopping. Not like James who has to actually *go in* with the platinum credit card and make a purchase! Some of us can actually just browse the goods on offer, or at least draw up a hire purchase agreement!" she says, sarcastically.

"How are things?" I ask, as sensitively as I can.

"I'm alright, Helene. Just alright," she says, stirring her coffee. I wait for her to continue. "James and I are going to marriage counselling. It's not easy but it's helping I think. He tells me he still loves me and that he felt that I was putting our daughters before him. I don't know how he thought that at all, I thought he was putting his work before me and the girls! Anyway, we are working through all our *issues,* as they say in America. Jesus, this therapy business would drive you cracked, not to mind broke! He is in the spare room for now but I believe him when he says he is not seeing that cow, Leanne, anymore. I saw her at mass this morning with her husband and her kids. I could swear she blushed madly when she saw me. I could be imagining it though. The heat was on full blast as it's so bitterly cold today, isn't it? Anyway, enough about me. How are you? Missing lover boy Dan by the sounds of things?" Caroline says.

"If only it were that simple," I say and launch into the entire story of Peterson & Co. Caroline's mouth is wide open by the time I am finished.

"For God's sake Helene. Why didn't you say something earlier? You must have been going through hell these last few weeks. What a disaster! You poor, poor thing," she says, sincerely.

"It's going to be all over the papers tomorrow, Carls, I don't know if I can bear it!" I exclaim so loudly that even the all-over-each-other -couple beside us glance in our direction inquisitively.

"Such a shame Dan is still away. Would you not ring him later and tell him everything?" Caroline probes.

"I don't want to be worrying him when he is in the middle of this deal," I say, not entirely convinced that that is the whole reason. "There is nothing he can do from London anyway. I know he never gets to so much as glimpse a newspaper when he is working so I'm banking on him not finding out anything until he gets home."

"So, let me get this straight. Due to no wrongdoing on your part at all, Andrew Peterson could potentially bring you down with him?" she reiterates.

"Ostensibly, yes."

"That's so unfair, Helene!"

"Life's unfair," I say.

What more can I say? How can I explain this madness to someone else? It is more than unfair. It's treason! The biggest betrayal ever! Judas Iscariot, eat your heart out. I think of all the clients of Peterson & Co., how they will all suffer at the hands of Andrew's self-serving ego. People might, (what am I saying *might*) people *will* lose their homes because of his actions. Families *will* be made homeless, investors *will* lose their life savings. If their rainy day comes, they will be soaked to the skin. There will be no umbrella to shelter them from the relentless downpour.

"I guess no one ever said life is *supposed* be fair," Caroline says, her eyes watering. "I don't know if James and I will make it" she says, candidly, out of the blue.

"Oh Carls" I say, moved. "But you are going to counseling now, that might help?" I say, stabbing in the dark.

"I think the counseling sessions are nearly bringing up more skeletons out of the closet! I mean, you'd want to hear some of the stuff he is coming out with about me. He's the one who had the affair, again! Not me!" she says, indignantly. "Some of the things he says are so hurtful, like he is looking for a reason to justify his latest affair. I've told him there is no point being with me if that's how he feels. I'd be long gone if it wasn't for the twins, you know," Caroline says, pointedly.

"No, you wouldn't," I say, epliptically. "I know you love each other. There's just a lot of hurt there. Open wounds to be healed."

"I suppose," Caroline concedes. "I'll stick with this counseling malarchy for the moment anyway. I'll try and give it my best shot. It's just not as easy as I thought it'd be," she adds, grimacing.

"Healing never is," I say, like I know anything about it. "But it'll be worth it in the end. I'd say too many couples walk around with blinkers on. At least the two of you are brave enough to confront your demons and sort everything out. I think you're amazing," I say, believing it sincerely.

"Thanks Helene. I'll keep you posted," Caroline says, "and remember I'm here for you too."

"I know you are, hon. You always are," I say, grateful for her support in return.

I sleep only intermittently on Sunday night. I dream of a Mephistopheles-type Judge banishing me from the island of Ireland to live in a pit of snakes, forever lost in a lair of hell. He barks his bleak prophecy for all ears to hear: Eventually I succeed in falling asleep just when I am due to get up for the day. I text Conor, who I have arranged to meet in the canteen of the Four Courts, telling him that I'll see him in court instead.

All the partners of Peterson & Co have been served with a court order to attend today's hearing. I cannot afford to disobey this order and risk being in contempt of court. It's the last place I want to be this Monday morning. I really cannot understand why since the Judge is going to take the peremptory step of freezing all the Firm's accounts and suspending our practising certificates, pending a thorough investigation. Of that I am sure.

I am not even objecting to the application and nor are any of the other partners. There is nothing to gain by doing so! The accounts are going to have to be closed down for a period of time anyway, to allow the Law Society accountants figure out the extent of the fraud. In the meantime we will be doing everything in our power to defend our innocence, to retain the right to practice as solicitors. Oh the joy of it all!

I make my way into the Four Courts, passing by the public entrance and using my solicitor's ID card to gain entry swiftly. Why the courts services should trust their own flock over Joe public is beyond me? We are clearly as dangerous as lay people. I could be armed with a 63 calibre gun to shoot Andrew Peterson down at point blank range. I could swan through security, produce my weapon from my expensive attaché briefcase in the commercial court and let loose a flurry of bullets at my target. A sweet revenge assuaged. Lucky for him, that's not my style. I am too cowardly.

I leave my coat and brolly in the solicitor's writing room and take the lift up to commercial court number nine. It is eleven o'clock. I take my seat beside Stephen, David and Conor who hardly acknowledge my entry. Each one of them lost in their own thoughts, probably wondering how on earth the pendulum is swinging so resolutely in our disfavour. The registrar, who sits in front of the Judge, is calmly reading out the various applications at this morning's call over.

The president of the High court, the venerable Justice Smythson, seems in an irritable mood. I don't blame him when the majority of matters seem to be applications for adjournments.

"Is Andrew here yet?" I whisper to Stephen.

"No such luck. Conor wants his guts for garters," he answers, in hushed tones.

"Who doesn't?" I say.

"I hear you," Stephen sighs.

"Number eighty two," announces the Registrar. "The Law Society *and* Peterson & Co., Solicitors, Andrew Peterson, David Burns, Stephen Carey, Conor Carroll and Helene McBain."

I take a deep intake of breath. There is silence. Slowly, a bewigged and cloaked Barrister, whom I recognise from his stance as John Everett SC, makes his application on behalf of the Law Society. Firstly, he asks if the Defendants could rise and identify themselves. Each one of us does so, feeling more akin to an accused than a defendant.

"My Lord," states Mr. Everett. "I would respectfully suggest that the non-attendance of Mr. Andrew Peterson, on foot of a court order, could be deemed to be a criminal matter. I would again respectfully' suggest that this matter be referred to the DDP to decide whether or not criminal charges should be brought."

"Hmm. Yes, I agree. Mr. Everett. These matters are serious indeed," Justice Smythson opines cantankerously.

"Quite, my Lord. Quite," Mr. Everett nods gravely.

"As you are aware, my Lord, from the comments made by Mr. Justice White, there would appear to be an alleged €100 million deficit in the client account that has not yet been resolved. In separate proceedings, BCC Bank, SBS Building Society, First Action Building Society, are, *inter alia*, proceeding to seek judgment orders in this court, your Lordship, for some €120 million against Mr. Andrew Peterson arising from loans made to him over a five year period for property and other investments..." Mr. Everett's words merge into one, sounding like a sustained litany of crooked swindling.

The atmosphere in the courtroom is tense. All in attendance strain to hear every morsel that falls from Mr. Everett's lips. I note a shrewd journalist in the back pew of the courtroom, writing shorthand in her wiry notebook. We had been forewarned, of course, that it was to be an open court today. It was still unimaginably tortuous to know that your name will be splashed across all the newspapers. The Law Society has specifically applied to allow the media and the public to be present. Wanting to make an example of us, no doubt. Funny how only the innocent turned up in court today? Where is the guilty man himself? What kind of country is this where he can abscond so easily, his whereabouts unknown?

I do know that if criminal charges are brought against Andrew, it would enable the State to seek his extradition, if he is found outside the jurisdiction. It's a small comfort but a comfort nonetheless.

"I am satisfied, having read the papers before me and from hearing the application of Mr. Everett on behalf of the Law Society, to direct that all accounts pertaining to Peterson & Co., solicitors of Highfield house, Quill Street, Dublin, be frozen with immediate effect. I furthermore direct that the Practising certificates of all partners will be temporarily suspended until this court directs otherwise. I accept into court the written undertaking from Mr. Andrew Peterson, which has mysteriously found it's way to my registrar, in which he furnishes an undertaking to the High Court that he will not practice as a solicitor without permission from the court," Justice Smythson orders.

At this juncture the court erupts into a frenzy of cheering and even a wolf whistle permeates the sombre air.

"Quiet please," hushes the flushed registrar.

"I also direct that Mr. Andrew Peterson's assets and those of his partners, his co- defendants, David Burns, Stephen Carey, Conor Carroll and Helene McBain be frozen. This will protect clients' monies and prevent further misappropriation," the honourable Justice Smythson decrees.

Again, the court erupts into a spontaneous cheer, and clapping commences in the front benches. The registrar struggles to keep order in the High Court. Most of those in attendance this morning are solicitors and/or their trainees, barristers and/or their devils. They are simply displaying their outright disgust at another colleague for breaching the ethical code, the core of the teachings of Law. Their anger flares at the ability of just a few to bring the entire profession into disrepute. They cannot even imagine, in their wildest dreams, what we, the alleged accomplices, are feeling. We cannot even articulate it ourselves!

"It would appear, my Lord, that Mr. Peterson and his co-defendants, have four hundred and three properties between them in countries including Romania, Portugal, England, Japan and Slovakia. It would be anticipated that Mr. Peterson and his co-defendants must now draw up a list of all their properties, their addresses and their mortgage status. Those properties that are free of mortgages will be made available to meet their liabilities," Mr. Everett continues in pragmatic tones.

Stephen and I look at each other, knowing full well that we can count the properties the other 'co-defendants' own on one hand! The scale of Andrew's greed is unprecedented.

"Lastly, I would respectfully suggest, my Lord, that suspending the Defendants' certificates to practice as solicitors might affect their insurance," Mr. Everett proposes.

"In that case, Mr. Everett, I will leave the practising certificates in place until the insurance situation is clarified. I will mention this case in a week's time to see what progress has been made."

"I am obliged, my Lord," says Mr. Everett as he resumes his seat calmly, his application undeniably successful.

The registrar moves on swiftly to the next matter on her list. I am aware of the eyes of the court on us. I make to move out of my pew when I feel a hand on my shoulder. I turn around and come eye to eye with Murdoch.

"See you on Wednesday," he whispers. "Don't worry, we'll work this out," he says re-assuringly. This gesture of kindness means a lot to me and I feel the tears well up as they tend to do these days.

"Keep yourself together, Helene," Murdoch warns. "The press are here watching your every move. I don't care about your partners but I care about you. Don't give them any fuel for the fire. They don't take any prisoners."

I simply nod and brace myself as I walk out of the courtroom. Conor, Stephen and David are all out in the corridor already. David is barricading himself from a wiry, bespectacled female journalist who appears as if she is about to pounce on him.

"No comment," David repeats for the second time.

"Do you not understand English?" Conor barks at the Journalist as she thrusts her card at David, asking him to contact her if anything occurs to him in the future.

We depart crestfallen by this morning's events. We did not anticipate that our own personal assets would fall into the mix. We berate ourselves for not being represented, then concede that it would not have made any difference. It's not as if we are not trained lawyers. We have a fairly good grounding in how the system works.

"But not enough to spot what that Andrew git was up to!" Stephen says, his words stinging our ears.

We are all singularly accosted by individual journalists as we attempt to leave the Four Courts building. Word spreads fast. I am only grateful that there are no TV cameras waiting for us. From now on I will have representation at these hearings and will do my best not to have to be in attendance in person. It is only going to get worse. I think of my Grandfather when he used to say, "The snow falls, each fleck in its appropriate place". How can this be my appropriate place? Who is controlling my fate? Is it me? Is it the Law itself?

CHAPTER 14

I clamber into my bed when I finally arrive at the sanctuary of Banville Road. The nervous energy pumping through my body is now spent. The inside of my mind is wallpapered with jagged photographs of Judge Smythson, the commercial court and an array of familiar yet forbidding faces.

Dan calls me periodically over the next day or so. I am dismayed that he never seems to have enough time for a proper chat. I begin to feel like an afterthought then I realise I may be paranoid, having too much time on my hands to think. I know he is busy at work and as far as he is concerned I am too. Truthfully, I have never needed him as much. I am lonely and scared. Caroline checks in with me every now and then and my parents are hugely supportive but it's not the same.

I spend far too much time wallowing in self-pity and sloth so it is with welcome relief that I set out to meet Murdoch Pierce. I hope to glean some sagacious words from him. I am hoping he will throw me a life raft and pull me into shore. I hope he can rescue me from the wreckage, which I am precariously clinging to by my fingertips. We arrange to meet at seven in the evening. I would meet earlier but he has a post-court consultation that will keep him engaged until seven. We meet at Raffles private member's club offGrafton Street.

I give my name at the door and am ushered into a small yet tastefully decorated room with an impressive Fireplace and roaring log fire. The waiter brings me over a Kir Royale before I have even settled into the crushed velvet armchair. Other than a solitary bald-headed man reading a newspaper, his feet resting on a large pewter-coloured poof, there is no one else in the room. I watch the flames dance in the grate, my cold hands thawing from the heat and the soft background music pacifying my active mind.

"Hello, my darling Helene," Murdoch says as he kisses me on both cheeks. "Sorry I am late, I grabbed ten minutes to shower and change. I couldn't bear to be in my court attire any longer. Forgive me," he says, smiling.

I note that his blue shirt brings out the blue pigment in his eyes. With his rust-colour hair and freshly shaved face, he reminds me in a familiar way of Robert Redford or Ryan O'Neill.

"Not at all," I say, self-consciously, aware for the first time that there is an attractive man sitting beside me. I never noticed that before. God, Dan really has been away too long. I need someone here with me. I'm not good on my own, especially not with this calamity unfolding around me.

"Nice headline," Murdoch remarks and inclines his head toward the newspaper that the bald-headed man is reading.

"CELTIC CHEETAH ON THE LOOSE!" screams the title across the front page of the popular daily newspaper. My heart skips a beat.

"HIGH-FLYING LAWYER SELLS HIS SOUL!" is written in smaller capital letters underneath. I cannot even imagine what the red tops have written.

"I've already checked the newspapers today, Helene," Murdoch confides. "I garner from your reaction that you haven't. I'm not going to lie to you. You are named as a possible *accomplice* so-to-speak, together with the other partners of Peterson & Co. The main focus is, however, on Andrew Peterson himself. At least that's something."

"For what it's worth Murdoch," I say desolately. "This whole thing is really tearing me apart. My head is such a mess." Murdoch squeezes my hand momentarily as if in empathy of my predicament. I am grateful for this gesture of kindness. I have never felt as vulnerable.

"Did you get all the papers I sent you? I posted out a copy of the partnership agreement I signed along with a few other documents I thought might help?" I say, quizzically.

"I did, Helene," Murdoch answers as he orders us another round of Kir Royales. My stomach is in a knot, my head already light from imbibing the champagne with an unquenchable thirst.

"Look, and I don't want to bore you with what you already know but I have to spell this out for you, plain and simple," Murdoch says authoritatively. "In cogent terms, if you like. Section thirteen of the Partnership Act 1958 specifically deals with liability of partners. Unfortunately you were not a limited partner. You, and indeed all your partners, signed the partnership agreement as a full partner. There is no way around that."

"None at all?" I say.

"None," he replies. "Section thirteen states that every partner in a Firm is liable jointly with the other partners for all debts and obligations of the Firm incurred while he is a partner," Murdoch says, pragmatically. "There is very little room to manoeuvre here, Helene, if at all. I'll do my best for you. I've been perusing the obvious high profile cases from the past for any loopholes I can find. I'm afraid I haven't been successful thus far," he says with conviction.

"But surely a criminal case against me would be different to a civil case?" I plead hopefully. "I mean, in a civil case they have to prove their case against me on *the balance of probabilities*, in a criminal case it's *beyond a reasonable doubt*. There's a big difference?!" I say, exasperated.

My third glass of champagne arrives, serving only to pump the adrenalin faster through my veins. I alternately press the cold glass on my flushed cheeks, temporarily releasing them from the volcanic heat. I feel like Mount Vesuvius finally permitted to erupt after centuries in a lava straightjacket.

"Helene, calm down. You won't go to jail over this. There has been no mention of criminal proceedings being brought against you. The worst that can happen is you get struck off the roll of solicitors," Murdoch says, gazing at me directly.

"That's all?!" I cry. "Oh sure that's grand so. Nothing to worry about at all!" I bleat sarcastically.

"Helene, we will appeal any application to strike you off all the way to the Supreme Court. Personally, I can't see you being struck off unless the Judges really want to make an example out of you or if they can show that you *did* actually do something to enable this fraud. Nevertheless, it is going to be difficult to prove that you and your partners had no idea that there was a hundred and eighty million fraud going on in front of your noses! He even ran his property business, Peterson Holdings, out of the same offices so you can see why some might be dubious, can't you?" Murdoch says.

"Yes, I can," I say reluctantly. "I can't believe how stupid we all were. I concentrated too much on the practice of law and not enough on the business of law. More the fool me!" I exclaim.

"Oh come here to me," Murdoch says, and before I know it he has me in a bear hug. I rest my head on his shoulder. I am pleasantly surprised by how delicious he smells. I am unpleasantly surprised by why I am noticing this at all. I feel slightly dizzy when I pull back from him. Perhaps it's the champagne, perhaps its just lust. Oh God, how can I possibly fancy this guy! He's married for one thing and he is most certainly not my type! He is far too confident, practically verging on the arrogant. Yet he can be incredibly sensitive and protective. Murdoch departs to reserve a table for two in the fine dining room as I sit rummaging in my head for a good reason why I should not be joining him. He is my legal advisor, after all. There is nothing wrong with going for dinner with my own legal representative! Married or not, this is strictly business. Yeah right! I hear a voice say but I choose to ignore it. Instead I take Murdoch's arm upon his return, and allow him escort me into the dining room.

Murdoch and I discuss little of my own situation for the rest of the evening. He regales me with the funniest stories of his colleagues at the bar, a prominent Judge caught in a compromising position, a female barrister baulked out of it in court for wearing a trouser suit and not a skirt, a respected Master having a mid-life crisis who follows his attractive devil around like a puppy dog and plenty more side-splitting anecdotes.

I am having such an enjoyable time that I forget our respective, separate lives and am wrapped in a time warp where it is just Murdoch and me.. There is nothing sexier than a man who makes you laugh. Murdoch, despite his failings, can make me laugh out loud like no other man I have ever met. He has the sharpest wit, an agile mind that shines when he has your attention. I think I'm in love with his mind, his words and his intellect. We are fellow bibliophiles and dissect book after book in the literary stratosphere. I am having such a great time!

"More wine, Helene? Or what about a nightcap?" Murdoch asks casually.

"Em, well, I don't mind but don't you need to be home at a reasonable hour? I know you have a case in the morning, don't you?" I say, giving him a get-out clause. I really don't want him to leave, I don't want to be on my own again. I'm enjoying his company. "I, on the other hand, am a lady of leisure at the moment..."

"Yes," Murdoch says, "and the night is just a pup so let's retire to my favourite quarters."

I am conscious that I am slightly wobbly on my feet as I get up from my chair, the heady mix of wine and stimulating conversation accelerating my penchant for excitement, for adventure.

"And where, may I ask, are your favourite quarters? You sound like a character out of a Victorian play...Mind you, you are an antique relic of the bar at this stage!" I tease.

"Come, come, Madam!" Murdoch acquiesces in his role, "Take my arm and I shall lead the way!" We giggle merrily with our silly repertoire of formal banter.

We walk up only a few wide steps of stairs and are in convulsions of laughter when I nearly trip on the last step. Murdoch's dextrous footing saves my fall and he steers us down a narrow, dimly lit corridor. His head is almost touching the mock tudor beams on the ceiling. I find this, of course, hysterically funny as he stoops by degrees the further along the corridor we walk.

"This is terribly discombobulating altogether!" he protests, causing me to shriek with laughter.

All of a sudden we find ourselves at a dead end, the beams above intertwining around us, the two of us giddy from the silliness of it all. I turn to sit on a small window seat to compose myself when Murdoch pulls me close and kisses me passionately. I am consumed by desire, by flirtation. I do not resist. I surrender uncontrollably to this master of seduction. We cannot get enough of each other. I forget all thoughts of responsibility, of duty, of practicality. I am lost in the moment, his kiss an outlet for my inner fervour.

Murdoch is urgent in his desire for me and me for him. He finds the bedroom which, of course, has been pre-booked just in case. He needn't have worried. I am an easy target. The room is like a boudoir, all regal and plush. I spot a bottle of champagne chilling in an ice bucket, I hear the tunes of a familiar melody, and I see his suit hanging outside the wardrobe. I don't care if this entrapment is pre-meditated. I just want to be consumed. I want to consume him. We undress each other with verve and enthusiastic ardour. I am eager for his love, his scent, his rapturous mind. He is a generous lover and I lose myself in waves of ecstasy. He tells me how beautiful I am, over and over as his body sighs in gratitude every time we make love. Our lovemaking is tactile and affectionate. He never stops kissing me, not for a moment. I feel like the sexiest woman alive. Murdoch is an illicit drug, a habit that if nurtured, I don't know if I could break.

Early in the morning I wake to find breakfast has arrived on a silver tray. Before I can say anything, Murdoch is kissing me again. I think I have been kissing him all night. He brings me into the beautiful marbled shower and we make love again, the water cascading our bodies, the urgency of the night before still strong, still not satiated. I have an all-consuming zest for him. I am in lust with him.

Later, he kisses me goodbye and tells me he'll call me later. I lie in bed relishing the memory of him, re-living the touch of him, the way he makes me feel. I smell him on the pillow and inhale it into my heart. I do not mind the walk of shame to a waiting cab to bring me home. Because I am walking on a cloud. I do not mind wearing the same clothes that I wore the night before. Because I'm sailing into the horizon. Murdoch Pierce has given me wings.

It's only when I get back to Banville Road that the consequences of my actions sink in. Five missed calls from Dan and two from my parents. I am alone and in withdrawal from the intoxicating drug that is Murdoch. Pierce. I ache for him. Worst of all I know I shouldn't ache for him. I am a sinner of the highest order! I should be the penitent in Dante's *Purgatorio*, walking within flames to purge myself of lustful thoughts and feelings.

What am I doing?! This is insane! It's not as if things aren't bad enough, I don't know why I am intent on making it worse. I just couldn't resist Murdoch. I didn't see it coming at all. I never, ever expected that to happen. The guilt torments me yet I get a warm, fuzzy feeling every time I think of him.

What is it about Murdoch? Can I not just be content with Dan? I love Dan. I fancy Dan. How can I fancy two men at the same time? As Mae West said too many men, too little time. The problem is I am not Mae West. Nor will I ever be! I'm just going to have to forgive myself and move on. Maybe I'll never hear from Murdoch again. Even when I say this to myself, I know I'm being duped. If he felt even a quarter of what I felt last night, he'll be ringing me as fast as a bullet out of a gun. What a night of passion! See, there I go again. I am immature and selfish. I really need to cop on and age gracefully, not disgracefully!

I call Dan and make some pathetic excuse about leaving my mobile in my parent's house. He doesn't doubt me for a second. Why would he? He loves me as I clearly love him! As the day comes to a close I am aware of checking my mobile every few minutes. I want Murdoch to ring me and I don't want him to ring me. I am torn between myself and my alter ego. The good and the bad. The angel and the demon. The phone rings. It's Murdoch. I don't hesitate to answer.

"Hi," I say bashfully.

"Hi, darling." he says, "how has your day been? I've been thinking of you all day. Can't get you out of my head."

"Me neither," I admit.

"Can you meet me later?" he asks

"Where?"

"The Lawless Hotel? Seven O'clock in the foyer. I'll be waiting for you."

"Ok."

"See you then," Murdoch says, "Oh and Helene?"

"Yes?"

"No need to bring your pyjamas. You won't be cold."

"I hope not," I say.

I put the phone down and run upstairs to shower. I can't wait to see him. I can't wait to make love to him, to touch him. I just want to devour him.

CHAPTER 15

My mobile beeps again with yet another message. My voicemail is full. Some are from members of staff of Peterson & Co abusing me for swindling them out of a job, some are from clients divided in their loyalty and some are from friends anxious to see how I am, none of them doubting my scruples. My name has apparently been lambasted in every daily newspaper, dissected on national radio and I even secured a mention on prime time news. I am a private person and this level of intrusion akin to a magnifying glass into my soul, catapults me even further into my shell. Intimacy is not my forte.

As I ride in the cab taking me to the Hotel I receive a text from Murdoch. It simply says, "room 221". I have a sense of déjà vu from the Caroline and James Christmas saga, namely the text Leanne sent James. For all my pontificating, here I am doing the same. I am a degenerate reprobate! I may not be the married party in this *liaison* but I am freely facilitating this affair with a married man. I promise myself that tonight is the last time. I just can't walk away yet. Murdoch's charisma is too powerful, too sensual. He has an inexplicable hold on me.

I take the lift to the second floor and knock once on the door of room 221. Murdoch opens the door and opens his arms which I fall into in one fell swoop. We kiss, our lips remembering each other, our bodies recognising each other. Murdoch undresses me gently and skillfully. The intensity of our lovemaking takes my breath away.

"You are such a sexy woman," he says softly, "I've wanted you for so long. Now I'm never letting you go."

I surrender a smile to him but we both know that we are living in fairytale land.

"This can't last Murdoch," I say as he leaves to run the bath for us. "We both have responsibilities."

As I drape myself in the Hotel's fluffy bathrobe, Murdoch comes over to the bed and takes my hands in his.

"Helene, you don't understand. I know you think me crass and uncouth at times" – I raise my eyebrow indicating my agreement– "but as clichéd as it may sound, you make me feel alive again!" I shift slightly, propping up the pillows on the bed. "Look, I've been married nearly twenty years." Murdoch looks away briefly. "Frances and I have nothing in common anymore. I love her but I'm not in love with her. If it wasn't for the children, we would be long separated. It's no wonder I am such a workaholic!" he surmises, "Anything to avoid pretending to play happy families! There, I've admitted it now…so you see Helene as Oscar Wilde once said, the pure and simple truth is rarely pure and never simple!" Murdoch quotes as he kisses me warmly on the mouth.

"He also said that in married life three is company and two none," I quote back, mischievously. "That's why I'll never get married myself. I couldn't take the risk of it all going pear-shaped. I think I'd get bored anyway."

"Who hurt you?" Murdoch asks me unexpectedly.

"Pardon?" I answer, not really comfortable with his line of inquiry.

"Well, in my experience, most young girls grow up wanting a knight in shining armour to whisk her off on his white horse into the sunset to live happily ever after! How did you become this cynical? It couldn't just be because of your dealings as a Family Law solicitor. You are too professional for that, am I not right?" he says, mapping my face with his eyes. "My guess is that someone hurt you, he broke your heart and you've never really got over it," Murdoch continues.

"You have built a wall of protection around that heart of yours but no one is ever going to get too close. You never want to risk putting yourself in a place where your love could be rejected. If you don't love, then how can you be hurt? Isn't that right? That's why you are here now. You might love Dan, be in love with him even, but he'll never cross the bridge fully. Do you not believe in what Tennyson said 'Tis better to have loved and lost than never to have loved at all?" Murdoch asks, deflating my mood instantly with his punctilious pearls of observation.

"I don't want to talk about it," I stammer as I pour myself a glass of wine from the mini bar. "With all due respect Murdoch, I have enough things going on at the moment. You are not exactly perfect yourself!" I almost shout at him.

"None of us are perfect Helene. Look, I didn't mean to upset you, it's just that you are still young with your whole life ahead of you." Murdoch stands behind me and wraps his arms tightly around my waist. I can't cope with this psychoanalysis at the moment. "Don't let one man ruin your view of a happy ending and don't look at me as if I'm a married man who has an affair every day of the week," he says. "I don't."

I feel the prickly heat of water welling up behind my eyes.

Murdoch's phone rings as he walks into the bathroom to turn off the taps. He ignores it until it rings again. "It's my daughter Vanessa. I better answer it. Sorry about this," he says apologetically. I am simply relieved that the focus is off me. Talk about saved by the bell. I listen to the intonation in his voice rising as he talks to his daughter. I can tell that he is surprised about something. "I'll be there in ten. So sorry love. I just got delayed," he says.

"Helene, I feel terrible about this but I forgot I arranged to meet my seventeen year old daughter at Festoon Art Gallery this evening. She wants to go to NCAD and is looking for inspiration for her portfolio. I managed to secure two tickets to this event tonight. They are like gold dust. Brady Finnan. Have you heard of him?" Murdoch asks.

"No," I say.

"He's *the* artist celebre of the moment. His paintings are magical! He's expensive but what an investment they will be in a few years!" he says, enthusiastically. "Sorry, I tend to wax lyrical when it comes to art. Why don't you make the most of the bath while it's still warm? I should be back in a few hours. I'll drop Vanessa home and tell Frances that I need to work through the night on an urgent matter. She won't know any different."

After a quick shower Murdoch is dressed and ready to leave. He kisses me lightly on the forehead and is gone.

I should be luxuriating in this magnificent bath but my mind is in turmoil. I give in to feelings of despair and guilt. To say I am confused is an over simplification of how I feel. Why when I have the man of my dreams in my life do I choose to be reckless with that love? I will not be here when Murdoch returns. I will never be with him again. Yes, his magnetic pull is addictive but there is no future in this. I do not want to be the cause of his marital breakdown. Have I not met enough clients whose lives have been destroyed through separation and divorce? I do know that despite adultery being the trigger to a marriage split, it is rarely the cause. Still, I don't even want to be the trigger. What would Frances think of me if she knew where her husband has been the last two nights?

How utterly selfish of me! Wanting everything and giving nothing.

Murdoch's words chime in my head. *"Who hurt you? Who hurt you?"* This resonates deep inside me, to a much younger woman. She entrusted her heart into the hands of another. He tore out her heart, sliced it in half and diced it into little pieces. Her best friend put the pan on high and piece by piece fried each raw, tender morsel. John and Rebecca.

They destroyed my life all those years ago. I loved them both more than anything, maybe more than myself. John, a childhood sweetheart. Rebecca, a childhood friend. They mirrored each other in their love for me, or so I thought, until I caught these butchers in my bed that fateful day. The room spun around in that instant. I was caught as if directly in the eye of a storm, no way back and no way forward.

We had grown up together, us three musketeers. We lived in each other's houses, playing every type of game imaginable. Becky and I were die-hard tomboys, racing with John up and down the garden, climbing trees and causing a general sense of pandemonium every where we went. My mother would be shocked at the dirt under my fingernails, the grass in my braided hair and the cuts and scuffs to my soft skin. After school in the autumn evenings the sound of our laughter would fill the small laneway where we lived. We would yank at the branches over- burdened with golden leaves, coaxing them to fall at our feet. We would needle each other over who had the biggest pile of leaves, nit picking over invisible boundaries and kicking our feet in buoyant delight, causing the leaves to firework into glistening tapestries of crimson, gold, orange and yellow. I can still smell the damp brightness, see my breath as I exhale, and hear the joyful hoots of laughter.

But the past is a foreign country, they do things differently there.

We made a concerted effort to keep in contact as the years passed us by. I left the shores of Devon, where we grew up, to come to Dublin and read law in Trinity College. Both my parents are Irish and although my outward imprint may appear English, my DNA is undeniably celtic. Dublin was a shock to the system. Much more cosmopolitan, way more driven. I missed Devon so much, mainly because my heart was there. I went back every other weekend to meet up my parents and Rebecca and John. We always had such a great time.

During one of these weekends John and I realise we are more than just friends. Rebecca was out for the night, at a concert. Bach recital. She is a free spirit, a musician who relishes every opportunity to savour her musical passion, no matter in what guise it comes. . John, on the other hand, is a resolute left-side of the brain man. Not surprisingly, a chartered accountant by profession. I think I fall somewhere between the two of them which is probably why we all got on so well together.

John and I are sitting on the terrace of a picturesque Victorian villa, with a beautiful view across the wide sweeping bay of Torquay. We have taken a day trip here as the sun smiles on the bustling harbour and the sparkling yachts in the marina. John is chatting animatedly about his new appointment to Rogerson, Mills and Young, chartered accountancy Firm. It is by far the biggest and most successful accountancy Firm in Devon. John is far too much of a home bird to have ever moved far from the place of his birth. Nor is he going to stretch too far in his choice of girlfriend.

"Do you love me, Helene?" John asks out of the blue as we drink our coffee.

"You know I love you," I answer.

"Are you in love with me?" he asks, gazing at me intently.

I can tell that he is in love with me. I have felt it for a long time. I have been too scared to cross that potentially destructive line from a great friendship into a disastrous relationship. It is a big risk.

"No," I say, transparently unconvincingly. I stifle a smile.

"I think you are," he says. "In fact I know you are. I know you too well. If it's any consolation I'm in love with you too."

And that was that.

For seven years we commuted between Devon and Dublin,

always planning to settle down in the former town or the latter but never actually committing to it. I loved him with all my heart and soul. No other man ever stood out in my radar. John was a hopeless romantic, a wonderful lover and the truest friend. I surprised him one Saturday afternoon, arriving unexpectedly on a windy March day, letting myself into the house we had purchased together. There I witnessed a sight that would be etched in my memory for years to come. I still have a lump in my throat when I think of it. Such a betrayal I had never experienced before for each betrayal begins with trust. I trusted John. I trusted Rebecca. The visual memories in my head play like a tainted roll of film, jarred with untruths and distorted perceptions.

John and Becky succumbed to their base instincts. Yet they say all is fair in love and war. I wonder this as I emerge from the en suite bath of a hotel room, after fornicating with a married man and in a committed relationship myself. Who am I to throw stones? Who am I to judge?

I finish the quarter bottle of wine as I dress. I make a promise to never find myself in this situation again. The shame and the guilt are too much to bear. There is no pleasure without pain, have I not learnt that already? My heart, though sealed from true intimacy, is not an impenetrable fortress. How I have let myself end up here with a man like Murdoch Pierce is beyond my comprehension. But like attracts like. Am I sending out signals of debauchery to the Universe? Are my thoughts that negative that I am attracting negativity back? I know I am vulnerable but what was left of my dignity and my self-respect has been annihilated purely by my own actions. I am the author of my own misfortune.

I take some paper from the bedside locker and write Murdoch a note.

I am sorry but I can't do this. Please understand. Please don't contact me again. H.

I get upset when I think of Dan and how utterly disappointed he would be in me if he knew. Not to mention angry and hurt. I know how that feels because I've been there. I should know better. It won't happen again. I swear.

I take a taxi back to the safe haven of Banville Road, shut the door and ring Dan.

Chapter 16

Dan's plans to bring me away for the weekend are scuppered. His work, as usual, takes precedence. We postpone it to the following week. After my recent behaviour this is a welcome relief. Guilt eats into my very marrow, sucking my bones dry.

"I am so sorry Helene," Dan says as he removes his shoes after the flight home from London. "I just couldn't get home any earlier than this. I promise I'll make it up to you."

He pulls me to him, his warmth and sincerity propelling an urge in me to scream. My guilty conscience is at the fore of my mind. Never again, I tell myself. Never again! I didn't realise how much I had missed him until he holds me. I feel safe and secure in his arms.

"A penny for them!" Dan says affectionately. "You seem a million miles away!"

I lie in the crook of his arm, my head resting on his chest. I am wondering how on earth I could have been unfaithful to this wonderful man. What was I thinking? I know that this is an opportune time to talk to Dan. There is no more time to waste as I have shut him out for far too long. It also serves the purpose of distracting Dan from wanting to make love to me. I have already indicated through my body language that I am not in the mood. How can I sleep with him when I slept with another man last night? I would feel like a whore. I just can't do it.

"Dan, there is so much I need to talk to you about," I say, bashfully.

"Has it anything to do with Peterson & Co.?" Dan asks bluntly.

"Eh, yes, it does actually. Did you read something in the

newspaper?" I reply, not totally surprised that this *exposé* has filtered through to Dan.

"No, but I noticed a big sign stuck up on the outside of your office windows on my way back from the airport. The taxi stopped briefly at the lights and I just happened to notice it. It said: '*This Firm has closed. Please locate another solicitor to assist you or if you are an existing client please address all queries to the Law Society*' or something to that effect," Dan explains.

"Why didn't you say something when you came in?" I say perplexed.

"Because I wanted you to tell me yourself. I knew something was up when I walked in the door. I know you too well Helene. I knew you were keeping a secret from me."

"Right," I say softly. "I see."

But I don't see at all, do I? What in God's name was I thinking of being with Murdoch? Haven't I got everything I could ever want in a man in Dan? The pressures of this bloody Peterson saga are taking their toll. I can't turn back the clock now! I'm such a fool. Dan would walk out the door if he knew what I'd been up to. I wouldn't blame him. I need to tell him about Andrew quickly. If he ever found out, he might show me some mercy if he knows how much stress I am under. Not that it excuses anything. Maybe I'm just trying to excuse myself.

I do know Dan would certainly *not* be be lying in bed with me at this moment! I have already received three phone calls from Murdoch since I left the note on Thursday night. I don't want to contact him again. It's too dangerous. Murdoch Pierce is everything I abhor in a man but the chemistry is undeniable. I have to avoid him. If it means retaining another barrister to represent me through the quagmire ahead then so be it. I cannot afford to continue seeing him as it would only end in tears. I feel a guilt I have never felt before; I'm deeply ashamed of myself.

"Tell me everything about Peterson & Co.," Dan says "and I mean everything Helene."

"Ok," I agree, relieved to finally explain everything. Maybe if I had said something to begin with, I wouldn't have done what I did. I need to seriously cop on here.

I embark on a lengthy monologue being careful not to leave out any detail, no matter how trivial, in order that Dan can assimilate all the relevant facts and any recent developments that have occurred. I try to keep my emotions hidden for fear it clouds the story. It's a relief to be able to tell Dan and now I feel ridiculous for not telling him earlier.

"Conor rang me on Friday to tell me that the accounts of Peterson Holdings Ltd and Peterson Overseas Property Law have also now been frozen and their websites closed down," I tell Dan. "Andrew was a director of Peterson Overseas Property Law. He would refer anyone investing in a foreign property to this company," I explain. "I mean, he even had the nerve to call for the selling of overseas properties in the Irish Market to be regulated!" I conclude, exhausted by my own story, my emotions coming to the fore.

"Surprise! Surprise!" Dan remarks indignantly. He mulls over the story in silence for a moment. "I just can't believe you kept this from me for such a long time! Why didn't you say anything? You must have been worried sick," he says, clearly confused.

"I'm sorry. I really just didn't want to worry you. You have had enough on your plate with your own work. I think I was hoping it would all just blow over." I say, attempting to rationalise my behaviour, if even to myself.

"Unfortunately it didn't. I still can't believe its happening. It's all such a mess!" I sniffle.

"Jesus, that Andrew guy is some crook Helene! I wouldn't mind but the grief he used to give you as well, breathing down your neck all the time. He really took you all for a ride, not to mind his clients. Don't worry he won't get away with it, we'll make damn sure of that! He had you all fooled, his colleagues, his clients, his family and the bankers! Bastard. He deserves to rot in hell."

"We can only do our best Dan. I don't really know what is going to happen. My most immediate concern is money really. We get paid monthly in advance and we all know it's the first of February tomorrow. I have savings but I don't really want to dip into them," I say truthfully.

"Hey babes. Don't be silly! I just closed the biggest deal of my career yesterday...we have more than enough money for the two of us. That's the last thing I want you worrying about! We'll work something out, ok? And if it makes you feel better we'll say it's a loan. Ok?" Dan says as he winks at me conspiratorially.

"Dan, I really appreciate the gesture but I'm alright for the moment. As I said I do have enough savings to last me a few months anyway. Hopefully by then this nightmare will be over and I'll be back earning again. Thanks though, what would I do without you, Dan Goodings?" I say, feeling emotional. I am grateful for his love. I need him.

I know I've messed up but I'll do my best to make it up to him. I just couldn't justify taking money off him. It wouldn't feel right.

"I don't know, what would you do? Hmmm, actually maybe don't answer that!" Dan laughs. "Look, we'll get some proper legal advice on this" he says, confidently. I have, of course, not even uttered Murdoch's name once. I don't want to even bring his name into our relationship. I have to put the past behind me and move on. What else can I do? "Let's just take it one day at a time," he continues. "Have no fear, *Desperate Dan* is here!" I picture Dan dressed up as a superhero and we both erupt into laughter. He never fails to cheer me up.

On Monday, the Law Society succeeds in having Andrew Peterson struck off the roll of solicitors and fined three million euro. All of this is being calmly reported on the four o'clock news on national radio. Have these news readers no idea how many lives are being destroyed by this man?

I learn that earlier in the week, three hundred and twenty bottles of French and Australian wines seized from Andrew Peterson's home at the behest of his creditors were sold off at public auction making a mere eight thousand euro. His Land Rover and Bentley have also been seized. I think of poor Tanya Peterson and her children in particular. They don't deserve this.

"That bastard will be facing jail after failing to turn up in court this morning. He didn't turn up after lunch either," Conor almost spits down the phone, his barrister contact feeding us all relevant information on a daily basis. "Andrew's whereabouts are still unknown. Apparently both his Irish and Spanish mobile phones have now been disconnected. Thankfully Justice Smythson issued a warrant for his arrest and ordered Gardai to place the bastard in immediate custody if caught. His legal team, who were initially instructed, successfully applied to come off record. They are dead bloody right. God knows when he'll come back to the face the music! The Garda National Bureau of Fraud will be investigating his affairs as well. I really hope he rots in hell!" Conor barks.

This seems to be the overriding sentiment being expressed towards Andrew Peterson. The Media are baying for his blood and I wonder if you can blame them? Every day there are stories of clients' houses that are mortgaged by maybe three or four different banks, leaving the banks with no option but to issue proceedings for re-possession.

The values of the majority of properties are not worth the paper they are written on. The properties are so encumbered that there is little, if any, equity left. Some of the properties are not even registered in the client's name at all. In other words they have paid thousands of euros for houses that they don't even own! It makes me feel sick to think about it! The trust these clients put in their solicitor! The Banks are preferential creditors and they get the first part of the left-over pie, that is, of course, if there is anything left over.

One elderly lady talks about her family home being now in a negative equity situation. She has no family and no income and no way of paying for a nursing home. Naturally she is beside herself with worry. The black and white photograph in the newspaper depicts an old woman with dark shadows under her eyes. She tells the journalist how she entrusted Andrew to do the conveyance on her house as he came highly recommended to her. The lady also says that she took an instant dislike to him and found his superior manner and condescending attitude irksome. My heart goes out to her.

She urges the public to follow their instincts and to complain to the Law Society if they are in any way concerned about their solicitor. She believes that all solicitors should undertake a 'personality' character test prior to entering Blackhall Place, to sort out the chaff from the wheat so-to-speak, as in her view written academic examinations alone are not enough.

"Did you read this part?" Dan asks me, engrossed in the evening papers.

"Which part?" I ask, weary with the media onslaught from all directions. I don't know if I can stomach reading or hearing anymore. Lots of journalists are attempting to track me down at my old apartment, luckily my tenants don't know where I live and therefore I escape their clutches. Thank God for small mercies.

"Well, we all know that at the height of Andrew's success he was a media darling, parading himself around the place, cajoling world-renowned sports starts into promoting his foreign properties," Dan says, by way of introduction. "Anyway, it says here that they have all now disassociated themselves from him. They are dead bloody right!" he adds. "Murphy, the hurling star expressed his 'disgust' at the debacle. And Jones, God I can't believe he had such a star behind him, has released a statement through his solicitor basically saying that his duties were to market the property and pass on the enquiries to Andrew, and that he had no further involvement," Dan concludes. "Can't see how they'll be rushing to support any future property exhibitions, can you? They must feel like awful eejits, even though they didn't do anything wrong," Dan surmises. "I tell you what Helene, you never really know anyone, you know that? Everyone got sucked in by his confidence, his wealth and his charm."

"Yeah, you're right," I say. I know that better than most.

"He really had a nerve," Dan says, closing the paper and talking animatedly on his new pet subject. "Do you remember when you had just started working on my divorce and we had a conversation in your Firm one Friday, a propos Andrew and his debut on the night time entertainment show on Irish TV?

"Yes, I do. I remember it well. It lifted the profile of our Firm no end," I say, recalling the successful fallout from the show.

"Didn't he jointly sponsor with Peterson Holdings the give away of a foreign property on the air to some couple from Leitrim or Laois?"

"That's right, he did," I say, as I recall the buzz and excitement around the office on the Monday after the show.

"Yeah, I remember that. He even flew them off to Romania for a few days to see the development. I doubt they ever saw a centimetre of concrete poured or a single brick laid! He just used them to endorse his property exhibition the day after the show. That property was supposed to be worth about two hundred thousand euro as far as I remember. The house might as well have been made of paper. He was a smooth operator alright that Andrew Peterson. He has left a web of deceit behind him. He'd make your blood boil! We'll fight your corner Helene, don't you worry about it!" Dan says encouragingly.

"I wish it was that simple Dan," I say "but you have no idea how much I appreciate your support."

"You'll always have my support Helene. We'll get through this. Believe me I've got through worse!" he laughs.

"Thanks Dan," I say, grateful for his no nonsense approach.

We are sitting on the living room couch, our feet horizontal on the leather poof as we watch the spray of rain shower the window panes. I am just thinking how cosy and snug we are in our warm cocoon when my Blackberry vibrates on the coffee table. On reflex Dan stretches out his hand and gives it to me.

"Who's Murdoch P?" he says as I hold my breath. Luckily, I have a few seconds to gather my thoughts as without warning my Blackberry silently switches itself off. "What happened?" Dan asks.

"I don't know. It was fully charged!" I say, genuinely puzzled.

"Is it a work phone?" Dan asks.

"Yes. Oh, you're right. That's what it is! Obviously I'm not entitled to use this Blackberry anymore. If there is no Peterson & Co. then it follows that there can be no Peterson & Co. mobile account. Don't know why I didn't think of that! It's so annoying. I'll just have to get another phone tomorrow and pay it myself. Anyway, it's probably no harm as I've had so many calls from people, and not all of them supportive!" I ramble on, hoping I don't look flustered.

"Was that one of the nasty callers?" Dan asks innocently.

"Ah no, he's just a barrister. He has worked on a few cases for me. He's probably just wondering what solicitor is representing the clients now. Like I have any idea! The Law Society will have their work cut out for them, dishing out the correct files to the correct clients. I don't envy them. And it's all because of that elusive fugitive Andrew!"

"That's a pretty polite way of putting it!" Dan says, stating the obvious.

"You know, I was just thinking that really the way in which solicitors draw down mortgages for their clients needs to be radically overhauled," I announce, the idea just occurring to me. "I think the current procedure is too tempting for the likes of corrupt solicitors like Andrew to take advantage of the system."

"No shit Sherlock!" Dan says sarcastically.

"I'm serious Dan!" I protest.

"Look, the Lending Institutions should insist on a *three way closing*," I say, animatedly. "A solicitor for the bank should be present as well as the purchaser and vendor's solicitor. This would ensure that thieving solicitors can't go off and certify the title to other Lending Institutions who are none the wiser," I explain. "As well as that the sale wouldn't close if there were question marks over the title," I say, wondering why I hadn't thought of this before.

"Sure that's the way it used to be done Helene!" Dan says. "I remember buying my first investment property in Dublin, maybe fifteen years ago, and it was a three way closing. The only problem was that as the purchaser I had to pay for my own solicitor and the Bank's solicitor so it worked out really expensive! I think that's probably why they stopped it. I'm sure they wish they didn't now! Andrew isn't the first rogue solicitor and he won't be the last, you can bet your bottom dollar on that!" Dan says, testily.

"What did you just say?" I tease. "Did you just say 'bet your bottom dollar'?!"

I crease up with uncontrollable belly laughs.

"Hah! Hah! Very funny!" Dan says, not liking being the butt of a joke.

"Were you an *Annie* fan when you were growing up?" I snigger, desperately trying to get the words out between laughs. "I didn't think musicals were your thing?!" I am in convulsions.

"Very funny Helene!" Dan laughs now himself and tickles me until I can laugh no more.

CHAPTER 17

Although Dan has the best of intentions, his kid glove treatment of me over the next few weeks does nothing to make me feel any better. I realise that I am acting like an ostrich, burying my head in the sand but there is really very little I can do about my situation. The court process is tedious and slow. Most of the applications are made in relation to Andrew Peterson himself. The rest of us partners remain in a state of limbo for the most part. We retain Frank McGrath SC as our legal representative in all proceedings. We put up a blanket defence to any aggressive applications against us. None of us have committed any wrongdoing, not that it seems to make any difference. All I can do is sit and wait. It's total torture!

Dan is probably wondering what sort of girlfriend he has taken on. I am lethargic and unnaturally tired most of the time. I am usually full of boundless energy and he must find this transformation in me somewhat unsettling. We have not slept together in a few weeks as I am either too tired or my libido is on vacation. Dan, being the gentleman that he is, has not even referred to this sudden absence in his life. I really don't know what is wrong with me. One afternoon I sit apathetically on the couch, yet again, and turn on the one o'clock news.

The woman who appears on the television screen is a shadow of the woman she once was. Tanya Peterson appears downbeat despite the remnants of her previous glamorous life still protesting their worth. She is wearing Chanel shades and wearing a Jackie O style shift dress in black. The dress simply hangs off her gaunt frame, her once voluptuous figure simply disappearing under the strain. She attempts to shield her face from the barrage of camera flashes as she comes out of the Four Courts building. The reporter informs the viewers that this wealthy socialite, and wife of Andrew Peterson, has to suffer the ignominy of having her affluent lifestyle exposed as a sham. He tells us that although they are still married, Ms. Peterson has told the High Court this morning that she still does not know the whereabouts of her husband. I can't help but feel for her.

The Reporter tells us that Ms. Peterson has been reduced to asking for clemency to care for her family. Entangled in Mr. Peterson's frozen riches is Ms. Peterson's domestic, household bank account. Her lawyer told the High Court this morning that the family account held in both their names pays for the ordinary household expenses. Ms. Peterson sought to vary the order made a few weeks ago to meet the expenses of raising her five children under the age of ten. The impartial reporter raises an eyebrow in disbelief as he informs us that Ms. Peterson looked for expenses of €6,000 per week to care for her family. That won't do her any favours! I think to myself, some families only get that in six months or more, not to mind one week!

Most people in those circumstances would find the humiliation acute. Poor Tanya has the added sting of having an audience, having paraded her very desirable lifestyle in the society pages. Diary items constantly reported her efforts for charity balls, galvanising celebrities and getting nominated for style awards. Her debonair husband was an ever present sidekick at such functions. They epitomised the Celtic Tiger and with more than a hint of a recession in Ireland now, Andrew's downfall will come to symbolise its demise.

According to the reporter, Tanya is battling the fallout of her husband's greed. Even their trophy home in the chic Mount Merrion environs was financed on the back of fraudulently obtained loans – four different banks stumped up eighteen million euro! Tanya insists that she was an innocent drawn into the fraud and that Andrew forged her signature too. The Banks are aggressively pursuing their right to repossess the family home. I've no doubt that Tanya and her family will lose their family home. I cannot even imagine how heartbreaking this will be.

The reporter finally announces that Tanya's application for expenses was denied this morning. Andrew's wife and children are at the financial mercy of their own family relations. I certainly wouldn't like to be in Tanya's shoes! No doubt some of her family were duped by Andrew's web of deception too. Andrew was continually boring us all with stories about the golf junkets he attended with his brothers-in-law. It's bad enough to rip off innocent people but surely to pull the wool over your own family's eyes is unforgivable?

As the news bulletin finishes we are informed that a special feature on the rise and fall of Andrew Peterson follows shortly. I don't want to watch this. It's like spectators at a horror movie, they don't like what they see but their human instinct compels them to stare all the same. I find myself glued to the couch, gradually rendered immobile.

The Narrator tells us that it is common knowledge that Andrew grew up the second youngest of eight children, all of whom basked in the light of his rays. They hero worshipped him. From humble beginnings in County Carlow, Andrew excelled academically in primary school and in secondary in the local Gael Scoil. His Father was principal of the Gael scoil and Andrew, in particular, found this embarrassing. No child likes to stand out in school, the Narrator explains, and Andrew went out of his way to remain out of his Father's radar. He won a scholarship to UCG obtaining straight A's in nine subjects in his leaving certificate including applied maths and physics. His mother was a religious woman and believed in living frugally. Oh the irony of it! I think to myself. Both his parents are deceased. They'll be glad they are! I say out loud.

I listen to the details of Andrew's rapid ascent into the high life. His extravagant lifestyle, his demand for respect amongst his colleagues, his flamboyant dress sense and his insatiable desire for even more success are just examples of this man's colossal ego. 'Far from that you were reared!' my mother would have said to him with disdain. It is said that you cannot be a slave to two masters, the masters being either God or Money. It is evident who Andrew was serving all this time. Who do I serve? Am I a slave to both? My Father used to warn me to never give the devil a ride, for if it pleases him, he'll eventually want to drive... I cannot deny that there is not a grain of truth in this.

My mind spins with a cornucopia of moral dilemmas about life and what it is all about. The enigma of the meaning of life! I clearly have far too much time on my hands!

Dan is bringing me somewhere romantic this weekend. Just the two of us. I think a change of scenery will do me good. I am spending far too much time moping around Banville Road. Thankfully Murdoch does not have my new mobile number. I am under no illusion that he could find me if he wanted to but at the moment I feel safe. Part of me hopes he will move on to his next conquest and part of me knows we had something special. Yet how can I ever justify that? or explain it? No one would understand. I just have to move on and put the whole soap opera behind me. Life is too short.

I spend the next few days in domestic bliss. I arrange flowers, I tidy out presses and cupboards and I have an appetising dinner ready for Dan every evening. I cannot quite believe how dramatically my life has changed in a few months. I was an ambitious partner in a busy law Firm and now I dig out weeds in the garden and marinade duck! I have never spent this much time alone. I am not lonely but I miss the work camaraderie and the jovial banter.

I miss that elated feeling in litigation when a case is won fair and square or a settlement is reached to the delight of the Plaintiff. I yearn for my role as peacemaker in the extensive amount of mediations I undertook and the skills I used to steer couples to reach viable proposals. I reminisce over all the divorces and separations I have handled over the years.

Some were fought tooth and nail and some clients even went for a drink together after the decree was ordered! Sometimes I catch myself becoming maudlin as if my life has changed forever. I struggle then to remind myself that this is just a temporary interlude, that all will resume as it once was and that I will be, once again, the solicitor that I am. I have served justice all my working life, now justice must serve me. The Law must protect me as I have protected it. *Nemo dat quod non habet*. Yes, but I will endure this! My name will be vindicated and this momentary notoriety will be forgotten.

"Hi Conor. How are you?" I enquire of my partner-in-crime.

Anyone would think we had committed some sort of *folie-a-deux* due to the amount of time we spend discussing our defence.

"I've been better Helene. I don't want to frighten you but I've received some fucking awful death threats and I'm not joking!" Conor says and I can sense he is not. "One bastard put an unused bullet in an envelope with my name on it through our letterbox!

Megan, who only just turned three, opened the bloody thing and came into the kitchen with a bullet in her hand! You can imagine my wife's face!"

"Jesus, Conor!" I say, shocked.

"Yeah, and then some other prick placed a note under the wipers of the front window of my wife's car. Whoever it was cut random capital letters out of newspapers and stuck them on with glue onto the page. It reads 'CONOR CARROLL, THE SCUMBAG LAWYER, IS DEAD!'

"Jesus. I presume you went to the Gardai?" I ask, shook by Conor's revelations.

"Yeah. They don't think either threat is connected," he explains, "That makes it worse as far as I'm concerned. The wife wants to move, like yesterday!"

"I can't say I blame her Conor! I'd be terrified to stay in the same house after that!" I say, empathising with the poor woman.

"I told Frank McGrath and he said that I should put in an affidavit of medical evidence as well as a garda report concerning these threats to my life. I swear to God, Helene, I'm on anti-anxiety tablets and sleeping pills. The works! I'm living a Goddamn nightmare and all because of that selfish bastard, Andrew. If it wasn't for the wife's family, we'd be in dire straits. Luckily they are not short a penny or two and are giving us a dig out. I'm not even sure they totally believe me, you know. No smoke without fire and all that. I can't believe how stupid we all were!" he sighs, patently upset by how the dice is rolling in his life.

"We were, weren't we?" I exclaim. "We just took our eye off the ball and trusted Andrew to do his job to the same high standard we were doing ours. I mean, to think we thought he had such a sharp legal mind! He had a sharper criminal mind, that's for sure! What galls me is that he has fucked off, excuse my language, to some far flung place like Timbuctoo and left us and all the staff at Peterson & Co. and clients and investors and even his own *family* to pick up the pieces! What a coward!" I say, angrily.

"You know, I googled my name yesterday, don't ask me why, and guess what was the first fucking frame of reference to pop up?" Conor asks.

"Go on, enlighten me!" I say, afraid to hear the answer.

"This bloody mess, of course. All the twisted articles and court reports on our involvement in this travesty! No mention, naturally, of all the bloody hard work I have put in over the years. All the years of study, all the fucking hours in that office, tied to my desk or how I worked my ass of to be made partner. All of that simply wiped out overnight. It's a fucking nightmare this Helene! A fucking nightmare!" Conor breaks off and I hear him weep heavily down the phone. I have rarely seen or heard a grown man cry. It is not a pleasant experience.

"Oh Conor! Don't worry!" I say, my heart breaking for him. "I've had my own share of tears, believe me. We'll all get through this somehow and I know it's not much of a consolation but we are all in the same boat. Frank McGrath is one of the best! I know he will prove that we didn't know what was going on in the Firm. We have to think positively!" I say, simultaneously trying to convince myself of the same thing.

"My concern, Helene," Conor says quietly, still recovering from his rare display of emotion, "is that we will be made the scapegoats here. After all, Andrew is not the first solicitor to dip into the cookie jar of the client account. There was public outcry after the last shower. They operated a secret bank account for years where they deposited millions but they still didn't get struck off the roll. I think the Judge is going to be out for the jugular this time!"

"I really hope you are wrong Conor," I say, feeling disillusioned. "There is no way I am going to be punished for committing a crime that I never did! Surely if the Gardai do their job properly and extradite Andrew back here, he'll give evidence that none of us knew anything of what was going on?"

"I wouldn't bank on it Helene. You wouldn't know what lies that Andrew will spin! Anyway, thanks for listening, I better go here. I promised herself I'd unload the dishwasher. I'll talk to you soon. Bye."

Conor unloading the dishwasher? God, things have really changed!

Either I get up from the couch too quickly or I have caught some kind of bug but it takes all of my resolve to make it to the kitchen sink without throwing up all over the floor. Its no wonder I have been feeling tired of late, this illness must have been festering inside me. I grip the sides of the Belfast sink as I dry retch twice. My hands are clammy and I am overcome with dizziness. I turn around and slide my body down to the floor. My back leans against the kitchen press and I put my head between my knees. I still feel nauseous but I know there is nothing but bile left in my stomach. Maybe I have food poisoning? Dan and I ordered a Chinese take away the night before and I had my usual prawn stir-fry. That's what it is! You have to be incredibly careful with seafood. It only takes one bad prawn.

I walk like a toddler up the steps of the stairs, holding on to the wooden rail and taking one step at a time. I think I am going to throw up every thirty seconds. At the midway point an overpowering wave of nauseousness almost makes me lose my footing. I sit slowly, straddle two steps and wait for this bout to pass. Jesus, I'm never ordering from that Chinese take away again! This is total torture! My mouth is dry and my throat stings but I don't think I am capable of even holding down a sip of water.

I curl up as tight as a ball of knitting wool, rest my head on the pillow and put on my velvet lavender -scented eye mask. I cover myself with the mohair rug, which I always believed was superfluous to the practicality of the bed, but not now. Oh not now! I am cold and shivery but grateful for the refuge of my womb-like cocoon. I close my eyes, appreciative of the reprieve my body has afforded me. I doze for a while, dipping in and out of sleep in short spurts.

I dream of Tanya Peterson. She can barely stand upright, her loose skin hanging off her toothpick limbs, as she clings to the barbed wire. Her head is shaved and her eyes dark and swollen stare listlessly into my own. She tries to speak but no sound comes out. I follow her gaze as it moves and focuses on something behind me. A single silent tear falls from her eye. I look back and see her five children being paraded in single file like cattle. Their tiny, frail bodies are painted into stripy pyjamas as they are herded to the smoking chimney.

I wake up disorientated and gasping for air

PART II

Chapter 18

"Hullo? Yes?" I whisper into the phone the next morning, noticing that my voice sounds hoarse and weak. The persistent ring of the phone jolts me reluctantly into a wakeful state. I slowly remember that I don't feel well. I still feel ill. "Yes, hello?" I say, irritated.
I am anxious to get rid of this caller and resume feeling sick and sorry for myself. I prop my head on my elbow and lean over the pillow, straining to hear a reply.

"Helene. It's me," the voice says, slightly muffled.

I am about to ask who *me* is when I suddenly feel a chill down my spine. *OmiGod.*

"Are you on your own?" Andrew says hurriedly.

"Yes," I reply, automatically. I can't even think straight for a few seconds. "What are you doing ringing me? And how did you get my number?" I stutter angrily, lowering my voice even though there is no one else home. "What the hell have you been up to?" I hiss venomously into the phone.

"Helene, please listen." Andrew replies quickly but calmly. "Please listen for a minute!" he pleads.

I hold my tongue wondering how on earth he managed to get the upper hand as if I'm the one at fault! My stomach churns with a fresh bout of nausea and I don't know if it's me or my reaction to Andrew's call. I lie back on the pillow, putting one hand on my forehead and holding the phone in the other. I close my eyes and listen.

"Thanks Helene," Andrew says gratefully, aware that I have resigned myself to listen to him. I feel too sick to argue. "I need your help," he continues.

The nerve of him, I think to myself.

"I have been following the press releases in the Media," Andrew continues. "I also have a source that tells me that Tanya and the children are in an awful way financially and I need to help them out except that I can't do it myself," he says, and I can't help but think he seems to feel a bit sorry for himself.

My heart bleeds.

"All my accounts are frozen but I do have some cash, well eh, let's say put away for a rainy day. It's quite a substantial amount..." he says, pausing momentarily. "The only problem is that the money, well the cash, is in a box in the walk-in safe in the back of the office building. I mean, of course, at the back end of the building where Peterson & Co. is, " he says by way of explanation. "Helene, I can't ask anyone else because I don't trust them. I know they would keep the money for themselves. You, on the other hand, have a conscience," Andrew says, using his flattery to massage my ego. "I'm not in contact with Tanya. It's too risky. I'm sure the cops have tapped the phones and I can't afford to be caught. They'd never suspect I'd call you," he adds as I feel pale inside and out. "Also, I need someone who has access to getting in and out of the building and before you say anything I know that the offices have been shut down temporarily but I also know that you and Conor *will* have your solicitors practising certificates reinstated pending a thorough investigation. In other words you will be able to be back working in the Firm before you know it..." Andrew talks authoritatively as I struggle to concentrate on what he is saying.

What does he mean we'll be able to practice under supervision? I can't believe he is calling me... where is he? I can hear the faint sound of a cuckoo clock in the background. Lots of indistinguishable sound in the background. Indecipherable white noise.

"...so I need your help. I need you to take this money out of the safe. It's hidden in there. I'll ring you again with the code. I want you to give it to Tanya and our children. I'm asking you as I know you are a good person and I'm urging the better side of your nature to do this on my behalf. You know she is innocent in all this. I know you know that it wouldn't be fair for her and the children to be suffering as a result of my wrongdoing. It'd be a charitable act on your behalf, wouldn't it? I'll help you and you'll help me."

There is silence for a moment as Andrew allows this sink in.

My head is pounding.

"I'll call you again soon for your answer" he says as he hangs up.

The manipulative bastard, I think to myself as I crane my neck over the side of the bed to put the phone down.

I stand up hesitantly and make towards the bathroom. I lurch over the sink and dry retch. I am seething inside. I can't believe I didn't even get to say anything! I let him dictate to me like he always has! I never even got to tell him what I think of him. Yet I am more angry with myself than I am with him.

What the hell do I do now?

This is a blatant attempt at emotional blackmail yet something stops me picking up the phone to report his call. Why am I protecting him? Surely the Gardai will be able to trace his call? Mind you, knowing Andrew he has probably covered his tracks. He has used enough surveillance tactics himself in his career I've no doubt he knows what he is doing. Dan will freak if I tell him. I don't want to put him under that pressure. Anyway, I don't know if I could trust him not to blab to Walter or his parents. Andrew's vanishing act is that topical he mightn't be able to help himself. He finds it near impossible to keep a confidence as it is. I can't tell Murdoch either even though I crave his advice. I need to wean him off me and don't want to encourage him. I have to keep things simple. I need to be careful with this one. I can't afford to make any rash decisions now. I'll think it through but first I just want cure myself of this horrible sickness. It is completely debilitating.

"Hey Conor," I answer the phone as it rings for the second time this morning. "What's up?" I say as the room swirls in front of my eyes.

"Hi Helene. I just got a call from Frank McGrath. It appears the Law Society want us to finish off certain files in the Firm. The accounts will still be frozen but we'll be allowed assist in the progress of certain cases under the supervision of the Law Society. What's strange about the whole thing is that you and I are the only partners who'll have our practising certificates re-instated, for a while at least. The Law Society are so anxious to have some of the files sorted out that they are willing apparently to indemnify us if the SMDF refuse to provide us with insurance. They seem terribly eager. I don't know what the story is with David and Stephen? I hope to God this means they have some faith in our integrity but I don't know why the others aren't being allowed the same treatment...Helene? Are you still there?"

"Eh yeah, sorry, Conor," I reply faintly "I'm feeling quite sickly this morning again. I don't know what's wrong with me," I say perplexed.

"Anyone would think you were pregnant!" he remarks deadpan. "The wife's like that at the moment too. Mind you she is used to it at this stage, her fourth pregnancy and all that. Anyway, this is a bit of good news isn't it, Helene? Though I can't say I find it all very odd, I'm not complaining! Look, I'll talk to you later when you are feeling a bit better."

Conor hangs up as I sit on the side of the bed. I wonder which part of the knowledge he has just imparted to me is the most shocking. Without showering I change quickly into jeans and a shirt. I run downstairs, stopping to put my hair into a ponytail at the hall mirror, grab my coat and keys and leave the house. I walk straight to the pharmacy which is two hundred yards away and purchase two digital pregnancy tests. Apart from the obvious urgency I also hurry for fear I bump into someone I don't want to bump into. I rush home, my breath catching in the back of my throat. My hands shake as I hold the plastic pregnancy test in my hands. It looks like a thermometer. I read the instructions on the box, pee as directed and sit and wait. *Three minutes.* It feels like an eternity. *Pregnant.* I stare at it with such intensity that the blue letters start merging into one another. *Sweet Jesus!* I sit motionless for a few minutes. It all makes sense now. I tear open the other packet in such haste that the foil-covered test falls onto the bathroom floor. I go through the same procedure again as if in a ground hog day. I pace up and down during the required three minute process, like a nicotine addict trying to wait out a craving. *Pregnant.* A blue-lettered blur. *Great!*

I text Caroline on my new mobile phone to tell her the news. She calls me back immediately and shrieks with delight until she notices the note of concern in my voice. I can't be sure who the biological father is but I don't say this to Caroline. How can I explain that one? After all my pontificating about James, I went ahead and did the same thing. Ok, I'm not married but the principle is the same, is it not? From the goodness of her heart Caroline assumes that I am just scared.

"Seriously, Helene," she says, calmly. "I know it mightn't seem like it now but this is probably the best thing that has ever happened to you. Trust me. Kids aren't easy but they bring so much joy to your life. It's so worth it. You'll never know a joy like it," she says as I silently scream inside. "Oh and eat some cream crackers. They are great for morning sickness," she laughs "and don't worry I'll keep your news to myself for the moment. Wait till you see though, Dan will be thrilled!" Caroline predicts.

It's not him I'm worried about I think. I'm emotionally attached to Murdoch already. The last thing I want is his baby growing inside me. If it is his baby, that is. I make another brief visit to the pharmacy later and ask their advice on morning sickness and how to alleviate the symptoms. I come back to the house armed with all sorts of medicines including folic acid and other multivitamins to take during pregnancy. I spend the rest of the day lying in the foetal position on my bed, physically feeling nauseous and mentally feeling sick with recent developments.

"Are you still that sick?" Dan enquires softly when he comes home unexpectedly early that evening. "I didn't think you were *this* bad. I was hoping to bring you off for a romantic weekend but I suppose the main thing is that you get better–" Dan stops abruptly.

I look up at him and follow his eyes which are fixated on two discarded pregnancy testing kits jutting out of the en suite bin. *There's no going back now.*

"Are you–" Dan whispers, the colour draining from his cheeks in front of my eyes.

"Yes" I interrupt him. "Yes, I am," I say and I start to cry which takes me as much by surprise as it does him. I can't even look at him.

"Oh Helene, that's wonderful news! A shock but still wonderful!" Dan says, his voice quavering as he sits by the bed and puts his arm around me.

"I must have missed a few pills or something," I say, by way of explanation. "I can't think how else it happened," I say again. I don't elaborate on the possible issue over the paternity of my baby.

"Don't be crying, Helene. I know it's probably the shock, not to mind the hormones! We'll be great parents," Dan says quietly, clearly moved by this turn of events. "How long are you gone?" he asks, innocently.

"I'm not really sure. *Fuck*. It's only a matter of weeks anyway," I say, trying to brush it off. "I'll get an appointment with an obstetrician and find out soon enough."

"Great,"Dan replies animatedly, "because I can't wait to tell Mum and Dad they are going to be grandparents. They'll be so excited."

"Just wait a while yet," I say, in a concerned voice. "At least let me get over this nausea. The medicine the pharmacist gave me seems to be working somewhat but I still feel horrific."

"Of course," Dan says as he kisses me on the forehead, pulling up the duvet cover and tucking me in. "I'll bring you up something light to eat later. You just rest for the moment."

An hour later Conor rings. He tells me that Judge Symthson has ordered the two of us to return to Peterson & Co. in the morning to assist the Law Society in finishing off certain files and in unravelling the labyrinth of lies left behind in Andrew's files.

"It's a very unusual move, isn't it, Helene?" Conor says, clearly confused. "What's more is that they will be putting out a press release to that effect so that the public-at-large will be off our backs. It's kind of like they are exonerating us from all liability already, even though there hasn't been a proper investigation. There is no precedent for this. How can they be so sure that we haven't done anything wrong? I mean, I *know* we haven't but they don't know that, do they? I was on to David and Stephen earlier and they can't understand why their practising certificates are not being temporarily re-instated but ours are. They were very upset about the whole thing. Stephen was really distraught. He kept wondering how Andrew could do this to him. Anyway, it's all very odd but as I said earlier I'm not complaining, even though I do feel bad for David and Stephen. You sound much better anyway, not up the duff then, huh?" Conor says, teasing.

I just laugh it off good naturedly. I can't risk telling anyone else for the moment as I don't want Murdoch finding out just yet. I need to get my story straight.

"This is so weird." Conor says at eight the following morning as we walk into the imposing lobby of Peterson & Co. I'm just grateful I can walk without feeling I have to retch at any given moment. "I feel like I've been mitching off school or something coming back in here," he says chuckling to himself.

"I wish it was that simple Conor but to be honest it's not really funny. The Law Society could be just using us to sort our their crap and then strike us off the roll anyway. How the hell do we know what's really at play here? We are totally at their mercy," I say, solemnly. I'm also thinking of my telephone conversation with Andrew but I keep it to myself.

"I know, Helene. I'm just trying to retain a sense of humour," Conor replies defensively, nudging me at the same time. "Don't look now but isn't that the investigating accountant Barnaby Walsh of the Law Society? I'm not getting stuck in an escalator with him. Let's take the stairs."

Conor and I slink over to the Emergency Exit staircase, looking like a couple running the three-legged race. We split our sides as we mock our ridiculously childish behaviour.

"Conor, stop! I've a pain in my side. I can't laugh anymore!" I exclaim as I put my hand out to steady myself on the stairway. We are in convulsions. It's a long walk to the third floor as we have to pause every few minutes to regain our composure.

"Good morning Ms. McBain. Mr. Carroll," nods Mr. Barnaby Walsh. "It's heartening to see you both in such good spirits at a time like this. If you wouldn't mind following me please to the blue boardroom and we'll have a debriefing on our roles here today."

It wouldn't take a Mensa student to detect the note of sarcasm in his voice. Unfortunately it doesn't take long for the seriousness of our predicament to sober up our mood in an instance. Mr. Walsh holds the door open for us as we enter the Boardroom. I am not expecting to see three other people sitting around the boardroom table.

What is going on here?

"Helene, Conor. Take a seat," says the Director General of the Law Society as he gestures us to sit. He shakes our hands and remains standing until we are both seated and Mr. Walsh has taken a chair to his right.

"As you know, I am Don Glennon, the current Director-General of the Law Society. I have met you both before under rather more pleasant circumstances," he adds, sweeping a well-manicured hand through his silver hair. "In case you haven't been formally introduced this is the Deputy Director-General Eoin Doyle, the President of the Law Society Garret Stone and the vice-president of the Law Society Teresa Butterworth."

It doesn't escape my notice that not one of them extends a hand or bestows a smile on myself or my colleague.

"You've certainly brought in the heavies!" Conor says, in a futile attempt to lighten the mood. There is an umcomfortable silence. Conor clears his throat, feeling as awkward as I do in the moment. I am rooted to the chair, feeling as if I am on trial for mass murder.

"Indeed Conor," says Glennon snidely, not hiding his distaste. "As you can imagine we, in the Law Society, are under serious pressure at the moment. The general perception of Joe Bloggs out there on street is that all solicitors are corrupt, slimy thieves." He lets this sink in for a moment before he continues. No one will catch my eye. "The actions of Andrew Peterson, are, to say the least, abhorrent. A full criminal investigation is underway but in the meantime the Disciplinary committee of the Law Society, on my recommendation of course, thought it would be useful to bring in the two of you to assist in cleaning up the mess, if you will. Fortunately our eminent Judge Smythson concurred with our recommendation and as you are aware your practising certificates have been temporarily reinstated. We, as in the Law Society, have agreed to make up the difference should there be any hit with regard to your insurance, which I'm sure there will be. I should warn you, however, that this does *not* mean that you are entirely without negligence in this matter but we have good reason to believe that you were not party to the appalling embezzlement that has been going on in this Firm. It's an awful pity, putting it mildly, that Andrew Peterson's passport wasn't confiscated but such is the situation we find ourselves in now. There has been a siphoning of monies on an unprecedented level!" Glennon says exuberantly.

Teresa Butterworth almost jumps off her chair towards the end of his sentence.

"We must conclude this investigation as soon as possible. Justice will be done and must be seen to be done! I have assured the Minister that we will leave no stone unturned and all facilitators and benefactors of this fraud will be punished accordingly."

Glennon continues.

The Minister?

"I will leave you in the capable hands of Mr. Barnaby Walsh who will outline the level of application expected from you. Needless to say we expect your discretion in this most sensitive of matters in the interest of the profession and of the general public as a whole."

Glennon waves a hand at Walsh who nods vigorously like an altar boy in awe of the ornately robed bishop standing before him. The Law Society figurehead leads the silent procession out of the boardroom door, leaving it and the mouths of those of us left behind wide open.

CHAPTER 19

"Helene, the Law Society would like you to deal, in particular, with the completion of these family law and litigation files," Walsh says agitatedly, gesturing towards a double filing cabinet against the wall of my office. "I believe that some of the papers in these files may not be in chronological order any more but rest assured that all the pleadings and correspondence relevant to each file will be intact. As you can appreciate we have had a team of people in here of late who have helped us with regard to this investigation," Walsh continues by way of explanation.

"What? Who else was allowed in to look at confidential files?" I ask, confused by Walsh's revelation.

This is all very odd.

"Ms. McBain I wouldn't be questioning an order that the Director-General himself has given which I believe originated from the Minister himself. I'm just presuming that this was what was done. I'm sure they know what they are doing. I'm simply following orders and if you could just do the same we'll get this all sorted as soon as possible. We simply want you to finish off these files as soon as possible. I will consult with you later with regard to your views on a realistic date to achieve this. I will leave you now as I want to have a word with Conor also."

He closes the door, turning the handle painstakingly slowly as if locking me into Alcatraz.

I survey my office in more detail and I can tell that everything has been turned upside down. On a superficial level an untrained eye would not notice that anything was amiss, but because this is or *was* my office, I can detect the subtle changes almost subliminally.

My solicitor's parchment is framed and hangs on the wall above my desk, in the middle of other academic achievements. Except that now it doesn't hang in the middle. It has been demoted to fourth place on the left. My annual desk diaries are no longer in chronological order. The drawers in my office desk bulge with papers, do not close and the key is missing. When I turn on my computer most of the content has been deleted save for the files I have been asked to work on, most of whom are clients who have loyally supported me throughout this showdown. *Why am I surprised?* Surely the Law Society or more likely the gardai in the fraud squad needed to trawl through all the offices of the partners and employees of Peterson & Co. to gather up evidence. It just seems to have been done in a very haphazard fashion. Apart from that Murdoch says I am going to go down in flames as a partner anyway so I can't understand how the Law Society have allowed me back or indeed *wanted* me back? If they knew Andrew Peterson had called me and I hadn't told them I doubt I'd be sitting here now. I'm just going to pretend to myself that it never happened, there's no other way.

I sit at my desk with my hands clasped protectively over my stomach. It's hard to believe a new life is growing inside me. I have every intention of keeping this baby, despite the real risk in time of Murdoch suspecting it's his own child. I'll just have to convince him otherwise if needs be. In the meantime I won't be divulging my condition to anyone other than Dan and Caroline and my parents in due course. I don't want Murdoch getting wind of it. Conor and Barnaby Walsh seem to have gone off down the corridor, probably to Conor's office. I get up and walk over to the first filing cabinet and take out a big red file with the name JANE MOORE written on it. I remember the thoughtful note of support I received from Jane some weeks ago. It was one of only a handful of kind letters I received. Since Peterson & Co has effectively ceased trading, I have no phone on my desk. I, therefore, take out my mobile phone to ring Jane. Walsh has told me that the Law Society will foot the bill for 'work-related' phone calls. I dial the number but it doesn't ring. *It must be a crossed line.* I hear a familiar voice on the other end. It's Andrew. *Again.*

"Good morning Helene. How does your office look today? Still the same?" he says, smugly. *How the hell does he know where I am?* I figure that he must have been ringing my mobile at the same time as I was trying to ring Jane.

"Stop calling me, Andrew," I say, in a forced whisper, darting a look at the door. I'm relieved it's tightly shut.

"I'm just wondering what your answer is?" he says quickly before I have time to hang up.

"Just leave me alone or I'll tell the Gardai and they can have this call traced to wherever it is you are hiding out," I say, fuming into the phone.

"Would you tell Murdoch too?" he says, casually.

I hesitate. "What's that supposed to mean?" I reply weakly as I feel a chill down my spine.

"Let's just say I have reason to believe that you and Murdoch have had a little 'liaison dangereux' if I can be so bold as to call it that," Andrew retorts menacingly. *Oh no! Please don't!* "I don't want to have to resort to this, Helene, but suffice to say that if your answer is not in the affirmative, then I will have no option but to arrange that your beloved Dan gets to hear about all these private club and hotel rendezvous with Mr. Murdoch Pierce SC," he says, calmly.

My entire body shakes. I cradle my left hand with the right hand to steady its hold. *How does he know about Murdoch?*

"So I'm assuming you will answer yes? What you will need to do is–"

I half-listen as I try to breathe normally. "The offices have been gone through with a fine toothcomb," I say, interrupting Andrew's instructions to mire me further into the depths of aiding and abetting a fraudulent criminal.

"Firstly, I seriously doubt that there are any monies, not to mind any cash, left in any of the safes. Secondly, the Law Society's Investigating accountant is here scrutinising my every move that there is no way I'd make it to the safe and out of the office and thirdly, how on earth do I get this money to Tanya without her seeing or knowing where it came from and fourthly, how do I know that *you* won't mention my involvement in this if and when you are caught?" I say, exasperated by the absurdity of it all.

"My, you have it all worked out!" Andrew laughs derisively. "Glad to hear you are on the ball as always," he says, smartly. "You're an intelligent girl so you'll work it out. Please ensure to tell Tanya that the monies are from the *Lord Leinster charity*. She'll know what you mean and will indicate that to you. Her reply to you will be the proof I need. I'll call you in a few days but in the meantime I'll text you a description and detailed whereabouts of the box. Oh and don't worry I don't intend on being 'captured' anytime soon!" Andrew laughs mockingly.

He is gone off the phone before I have time to protest.

OmiGod! This is a nightmare!

"Everything ok there, Helene?" Barnaby Walsh says, knocking and opening the door without waiting for a response.

"Eh, yes," I splutter tentatively, desperately trying to regain my composure. "It's just a bit overwhelming to be back at my desk, you know," I reply, hoping this red herring might divert his attention.

He could have walked in thirty seconds ago.

"I heard you talking on the phone. I'm sure Jane was pleased to hear from you," Walsh remarks as his eyes flicker over the file on my desk.

"Oh yes," I reply, lying already. "Most pleased. I'll just be getting on with sorting out a few matters here," I say decisively, pushing papers around on my desk.

"You've no secretary now so if you need anything photocopied or any assistance at all, just holler!" Walsh says good naturedly as he closes the door. *Has he had a lobotomy?* Random acts of kindness are not really advantageous to me at this time. Tears well up behind my eyes. I distract myself by calling Jane Moore and arranging to meet her at the case progression hearing in phoenix house on Wednesday. I fob off her words of support as they are likely to trigger an immediate downward spiral of emotion. I need to stay strong now. *This is serious!* I contemplate telling Walsh and/or Conor about Andrew's phonecalls. I dismiss this outright when I accept it as a probability that Andrew will tell Dan about Murdoch. I can't lose Dan and I can't have him doubting this baby's paternity either. *I just can't risk it!* I weigh up the lesser of two evils and decide that I have no choice but to do what Andrew asks. It goes against everything I've ever stood for but I can't risk the alternative. *Fuck! How in God's name did I end up here?* I sit with my head in my hands. I keep coming back to the same answer. Now I must devise a plan, a foolproof plan at that.

"What is the position on your client's inheritance from her mother?" Marjorie Price, the County Registrar asks me at Jane Moore's case progression. "I am anxious that there is no untoward delay in this case, Ms. McBain," she cautions pointedly as she lightly taps the desk on her raised platform. "This matter has already been before me on a previous occasion," she warns.

"Yes, County Registrar. I would be concerned in this regard also," pipes Barbara Dolan my opposite number, delighted for an opportunity to pounce. "I appreciate with all the, how can I put it, *goings on's* in the Respondent solicitor's Firm recently that some matters may have been put on the back boiler." *Thanks Barbara.* "However," she continues, "my client is extremely anxious to move forward to a hearing date as soon as possible. He has recently had to take a significant pay cut in his wages and wishes to have all issues resolved between the parties at the earliest opportunity. I note there is a new practice direction available to the Registrar and I wonder if this might be considered as an option at this juncture?" Ms. Dolan suggests tentatively.

"Registrar, if I might just intervene, here, before we progress any further," I interrupt, fully aware that mediation might be suggested. "I understand from my client that her brother's solicitor is dealing with the probate of their mother's estate. The grant of probate has been extracted and the solicitor is now dealing with the administration of the estate. I would respectfully suggest that a short adjournment, for say a period of four weeks, is in order at this stage in the proceedings. I am a firm believer in Mediation but I do not believe it is necessary at this stage. I will be in a position to furnish the court with all relevant details of my client's inheritance in a month's time," I conclude, outlining Ms. Moore's position.

"Fine. 20th March?" Marjorie Price dictates the date. Barbara and I nod in agreement. "This is peremptory, however, and the last time I'll allow this matter come before me," eschews the County Registrar.

As we are last on this morning's list Barbara and I have a brief chat after the case progression meeting. We decide it would be worthwhile to meet for without prejudice talks as soon as we know what monies my client will inherit from her mother.

"Hopefully we'll do business then," Barbara says, "but it'll just depend on what your client gets. We might even be able to set that off against your client's claim on my client's pension. It's the second biggest asset and if she is staying in the family home then there has got to be some kind of compromise on her part, surely?" she

162   NEGLIGENT BEHAVIOUR

quizzes, already attempting to settle the matter.

"Barbara, you know I can't possibly give any advice to my client until I know the inheritance details!" I tease good-humouredly. "I'll be back to you on it asap," I say, rushing off for fear she starts interrogating me on Peterson & Co and the recent shenanigans. I may be able to divert attention from myself through humour but my heart is breaking inside. I can't believe I have got myself into such a muddle with such serious ramifications.

Here I am off now to the High Court to defend an interim maintenance application for a "big money" client, looking like Ms. Professional on the exterior when everything around me is coming apart at the seams! I don't know where to turn. How lovely that Murdoch is the Senior Counsel in this case and my meeting with him unavoidable! I need to keep the Law Society on my side and can't afford to be refusing to deal with files just because I had an affair with the Barrister who may or may not be the father of the baby growing inside me! What fun!

I sit with my client, John L. McDermott whose cheeks are red from the exertion of walking up the flights of stairs to the fourth floor.

"I can't believe the bloody lift is broken!" he moans, sweating and breathing in and out like a large water mammal.

"Do you want some water?" I ask him, while dispensing some cold water into a plastic cup from the cooler. We talk outside the High Court as we wait for Murdoch. The Junior Counsel comes out of the Law Room briefly and checks in with us. Unfortunately there are no consultation rooms left so we are reduced to whispering for fear the other side might overhear our conversation. They too, are huddled together, further up in a corner of the corridor. I can hardly make out Mrs. McDermott for all the black-cloaked bodies around her. Barristers swarm around the euro notes parading in front of their eyes. I can just about decipher a well-dressed and exquisitely coiffed blonde, legs crossed and designer handbag by her side. With my client worth close to fifty million, I wouldn't have expected any less of a cliché.

"Thanks," John says, gulping back the water and stretching over to pour himself another. "My new year resolution has gone by the way side. It's 20th February and I haven't lost a pound. I've been comfort eating, I think. Would you blame me with a wife like that?" he says, grimacing and acknowledging Murdoch's arrival with a nod. I don't even raise an eyebrow. *I can't believe I have to do this case with him.* "I don't think she ever loved me, you know. She was only after my money. So obvious now, isn't it? How she has the gall to bring me in here and look for even *more* maintenance is beyond me. I refuse to give her a cent more. She's cleaning me out!" he says, looking at Murdoch for confirmation but Murdoch is busy looking at me. I pretend I don't notice.

"Well, that's not quite true," Murdoch finally replies, after a pregnant pause. "We will be resisting an increase in the interim maintenance payment on the basis that your wife has skills that she can use out in the workforce. She is twenty two with some hairdressing experience." *Twenty two. My client is fifty nine.* "We are going to insist she return to the workforce as soon as possible. The judge might allow a moratorium of say three to six months to allow her to do further training but at that point I think we should insist that she work for a living. Those days are gone where a wife can be expected to be maintained in the manner to which she has become accustomed." Murdoch concludes sanguinely.

"And about time too!" John remarks sanctimoniously. "She has a lot more experience than just hairdressing!" John says belligerently. "Look, I didn't want to bring this up before but I met Katja in a *lap-dancing* club," he whispers at an even lower decibel. She's what you'd call an *exotic* dancer. She's also been working in escort agencies since she was sixteen. Believe me, Katja is well able to earn a quick buck *turning tricks*, the poles are great for that, if you know what I mean, hah hah," John guffaws, elbowing Murdoch in the arm as if he is in the know and colouring my opinion of him simultaneously.

"I see," Murdoch says, evenly.

"Yeah, but I don't want the papers getting a hold of that info," John warns. "So it's only to be used if it means I have to pay her less than I already do. That woman would have feic all if it wasn't for me! She's gone up in the world now, don't be fooled by the look of her. I brought her to the best image consultants and personal shoppers. I even got her deportment and elocution lessons in English. She was desperate to fit in and I helped her do that. She mingles with all of Irish high society now on the strength of my grooming," he adds, steadfast in his opinion.

I am beginning to think he is talking about his pet.

Armed with this information Murdoch negotiates with the

Senior Counsel on the other side. We learn in return about John's penchant for fantasy sex games. In particular Katja's role as dominatrix and the not infrequent use of a ménage-a-trois. I attempt to keep the picture of this out of my head or I might risk a return of nausea. *Thou shalt not Judge*. Although both sides are aware of the in camera rule both are afraid of the media getting hold of this information. Thankfully we reach a compromise with regard to the maintenance and our client is given certain assurances with regard to his wife seeking employment in the future. We have the matter ruled after lunch and my client is as satisfied as he can be. I am starving as negotiations continued on through lunch and my stomach rumbles with hunger. *I am feeding two now.*

"All rise," the Registrar barks.

We stand as the Judge leaves the courtroom. I gather up all my papers, hurriedly stuffing them into my briefcase on wheels. I want to get out of here before Murdoch worms his way over to me. It is at times like this I wish I was a muslim wearing a *burqa* or *niqab*. To be able to blend chameleon-like into the background has its advantages.

"Come dine with me tomorrow night?" Murdoch whispers into my ear as we walk out of the court.

"Is that a joke?" I reply, irritated. There is no way I am going out for dinner with him.

"You are misinterpreting me, Helene," he says quickly, picking up on my discomfort.

"It happens to be visitors night at the Inns tomorrow and I thought you might be my guest. I couldn't believe it when you rang me to say you were coming down on this case today. I felt sure you were going to be struck off the roll," Murdoch says, puzzled by my sudden re-instatement back into what is left of Peterson & Co.

"I could still be," I say, deadly serious. *He doesn't even know about Andrew's blackmail.* "We need to talk anyway. You just left me high and dry and I haven't been able to contact you at all. You don't have to stay long. Please do me the honour. For old time's sake?" he pleads, using his own form of emotional blackmail.

"Alright!" I reply, exasperated by the day and too eager to get away from him to think about the consequences of my words.

Chapter 20

"I'm not sure if I like you back in that stressful environment," Dan says, protectively as he dishes out another helping of creamed carrot and parsnip onto my plate.

"If it means I stay on the roll of solicitors, isn't it worth it?" I say, feeling exhausted but starving as usual.

"I wonder," Dan retorts, "that Firm has brought you nothing but trouble as far as I can see."

If he only knew, I think.

"Thanks for the beautiful dinner," I say, appreciatively, changing the subject. "Food is definitely the way to my heart these days!" I laugh, being totally serious.

"Well, we never did have a proper Valentine's Day celebration so better late than never," Dan smiles, "and it's good to see you relishing every morsel. This baby of ours will be half-reared by the time it comes out!" he quips. "I've never seen anyone eat so much!"

I try to laugh but my mouth is full to the brim with food. I have to make a concerted effort to breathe and chew slowly so I don't lodge a piece of food in my windpipe.

"Hey smarty pants!" I tease, once I have recovered, "I'm just making up for lost time. That awful nausea had me practically anorexic at one stage!" I protest, as I cram another roast potato into my mouth. "That chocolate mousse is delicious" I say, salivating with every spoonful. "It's positively orgasmic" I swoon.

"Glad to be of assistance!" Dan says, clearly amused by my exuberance for food. I spend the rest of the evening on the couch curled up in the nook of Dan's arm, wondering what on earth I did right to deserve such a wonderful man. Not much recently anyway, that's for sure! *I have to do what Andrew wants. I've no choice.*

Dan is going to be a great Dad and there is no way I am going to take that away from him.

I have to get Andrew off my back.

I get out of the bath later that night only to be greeted by a cryptic text from an unknown sender, though I know exactly who it is.

"The code for the back safe if 899421. The cash is in a brown and white R-Kive Premium box marked 'Correspondence in [FR v LR]: 2004-2005/ Ref: AP/SM9204/627L'. The box is in the right-hand corner of the safe on the second shelf. In the box there are three red files and two blue files filled with correspondence. Underneath these you will find ten large white envelopes with cash. Get this money to Tanya. You have forty eight hours. The alarm code for the building is 4421 if you need it. Good luck."

I re-read the text again and feel like throwing the mobile and smashing against the bedroom wall. *This is a fucking joke! I need more than luck!*

If I refuse to carry out Andrew's orders I am in deep trouble. But if I do carry out his orders I am in deep water too. I don't doubt for a second that Andrew's threats aren't empty. Life with Dan as I know it would be over. But if I continue with his instructions I am embroiling myself further into illegality and crossing the line. But I can't lose Dan?! *How do I get to the safe and get the money out? And how do I get it to Tanya?*

My mind works overtime all night pondering different scenarios, all blocked by some angle or another. I eventually drift off to sleep, praying for the angels of guidance to come to me in my slumber and enlighten me. I can't believe the mess I have got myself into.

"That Law Society mole keeps breathing down my neck," Conor says the next morning, referring to Barnaby Walsh. "I feel like he is watching every move I make," he whinges.

"That's because he is," I remark factually. "That's his job" I add, by way of explanation.

Conor sits in the chair in front of my desk, turning around every now and then to ensure the door is closed.

"That may well be but I can't understand what we are doing here in the first place. This place is like a ghost town. Seriously,

Helene, you have lots of files to catch up on but most of mine have been ferried out to other Solicitor's Firms or the clients themselves don't want to deal with me. No smoke without fire as I said before. What the hell use am I here for? I am just going through all those old files no one has advanced in ages. Some Landlord and Tenant. Some Rent Reviews. Bloody tedious and bloody boring. I tried to ring David and Stephen last night to reassure them that it's not all it's cracked up to be, being back in the fold as such but I didn't get a reply. Usually they answer on the first ring," Conor says, looking perplexed.

"I hope they're alright," I say, languidly, but distracted by a sudden thought. "You know I could do with your help if you wanted to feel useful?" I say quickly, appearing nonchalant. "I need to get a file up from one of the safes. At least I think it is in one of the safes. I have a nullity case coming up and I want to go through some of the correspondence and pleadings in a case with similar facts, Frances Reilly and Laura Reilly. The husband managed to get a nullity in that case based on the fact that he was not capable of sustaining a normal marital relationship and that he was incapable of giving proper consent on the date of the marriage. It was also..."

"Enough!" Conor says, brazenly interrupting me, "I don't want to know the technicalities of someone's marriage breakdown, thanks very much. What is it? You need me to help you lug the file up here, is that it?" he asks, sounding like a husband tired of his wife's nagging. "Right, come on so and we'll ask the school principal for permission," Conor adds, sarcastically.

I follow him out the door and a short way down the corridor. Walsh isn't seated at his usual spot. His desk is strategically positioned a perfect distance between my office and Conor's office. Conor looks around quickly in all directions. He then makes an impetuous dart over to Walsh's desk. He opens a large white folder on top of the desk and flicks through it hastily.

"What are you doing?" I hiss at him, my heart racing. Conor doesn't answer but pulls open the binder rings, loosening some kind of document, dashes over to the photocopier and presses the button for one copy. My legs are shaking but I can't move. I don't know where to look. In the near distance I hear the distinct ping of an elevator. *Oh sweet Jesus! I think I'm going to lose my mind!* "I'm out of here, Conor!" I rasp at him, taking a step backwards, moving slower than I want to. It is as if in slow motion I watch helplessly as

168   NEGLIGENT BEHAVIOUR

Conor puts the original document back in the binder and closes it. He stuffs the photocopied papers into the inside pocket of his jacket, folding his arms over his chest.

"Have I kept you waiting?" Walsh says, on his return, wearing a bemused but slightly worried expression. His tone may be courteous but I can tell that he is put out. This man likes to think he is in control, needing order and rules to help him feel safe in this life.

"No, not at all" Conor replies, his voice marginally more high-pitched than normal. I notice he is struggling to keep his breathing even. "Helene needs my help to bring up a file from one of the safes. Maybe you could check in which safe it's located as we don't have access to that information ourselves," Conor continues, somewhat snottily.

"Indeed," Walsh says calmly, turning his attention to me. "And why is this necessary?" he asks, the lines between his eyebrows creasing harshly.

Don't fuck this up, Helene. "Well, I am working on a case at the moment which is coming up for hearing shortly..." I explain matter-of-factly, looking Walsh in the eye. I feel a red flush creeping up my neck and face but I keep up the charade as best I can. "It's not the end of the world if you can't locate the file," I say, flicking my hand. I'm desperate to appear casual about the whole matter.

"Having said that, I do think I would be in a better position to advise my client if I had a look through that particular file" I say, deliberately honing in on Walsh's love of due process.

"Indeed," he says again, mulling it over in his head. Then he taps away on his keyboard and announces he has located the file in a box in the back safe. *I could have told you that.*

"Grand so, I'll help you lifting it up," Conor says, grateful to be leaving the scene of the crime.

"I'll escort you both," Walsh says, pragmatically. "Anyway, you'll need the code for the safe and I want to make sure you locate the correct file," Walsh says, standing up and leading the way.

This is too much. I feel like getting sick. I veer left into the ladies, close the door of the toilet cubicle and violently dry retch. *I need to stay strong. I have no choice.* I take a few moments to compose myself, wash my hands and clean my face. Conor looks at me quizzically when I return. I make a brief apology, avoiding eye contact and we carry on towards the safe. *There is no going back now.* I put my hand over my belly, worried momentarily that this stress could affect my unborn child.

As Walsh is a taciturn man, the walk to the safe is heavy with silence. Conor is not bothered making polite conversation, his mind no doubt focused on the contents of the document in his jacket pocket. I am dizzy from the predicament I find myself in, not knowing which way to turn. *What am I letting myself in for?*

"Here we are," Walsh announces cheerily, as if we've arrived home after a long journey. "Feel free to root around until we locate this particular file. It may take you some time. I'll remain here and ensure the safe door remains open. We wouldn't want that to close unexpectedly, now would we?" Walsh jokes, more to himself than anyone else.

Conor asks me the name of the case again and we then embark on our search. Of course I know where the file is located but I can't make it that obvious. I can't believe I have been deliberately brought back into Peterson & Co for this purpose. *It must be for this purpose.* How the hell did Andrew get me back in here? Do the Law Society know something? *I just can't put my finger on it.*

In a daze I feign my surprise on finding the box after only half an hour.

"Wonderful" Walsh says, clearly delighted he hasn't to supervise us all day.

"Thank God for that," Conor wheezes. "My back is killing me already!" he complains.

"Well, if that's the case we'll just let Helene sift through the box and she can take out the relevant paperwork she needs. There's no need to bring up the entire box," Walsh orders as he starts walking toward it. *Please don't open it*

"Ah sure, it's no trouble at all," Conor says bravely, as if he is picking up on my subdued panic. *I am sure that letter is burning a hole in his pocket.* I steady myself, leaning on a dusty wall not knowing what is going to hit me next. Walsh doesn't dare protest as Conor balances the box in his bulky arms and directs his body towards the safe exit. *Nearly there, nearly there.*

Conor takes a break intermittently from carrying his dusty load. He places the box on the floor in front of him, puts his hands on his sides and gasps for air in theatrical spurts. At one point

Walsh urges that he and I pull out the relevant papers from the box there and then. I freeze with panic. Conor then startles him by disobeying him and insisting he is well able for the job. To make matters worse he asks Walsh if he is worried that he will hit the Law Society with a personal injury claim for back damage caused by lifting heavy items against his will.

"You can be my witness, Helene!" Conor jibes, roaring with laughter. Walsh just glares at him, clearly not amused.

By the time Conor has lugged the heavy box up to the third floor, Walsh has had enough of both of us. He sits down at his desk and starts typing into his keyboard almost immediately. Conor stumbles into my office, puffing dramatically, heaving the box onto my desk as instructed by me. *Now, what do I do? I'm selling my soul to the devil.*

"What in God's name were you doing earlier?" I say to Conor, straining my voice to keep it as quiet as possible.

Conor closes the door of my office. "There is something fishy going on here, Helene. I'm telling you. I know you think I'm a big oaf at times but believe me I'm no eejit. There is something going down here that we are not party to," he says conspiratorially, pulling the document out of his jacket pocket at the same time. I glance at the box on my chair as Conor sits on the corner of my desk, his eyes scanning the pages.

"Well?" I ask impatiently. "What does it say?" and I shake Conor's arm to get his attention.

"Here, read it," he orders, giving nothing away.

I take the document, which turns out to be a letter, and read it:

Minister of Justice's office,
Leinster House,
Nassau Street,
Dublin 2.

By Courier

15th December 2009

Mr. Don Glennon,
Director-General,
Law Society of Ireland,
Blackhall Place,
Dublin 7.

Strictly private & confidential

Re: The Law Society vs Andrew Peterson and Ors

Dear Don,

This letter is simply to express my gratitude to you and your office for meeting with me last Tuesday in respect of this matter.

Naturally as a Solicitor myself I am most concerned with the current public outcry at the scandal caused by Andrew Peterson's fraudulent activities over an extended period of time in Peterson & Co. His actions have been nothing short of abhorrent. No stone must be left unturned in unearthing the truth of this man's deceptions. The public are rightly incensed. Justice will be done and must be seen to be done!

On receipt of this letter (dated 10th December 2009) a copy of which I enclose for your convenience, which purports to be from Andrew Peterson himself, one can only surmise that he has no plans to return to this Jurisdiction anytime soon. I understand the Fraud Squad and Interpol are doing their utmost to track down his whereabouts.

It would also appear that there is tangible proof to surmise that both Stephen Carroll and David Doyle were also involved in these dealings. (I accept, however, that proper disciplinary procedures must be followed and it goes without saying that one is innocent until one is proven guilty). Nevertheless the references in Mr. Peterson's letter have already been cross-referenced and the proof would appear to be irrefutable.

In any event I would strongly suggest that the two remaining partners be re-instated back into Peterson & Co to finalise any outstanding matters and the public will also be reassured that we are taking this matter extremely seriously indeed.

In my humble view, it is important that the general public are made aware that not all of the partners and/or solicitors in Peterson & Co are guilty of negligent behaviour.
Furthermore, I would appreciate being briefed on progress over the next few weeks or months. I do not envisage matters should take longer than that?

You may rest assured that I will not forget your honourable action in this regard in the future.

Please do not hesitate to contact me should you have any further queries.

May I also take this opportunity to wish you all the compliments of the season.

Kind regards.

Yours sincerely,

R. Singleton

Robert Singleton
Minister for Justice

c.c. Eoin Doyle, Deputy Director-General Law Society of Ireland, Garret Stone, President of the Law Society of Ireland, Teresa Butterworth, Vice-President of the Law Society of Ireland

"Right, yeah. Well, Glennon did mention the Minister at some stage," I say quietly, not really knowing what to make of the contents of the letter. Conor is lost in thought, his arms crossed as he balances himself on the corner of my desk. "And come to think of it, so did Barnaby Walsh," I add, succinctly. "It's no wonder since he had this letter in his file. Of course, sure they are all kowtowing to the Minister. At least now we know why we are here!" I conclude, but not quite believing it. "Though it's a pity Andrew's note isn't attached as I'd like to have read exactly what he wrote in our defence."

I hand Conor back the letter and protectively hover near my illicit box of hidden cash. Conor stands up slowly and paces the room.

"I don't want to be pedantic, Helene, but I think you are missing the point entirely," Conor says gravely. "Why would the Minister bother taking such an interest in this Firm? Why would he suggest us being re-instated into the Firm? What loyalty does he owe to us? I know he is saying that it is in the interests of the public as a whole but since when has that ever happened? It doesn't make sense!" Conor exclaims animatedly.

"Well, he does say he is a solicitor himself and that..." I

suggest helpfully.

"How convenient," Conor interjects quickly. "I just don't buy it," he says, shaking his head with certainty.

"Neither do I," I concede, "but for what it's worth, it's not really our business, is it? Let's just get on with our jobs and Conor..."

"Yes, boss," he replies as he holds my office door open, gazing back at me wearily

"I'm begging you just to stay out of this mess," I plead sincerely. "We have already gone through enough. Let's just leave it at that."

Conor sighs as he closes the door, leaving me alone with the incriminating evidence in the brown and white box. *I can't drag Conor into my mess.* I open the lid, lift out the three red files and two blue files. There lies beneath countless tight bundles of purple €500 notes. *Hundreds of Thousands of euro.*

174   NEGLIGENT BEHAVIOUR

CHAPTER 21

"So you are dining with another man this evening, huh?" Dan teases me as he watches me put on my black patent high heels.

"Don't be dressing too sexy now," he jokes, "I want to keep you all to myself, especially now you are carrying my child," Dan says, patting my stomach protectively.

I hope I am carrying his child.

"At least I don't look too pregnant yet. I just look like I've put on a bit of weight," I say, hoping that my eyes don't fool me as I observe myself in the full-length mirror.

"You are just beautiful, darling," Dan says, admiringly. "It was great to be at the scan today. I can't believe the baby was sucking it's thumb. It was really mind-blowing stuff, wasn't it?" he says, clearly awestruck by the whole ultra scan procedure. I find it difficult to concentrate on what he is saying, my mind racing ninety to the dozen.

"It's in my interests to go tonight," I say, flatly, rationalising it to myself as much as to Dan. "I need to re-establish my reputation after all those vicious media reports," I explain.

"Fair enough," Dan replies, "but I just don't see how any Barrister can be your future employer?" Dan asks a genuine question.

"It's not who they are, Dan. It's who they know," I reply casually, only half believing it. "Now, where are those car keys gone? I'm going to take your car if that's okay. It means I can leave when I want, as early as I want. No doubt there'll be a shindig afterwards, upstairs in Judge's chambers. I want to be able to make a quick exit at that point," I say, sharing my strategy.

"Does this Murdoch Pierce know that you are pregnant and that you are in an intimate loving relationship already?" Dan teases as he helps me on with my coat. "I hope he knows I'm *a force to be reckoned with*," he says, putting on his superhero voice. Dan's laugh belies the seriousness of his words.

"He's only a man," I retort flippantly, walking out the front door.

"That's what I'm worried about," Dan shouts after me. But my mind is elsewhere. I have too much to do, too much to find out. I have only until the morning to get the cash to Tanya Peterson. I'll have to get it to her tonight.

"We're just on time," Murdoch says, breathlessly as we hurry through the imposing doors of the King's Inns. "Let's sit with Carey and Bowman. They usually hog all the wine," Murdoch adds as I follow him, sucking in my expanding waistline for fear he notices the new life growing inside me. That's the last thing I need. I look around the ornate hall and marvel at how grandiose it is. I notice many familiar faces at the various tables scattered around the hall. I squash in beside Murdoch at a table of male Barristers. No one even notices my arrival. We stand as we wait for the benchers to arrive. I glance over my shoulder and fleetingly catch the eye of Judge Smythson. He appears distracted by something his colleague murmurs to him, yet I can see he is digesting the fact that I am present. I notice some terse whispering between the benchers and the tip staff. No sooner have the benchers arrived than they leave and the oak double doors are once more closed behind them. There is a lot of clatter and hushed murmurs as we resume our seats. I could be imagining it but suddenly I feel about one hundred pairs of eyes on me.

"What's going on?" I mutter to Murdoch.

"I've no idea," he says, obviously baffled, "but something else has just occurred to me," he mumbles quickly.

"What?" I ask, hoping to God it's nothing to do with me.

"I think I got the night wrong," he explains gravely. "I don't think it's visitors night tonight. In other words, no solicitors are allowed," he says sombrely. "We'll have to leave."

Simultaneously I observe a small figure dressed in black walking towards me out of the corner of my eye. Now all eyes in the hall are on me. I just want the ground to swallow me up.

"Excuse me, ma'am," says the tip staff apologetically and smelling of cloves. "Sorry for the inconvenience ma'am but the benchers cannot enter the hall until you have left. I'm terribly sorry ma'am but they're the rules like. It's only them that's allowed dine here tonight. It's visitors tomorrow alright but not tonight. It's only them, the Barristers, that can dine tonight Ma'am," he explains kindly, pointing his eyes towards the double doors. I notice the protruding red capillary veins on his large nose. The silence in the hall is palpable. *I feel like a second class citizen.*

"I'll escort you out ma'am. Sorry about this," says the veiny red nose as he leads me towards the doors. I stand up, my chair squeaking on the parquet floor. *This is mortifying.* My legs feel like lead as I walk red-faced towards the doors. Murdoch follows behind. I am grateful for this act of solidarity. No one else utters a word, their silence confirming the rules of the club. *I am an outlier.* To add insult to injury I have to walk down the steps outside the doors as the benchers wait impatiently to enter their kingdom. I avoid eye contact bowing my head in shame. I've never felt this unworthy yet I balk at such antiquated traditions which surely stem from an elitist belief in one's profession. By the time I get to the outside doors, I am furious.

"You Barristers have such a superiority complex!" I rant at Murdoch. "Far be it for a lowly solicitor to grace your presence! We are all lawyers, you know. It's ridiculous!" I exclaim, feeling as if I am about to cry from the humiliation. "I was made feel like a criminal in there! And what you Barristers should remember is that *none* of you would have any work if we didn't give you the work. We employ you, remember!" I say, tears stinging my eyes despite my anger.

"Oh Helene! I'm so sorry about this. It's completely my fault. If it's any consolation I'm embarrassed too. I'll be the laughing stock of most of my colleagues at the bar for allowing this situation to arise. The rules are the rules, even if they are somewhat outdated. What could we do but leave? It's not their fault. It's mine. I'm so sorry, truly I am. Come on. Let's grab something to eat in town. My treat, of course," Murdoch pleads dejectedly.

"I just didn't need this now Murdoch. I've had enough unwelcome attention recently, as you know. I could have done without tonight," I say, wearily. *I've enough to do tonight.*

"I know," Murdoch agrees, clearly embarrassed by the whole debacle. "Look. Let's just head to *L'oeil du Loup*. I know you love their seafood chowder and their stilton cheeses," he says, linking my arm and his and opening the main doors of the Inns.

"Just for an hour," I say, knowing that I need to eat but also knowing that neither seafood nor stilton cheese will be on the menu for me.

"You are very well behaved this evening, Helene," Murdoch quizzes me, a look of disbelief forming on his face. "And you have even quit smoking?" he comments, glancing in my direction as he pours himself another glass of Chateau Marmont. "Anyone would think you were pregnant!" he surmises, as he concentrates drunkenly on smearing another bit of cheese onto a cracker.

"I need your help, Murdoch," I say, not even allowing time for a response to his wisecrack.

"You want me to help you finish off where we left off?" he asks, looking at me directly.

"No," I reply, my gaze unwavering, ignoring his unsubtle pass.

"You know that will never happen but I do need your help in something else."

I explain to Murdoch that there is a heavy file I need to bring home from the office. I tell him about the Nullity case I am working on and that I am anxious to go through another precedent case but that the box is too heavy for me to lift out of the office by myself.

"Of course I'll help you out Helene," he enthuses in his merriment. *Strike while the iron is hot.* "If every solicitor was as diligent as you, the world would be a better place!" he quips as he leaves a €200 note as payment of our bill, reminding me instantly of the task in hand.

Whether or not Murdoch's sentence is a back-handed compliment or not is really irrelevant to me at this moment in time. I just want to get him to Peterson & Co as speedily as I can while he is still under the influence. I cannot risk him changing his mind. I've no other way of getting that box out of the office. I clamber into the car with a very merry Murdoch as we make our way to Peterson & Co. Murdoch has always been capable of holding down a wholly intelligent and coherent conversation even while completely buckled. He will walk in a white line, touch his toes and recite the *ratio decidendi* of any judgement yet he won't recall a single thing the following day. After two bottles of his favourite robust red wine I'm counting on it.

I park directly outside Peterson & Co having already disabled the CCTV camera in the now defunct security room earlier. No one will even notice, of that I am certain. I deactivate the alarm with the code furnished by Andrew and urge Murdoch to keep his voice down in the lobby. Although I note there are no lights on in any of the offices, I am riddled with fear. My body shakes from the stark rush of adrenalin. Murdoch hums the national anthem as we ascend the elevator. It takes a few minutes to cajole him into actually lifting the box for me. I actually have to take out two of the top files and leave them on my desk as he moans that it is too heavy. *I can't remove anymore.*

Murdoch eventually obliges and we descend in the elevator with the box of cash. He walks almost upright through the half-lit lobby out to Dan's car.

"That's it, my darlin'!" he puffs, closing the boot of my car with a dull thud.

I instinctively jump. My head throbs and my hands shake as I try to put the key into the ignition. *I can't believe I have just done that. I am now a criminal assisting a fugitive! Sweet Jesus!*

"Now, where are we off to for that last drink you promised me? I miss you, you know," Murdoch says, a propos nothing, a firm hand landing on my knee. "You just upped and left without a trace," he moans softly.

"I think you need a good night's sleep," I say, part of me feeling wretched with worry, part of me feeling guilty for implicating Murdoch. *But he won't remember.* I wonder if I am actually capable of driving Dan's car at all, such is the level of tension in my body."By the way, what were those eejits David and Stephen up to in that Firm of yours? Seems Andrew wasn't alone in this theft." Murdoch says scornfully. *Oh God!* "Daylight Robbery! That's what it is," he pontificates as I try and breathe evenly.

"Murdoch, please shut up. I really don't need to hear that right now," I say, defensively. *What in God's name am I doing? I'm caught in the spider's web. No way out.*

I drive as calmly as I can to Murdoch's house having to endure an earful of well-meaning platitudes from my companion.

"Goodnight Murdoch," I say, hurriedly, anxious to him out of the car and to get my visit to Tanya over and done with. After he leaves I sit in the car for some time furiously attempting to restore some level of peace to my mind and to reassure my body, not least my baby, that I'm still alive. To all intents and purposes I'd consider throwing myself in front of a truck if it wasn't for this new life. I cannot see how I can get out of this. Now it's all about damage limitation. I just have to get on with it and get this money to Tanya Peterson tonight. Then maybe I can put this whole sorry mess behind me and move on with my life.

It occurs to me, as I input Tanya's address into Dan's sat nave, that she might not even be at home this evening. *Then what do I do?* As my mind thumps from the stress of over-analysis the sat nav informs me that I have reached my destination. I look across the road at the familiar ivy laden detached house. I don't need sat nav to find it. It still looks impressive. I've been here on numerous occasions. Christmas drinks parties. Celebrating my partnership. Andrew's 50th birthday party. Such glamour and frivolity seems a thing of the past. *What happened? Greed happened, that's what.*

I feel a lump in my throat as I recall the last occasion I was here. I remember looking up into the beautiful bay windows as I watch the silhouettes of the rich and influential mingle at ease. I feel privileged to belong to this group of high achievers. Not bad for a girl from Devon, my parents humble Irish shopkeepers. My father teaching his only child that perseverance and determination is the key to success. My work ethic, like my Father, is strong, diligent and honest. My scruples are solid, moral and steadfast. *Where did I go wrong?* I brush a tear from my eye before I become too maudlin. I've never felt this alone. *Time is of the essence now. I can't turn black the clock.* I drive up a little bit and park around the corner in a quieter cul de sac. I get out of the driver's seat and close the door. I spot two walkers and their dog coming through Mount Merrion church car park. They turn and go back the other direction. I open the back door of Dan's roomy car and slip inside. I open the canvas supermarket bag I've hidden under the front seat and take out the outfit I'd purchased earlier. It's just as well I am wearing black as it fits in perfectly under my black tunic and veil. My face is barely visible, framed as it is by a stiff white cowl which juts into my skin. A long wooden cross completes my metamorphosis into a traditional Irish nun. *Franciscan? Sisters of Mercy? I have no bloody idea.* All I know is that this is the only way I could think of getting the money to Tanya without her knowing that it's me. I doubt Tanya is up on the modern habit of the average Irish nun either. I put on the heavy rimmed glasses, the silver band on my right hand wedding finger and dusty greyish powder on my face. I scrutinise my reflection in my compact mirror. I am unrecognisable, even to myself. *This better work!* I open the car door, taking the plastic bag with me. I open the boot and with the aid of the torch I remove the remaining files from the box. I take a quick look around me. Then I start unloading the €500 notes in bundles of a hundred (as indicated on paper wrapper which fastens each bundle) into the canvas bag. I count 50k, 100k, 150k. The bag is full at 500k. *That's five hundred thousand euro.* I grab the second canvas bag which thankfully I had the foresight to bring. I start counting again. I hear my mobile ringing. It's probably Dan wondering where I am. I ignore it. The box empties and the second bag is full at 500k. *That's one million euro.* I look around again. Mount merrion is deathly silent except for a lone fox who saunters past, seemingly unperturbed by an insane-looking pregnant nun fumbling in the boot of a BMW. If I possessed any courage or had any sense I'd leg it now, abscond with the money, tell Dan everything and sail off into the sunset. Andrew, however, took a gamble on a sure bet. I'm not that devious. I'm not really a bad person. *Just caught up in bad.* I somehow feel like I am doing a good thing when I find myself carrying a canvas supermarket bag in either hand, tightly knotted at the top, up the driveway of Tanya Peterson's home. I may have lost all semblance of reason but at least I'll finish the job properly. *Never let it be said.* I knock on the door, having some sense not to ring the doorbell at nearly midnight and wake the innocent, sleeping Peterson children. Eventually I put the bags down on either side of me. There isn't a sound. I walk over to the window and try and peer through a slit in the curtains. The room is dark, not lending itself to much analysis. I decide to knock again, this time somewhat louder. I knock three times, using the wooden cross for extra gravitas. I wait. I even have the audacity to look through the keyhole. Slowly I make out a figure descending the stairs warily. *Here we go.*

There is a momentary pause and a light shuffling behind the door. I imagine Tanya is ruminating on whether to open the door or not. Nervous energy coarses through my veins. *Fuck.* Presently I hear a bolt being undone and the distinctive sound of loosening chains. The door is opened only slightly.

"Yes?" says a crisp voice. Her body is partly hidden in the dark. I cannot even be sure it is Tanya. I freeze. "Yes?" says the voice, even more impatiently this time. "Can I help you?" it asks, evidently irritated.

"Well, we, eh, I actually wanted to help *you*. Mrs, eh, Mrs. Peterson, isn't it?" I stutter self-consciously, feeling completely ridiculous and utterly stresses. My accent appears to have adopted an Anglophile cut-glass slant all of a sudden.

"What do you want?" Tanya snaps brusquely. For it *is* Tanya. She opens the door a little more and I can see her face clearly under the security light. Her skin looks dehydrated, her eyes slightly bloodshot. It wouldn't surprise me if she had been crying. Her hair is pulled back in a makeshift ponytail, highlighting the stubborn grey under the blonde dye. The salmon pink dressing gown pulled tight around her thin frame doesn't do her any favours. She looks wretched.

"Again, my apologies for disturbing you this late at night," I reiterate, the intonation sounding more like a question than a statement. "I represent the *Lord Leinster* charity and they asked me to give you these as a token of our support and goodwill," I say, remaining absolutely gobsmacked by the words coming out of my mouth. I take the two bags and thrust them onto the rug behind the threshold of the door. *I want rid of them!*

"I see," she says, intrigued.

She darts a sneaky glance at the bags. I think I detect a glimmer of a smile but I could be imagining it. I feel her eyes pointed at me.

"One moment please," she says politely as she pulls the door over slightly. I can hear the rustle of paper. I know she is mentally counting as if her life depends on it. I wait on the doorstep like a trick or treater. She opens the door again and stares at me for a moment. "And what a gay Lord Leinster he is," she says, in a monotone. *That's all I need.*

I turn to walk back up the path, forgetting or not caring to say goodbye. I don't look behind but I still feel her eyes on my back. I turn the corner as quick as my legs will bring me there. I wait in the car for a while until I think she has closed her front door. I don't want her to hear me turn on the ignition. *What ever difference that would make?* I don't know if she recognised me. I don't even care. I put my head in my hands and cry tears as big as boulders.

CHAPTER 22

I am sitting at my desk at 6.30am the following morning, having already carried the box which contained the cash, as well as the files into the building. It takes me three separate trips. I re-activate the security camera before I make my final trip up the escalator. I am exhausted. Being pregnant doesn't help. Just before eight my mobile rings. I know who it is. I wish I could ring Andrew's neck.

"I've done your dirty work, Andrew," I say, sharply. I can hear a cuckoo clock again in the background. *Where the hell is he?*

"Good," Andrew replies calmly. "And what did my darling wife have to say for herself?" he asks.

"She just said *'and what a gay Lord Leinster he is'* or something like that," I reply. There is a brief pause. Then I hear Andrew laughing heartily down the phone. He makes my blood boil. How he can laugh like that? I think, as if he doesn't have a care in the world? I can hear the Escalator doors open. Either Conor or Barnaby Walsh has arrived to work. My heart beats faster and I feel perspiration under my arms.

"Excellent news, very good. I'm proud of you, Helene. I knew you'd come up trumps," Andrew says condescendingly. "Let's just say your little secret is safe at the moment," he adds.

"What do you mean *at the moment?*" I shriek at him in a forced whisper.

"Cheerio for now!" he says before I have half a chance to quiz him. *Damn him!* I curse, shaking the phone for no other reason than to vent my frustration. This is over! It has to be over. I just want to get on with my life. Have I not done enough to make amends? I just seem to be propagating the mess. When does it end?

"Good morning, Helene," Walsh says, as he opens my office door without knocking.

"Good morning," I mutter, my eyes fixated on the file on my desk. If I look up he will see the anguish in my eyes.

"Ah, yes. You're all set for tomorrow then?" Walsh asks.

"Yes, of course I am," I reply curtly. I am running a High Court case in the morning. "It looks like I could be at hearing for at least three days. It depends if there are settlement talks," I say, wondering why I'm bothering to elaborate. There is an uncomfortable silence but I am in no mood for small talk.

"Rightio," Walsh replies, appearing preoccupied himself. "You might be interested to know that there is a special sitting of the commercial court at two o'clock today. Some matters to do with Andrew Peterson I believe. Just thought I'd mention it anyway," he says, scurrying out of the room as fast as he arrived. I try to concentrate on the file in front of me. I need to double check all my proofs for tomorrow's case.

"Morning Helene," Conor says, also opening the door without knocking.

"Does anyone around here actually know that you are supposed to knock first?" I say tartly. I'm in foul humour.

"Sorry, Ms. Grumpy!" Conor laughs, not taking any of my nonsense. "Walsh just told me about this special sitting in the commercial court later. It's as if we are being kept out of the loop now that the suspension on our practising certificates has been lifted. Frank McGrath seems to have fallen off the face of the planet. I'm going down later anyway. I want to see if anyone has any idea where the bastard is!" he says angrily.

"It's the commercial court, Conor, not the central criminal court!" I chastise, feeling flushed all of a sudden.

"Yeah, well, someone might have some information on how Interpol are getting on. I'm still getting nightmares after those death threats. I'll never forgive him for that or for fucking everything else up either," Conor says, his words gathering speed. He paces in front of my desk like a panther on heat.

"Ok. Look. Just let me work on this case for tomorrow and we'll head down and grab some lunch in the canteen before we head up to the commercial court, alright?" I say, diffusing any potential conflict. Conor leaves and I close my eyes as if to block out the world. After a while I ring my client and arrange to meet him and his wife at 9am at the Four Courts. I have a consultation room booked for the next three days. I concentrate on doing up the Schedule of Special Damages. It's the only item not yet sent to the other side. I'm slightly concerned about the loss of earnings and need to refresh myself with the figures.

"Hi Dan," I say, answering my mobile.

"Hi darling. Listen, are you free for lunch today? I'm not always in Dublin so I thought it might be a nice idea. I'll let you choose the restaurant. My treat," he says.

"I can't Dan. I've got to go down to the commercial court later. I need to be there at two. Sorry hon," I say.

"That's a shame." he says quietly. I've a feeling there is more to this phone call than just lunch. "To be honest I'm a bit worried about you, Helene. You were tossing and turning all night last night. You seem to be under lot of stress. I can totally understand that, bearing in mind what's gone on in the last few months but you are pregnant. You're half way almost. I think it's time you tell that Barnaby Walsh guy, that Barrister you were out dining with last night and everyone else working with you that you are pregnant. I know you are not really showing yet but that's because you are naturally slim. Will you do that?" Dan asks, his concern obvious.

"If you really want me to," I say, appeasing him. I know he is right but I also know it won't make a whit bit of difference to my stress levels. *I don't want Murdoch suspecting anything!*

"Yes, I do really want you to. It'd make me feel better Helene. You and our child are all that are important to me," he says.

"Ok" I say, "I will. See you at home later."

I forget sometimes that I am pregnant because I am constantly preoccupied with what's going on around me. If I'm not handling stolen cash and assisting a fugitive, I'm money laundering it to an associate, all while I act as an officer of the court! I'm an honest woman forced into fraudulent activities as a means to keeping my family together. Andrew is blackmailing me and there isn't a thing I can do about it. At least I can't see what I can do about it.

"Unless I'm imagining it, I think everyone in this canteen is staring at us," Conor says, his eyes darting around him.

"I know," I reply, feeling terribly self-conscious. "Sure what can we expect Conor after all the bad press? I'm sure half the solicitors in here think there is no smoke without fire. They'll be blaming us for their insurance policies skyrocketing even though we haven't done anything," I say, holding the flimsy egg sandwich in my hands. *Oh yes you have*, says a voice in my head. It unnerves me.

"Are you not hungry?" Conor says, noticing my reticence.

"Eh, I, eh, seem to have lost my appetite," I respond. *I have to hold it together.*

"Yes," I snap out loud, acknowledging my struggle within.

"What?" Conor says, looking perplexed. "Are you alright, Helene?"

"Come on. Let's get out of here," I say, suddenly finding the room oppressive. I feel claustrophobic. My hands are clammy and my peripheral vision is out of sync. *I need to get out of here.* I walk unsteadily to the door of the canteen. If I can just make it to the bench I'll be okay, I think to myself.

"Jesus, Helene! What the hell is up with you? You look like death warmed up," Conor says, following me armed with our coats and briefcases.

"I'm pregnant," I say, choosing the simpler explanation.

"Ah! Now that makes sense!" Conor says, his voice reverberating loudly around the corridor. *Please keep it down Conor.* "For a minute there I thought you might be having a panic attack. Take it from me, they're the pits. You poor thing. I'll get you a glass of water. Just sit here for a minute and I'll be back."

Conor returns with a glass of water and a banana which he insists I eat. He promises not to divulge my condition to anyone else for the moment. *Especially not Murdoch.* I wish I could tell Conor everything but I can't. All I do know is that if I don't find a way out of this mess soon I'm heading for disaster. I know he is anxious to get to the commercial court on time so I do my best to get myself together.

"No rush, Helene," he says, lying good humouredly. "No rush."

We take the lift by the Round Hall up to the first floor. The corridor is deserted, indicating that the court is already in session. Conor opens the door and we squash into a bench at the far end of the court. David and Stephen's absence is noticeable. Conor and I have both tried to contact each of them on numerous occasions but in vein. How they became embroiled in Andrew's fraud and how we weren't aware of it still amazes me. I trusted them both but hey who am I to talk, sitting here like Ms. Innocent! From the corner of my eye I see Tanya Peterson standing by the door. *I can't believe she is here*! She must have seen me come into the court with Conor. I feel my cheeks redden as my heart races.

"Mr. Forsyth. I will only ask you this question one more time. No one in this court seems capable of giving me an answer to this simple question, Judge Smythson says, sighing on the bench. "Why did the Bank sanction a loan of this amount to Andrew Peterson? And I am referring, for the sake of clarity, to the BND loan of €48 million specifically and not to any of the other loans. I have read the Affidavits and they do not assist me in any way in answering this question!" the Judge says, scornfully. He peers at Mr. Forsyth over his half-moon reading glasses.

The air is taught with tension. Conor and I sit at the back of the court, grateful to even get a seat. The court is packed but no one makes a sound.

"Yes, your Lordship. Well, if I may digress for a little and point out..."

"No, you may not digress!" Judge Smythson barks from the proverbial pulpit. "But I will! If only to point out that the use of flowery language in this court is unnecessary and frankly nothing but a time-wasting device to dress up Affidavits and submissions. You will have to admit, Mr. Forsyth, that the difficult to understand wording is a rather fancy way of stating obvious propositions?" he scolds rhetorically as Mr. Forsyth visibly shifts on his feet. "In any event please now get on with answering the question. I have called this special sitting today as I believe that the answer to this question is at the crux of Mr. Peterson's easy rise to the top, not to mind his swift demise. I have spent months pouring over these documents. I cannot find a single reason to validate the sanction of this loan to Mr. Peterson! Although this is not a criminal court we are all aware of Mr. Peterson's fraud. I am, however, attempting to ascertain the role of BND bank, if any, in facilitating this particular loan to Mr. Peterson. Now, Mr. Forsyth, do you understand the question or do you need me to spell it out again?" Judge Smythson glares at Mr. Forsyth who seems hapless in his predicament. "I might add" Justice Smythson says, interjecting Mr. Forsyth's thoughts, "that I am aware that Ms. Tanya Peterson is in court this afternoon to defend separate proceedings for the re-possession of the family home by your client and you can be sure that unless I receive an

190   NEGLIGENT BEHAVIOUR

adequate response to my queries from BND bank *that* application will be adjourned. Perhaps that might give you some food for thought, Mr. Forsyth,"

"Indeed, your Lordship," says Mr. Forsyth, clearly having no explanation for the Bank's cavalier sanction of the loan. "I'm at the court's discretion, your Lordship. I don't think I can put the matter any further. It's in the court's hands," Mr. Forsyth submits humbly.

Mr. Smythson ponders this reply momentarily.

"Yes. Mr. Forsyth. Many thanks for your clarity in this matter. Registrar, could you ask the stenographer to make an adequate note of this order please?"

"Yes, your Lordship," replies the Registrar. There is a brief pause while the Stenographer readies herself.

"It would appear that BND bank is declining to comment on why it sanctioned this particular loan of €48 million to Mr. Peterson. I have therefore no other option but to direct that under these special circumstances a file be set to the Director of Public Prosecutions (DPP). This is to allow a full investigation into the loan of €48 million sanctioned by BND bank to Mr. Andrew Peterson. This is also to include any bonuses paid by the bank to its employees. I direct that BND bank provide the DPP's office with all documentation to facilitate this investigation. I direct that this file be handed over to the DPP within fourteen days of today's date." There is an audible gasp in the court. "Registrar I will break for fifteen minutes, returning at quarter to three."

"All rise," says the Registrar as the eminent Justice Smythson stands and descends the steps of the court podium.

"Wow," whispers Conor. "That's unbelievable. Smythson obviously believes there is something strange going on in the bank not to mind with Peterson. I bet someone in the bank has been dipping into the cookie jar as well. This is mad stuff!" Conor says, echoing the flurry of activated voices around me.

I look to the left but Tanya has disappeared. "It's crazy alright," I reply, as I note four or five journalists scribbling furiously on the back bench. I really can't understand what is going on. Surely the Bank has been duped by Andrew and not the other way around? This whole thing just becomes more confusing as time goes on. *I just hope they don't come after me.*

"I mean, a Judge of the commercial court will rarely send a matter to the DPP unless he seriously suspects fraud. He's obviously suspicious of someone in the bank. I know I've said it before, Helene, but there is something fishy going on. I can feel it. Fortunately we can rely on the likes of Smythson to get to the bottom of what's going on. He won't rest until the truth is unearthed. He believes in justice, not like some people who use and abuse the law to suit their own ends."

Oh God, Conor! Rub it in!

"I'm really confused Conor, to be honest. I thought Andrew was the only one involved in siphoning monies from the banks. I didn't know David or Stephen were involved, and now the bank themselves seem to be up to something. I just don't get it at all." I say, at a loss to understand the world around me. I just know I want no more deceit myself.

"I'm confused myself, Helene," Conor remarks as we walk out of the court. There is still no sign of Tanya. She has probably made a quick exit, relieved to still be retaining the family home, at least for another short while.

"Something is not right but I just can't put my finger on it. It's really strange that the Law Society wanted us back in Peterson & Co at all, even if it is only to finish off some existing files and then the letter from the Minister only confused me further. I still don't get what any of this has to do with him really," Conor adds.

"Or why the Law Society would make allowances for us specifically. I mean they could have outsourced other solicitors to come in and finish off the files like they have done with some of them.

"I think the Minister is just covering his back," I say, none the wiser.

"Yeah, they all seem to be doing that," Conor says, "but now BND bank are thrown into the mix as well. It's highly unusual. Very strange circumstances indeed and none of it adds up. I just don't get it," Conor says, holding the door of the Garage open for me.

"Nor do I," I say, and I certainly don't.

"You're late," Dan says as I walk wearily in the door of Banville Road.

"I know," I say, exhausted. "I had to go back to the office after court and finish preparing some documents for a case in the morning."

"I'll heat the dinner up for you. You must be starving," Dan says, helping me off with my coat as I kick off my shoes.

"I am. I'm famished!" I agree, eyeing the plate of food being put into the microwave.

"So did you tell them at work that you are pregnant?" Dan asks, concerned.

"Yes, I told Conor anyway," I answer. I deliberately withhold the real reason for my admission.

"Right, well, hopefully they might go a bit easier on you with your workload. I don't want you any more stressed than you have to be," Dan says. "You seem to be enjoying the fish pie anyway. Your mum dropped it in earlier. She's a great cook. It's just as well as she wouldn't want to be relying on our culinary skills."

"Are you saying I can't cook, Dan Goodings?" I tease. "You'd be well advised not to be slagging off a hormonally-charged woman. You might end up with a frying pan on your head!" I laugh. "God, it's great to be home I can tell you," I say, putting my hand over Dan's, and feeling emotional all of a sudden.

"And it's great to have you home," Dan says. "And even better to see you haven't lost your sense of humour. I worry about you, you know. Anyway, I'll run you a bath and we can put on a DVD."

"Thanks Dan," I say, grateful for his kindness. In the harsh world of my dubious career, Dan's love keeps me grounded and helps me cope. I know I am being duplicitous in my behaviour towards him but I don't know what else I can do.

I lounge in the bath, resting my tired limbs but try as I might, I can't stop thinking of the mess I am in. Murdoch rang me three times today but I didn't answer his calls. I wish he would just leave me alone. *He is too dangerous for me.* I have to accept the fact that I will always be attracted to him but that doesn't mean I want to be with him. It's Dan that I love. Murdoch could have become a bad habit if I nurtured our affair but that wasn't something I was prepared to do. Especially now that I could be carrying his child. *Ow!* How auspicious that my baby decides to kick as if it can hear my mind working out the logistics of my life. *I'm sorry little one. I'm sorry,* I think as I massage my protruding belly lathered in suds. I promise I will lead by example from now on. I am determined to try and turn my life around and start afresh. If that bastard Andrew calls me again I'll ignore it. I don't want anything more to do with him. I am not going to let him ruin my life. He has already left a trail of destruction behind him. I'll be damned if he causes anymore. Conor phones me later to say that Don Glennon of the Law Society wants to meet us as soon as possible for a report on our progress with the existing files in Peterson & Co. That's all I need, another person on my back, watching my every move.

Chapter 23

"I do believe that the figure given for your future loss of earnings is slightly aspirational," Luke Callanan SC tells my wide-eyed client.

"That's not to say I am discounting the actuary's figures. I am simply saying that I don't know if they will hold up in court. I would be of the view that a Judge *might* find our claim for future loss of earnings just a little on the generous side," Callanan says, fixing his black gown as he sits on the consultation room chair.

"So, in short, and in reply to your question, no, I don't believe that any of the High Court Judges available today will give you the full whack of your loss of earnings as claimed. Look, this case isn't an assessment only. We have a full fight on our hands here. The other side haven't approached us yet but there may be some talk after the call over. We'll just have to wait and see," Callanan says shrugging his shoulders. "I'll talk to you later Helene," he says as he stands, gathering up his papers and exiting the room. "Let me know when the Engineer gets here and I'll have a word with him," he asks, glancing at me as he leaves.

"Of course," I reply, picking up my mobile to confirm our Engineer is en route.

I have all the Doctors on stand-by including the psychiatrist who has been treating my client, the Plaintiff, for post traumatic stress following the accident. My client was knocked down by a car whilst crossing the road at a busy junction in Ranelagh. Four years on George Mulvihill wants his day in court. He will be a difficult client to advise.

"I don't understand why the Senior Counsel is saying that about my future loss of earnings? I am a critically acclaimed sculptor. I was exhibiting my bronze sculptures all over the world before I was knocked down by that blind bat. She shouldn't have been allowed on the road!" George says, his nostrils flaring with anger.

"Yes, George. I appreciate where you are coming from," I respond gently but firmly. "The problem is that there is an independent witness who alleges that you had one too many, if I can put it like that. She says that you were walking haphazardly across the road. It will be very difficult for our counsel to discredit her character and there may therefore be some contributory negligence alleged on your part. It's unfortunate that we don't have any independent witnesses ourselves but…"

"I-had-two-glasses-of–single-malt-with-water," George says, enunciating every word aggressively. His wife Ita rolls her eyes. I get the impression she is familiar with these outbursts. "How many times do I have to say it?" he shouts. "I was celebrating winning the silver medal at the international festival in Oslo. I have never denied that I drank alcohol but to say I was staggering across the road is a complete exaggeration! *That* woman must need glasses as well. I'll cross examine her myself in the witness box!" he says, and I worry that he might have a heart attack on the spot.

"Look, I'm only playing devil's advocate here, George. You have a good case and suffered some awful injuries but I wouldn't be doing my job if I didn't advise you of the holes in it," I say, doing my best to placate him.

"I know you are only doing your job Helene," George says and I can see the tears welling up in his eyes. "It's just frustrating being stuck in this wheelchair. Between that and my mangled hand I'm no use to anyone, not even to my craft which is now almost impossible," he says quietly.

"He's been very stressed about this case," Ita pipes up then by way of explanation.

"I understand that," I say, nodding at her. "Don't worry, you're in good hands. I'll go to the call over now and I'll be able to see where we are on the list. It's at half ten. I'll come back to you immediately afterwards." George tried to commit suicide last year such was the level of his distress. I know that no money will ever compensate George for his loss now or into the future. Yet if we can get a good settlement for him he may be able to try and move on and let go of some of the anger and resentment. It might be some kind of closure for him.

I know that there are three important considerations in any case: knowing your client, knowing your opposite number and knowing the Judge. I am not convinced that my client will come across well in the witness box. He may hold his own under direct examination but if counsel on the other side cross examines him with any competency, I think he will fold. He will lose his temper and possibly lose the favour of the Judge.

As I make my way across the Round Hall I think I glimpse Murdoch darting into High Court 4. *Phew*! My mobile vibrates in my pocket.

"Hi Caroline. I'm just running into court for the call over. Can I call you back this evening?" I say, hurriedly.

"Ok, Helene. That would be great. I really need to talk to you. James and I...well, we're splitting up once and for all. I've had enough," she says, her voice breaking.

"Oh God. I'm sorry to hear that Caroline, you poor thing," I say, my heart breaking for her.

"Not as sorry as I am," she says softly.

"I'll call you later Caroline. Hang in there," I say.

By now the court is filling up, with only moments before the Judge arrives. Caroline's phone call has thrown me but I have to get on with the task at hand. I scan the Personal Injury list. Luckily most of the Judges available today are marginally pro- Plaintiff Judges. That is certainly no harm. It may nudge the Defendants into making an offer, even if they make allowances for their claim of contributory negligence. We are number 12 on the list which is ideal as in it allows us some room for negotiations.

"Thankfully there doesn't appear to be much of a backlog today which is a relief. If we don't settle today it looks like we'll be assigned a court in the morning, even if none of the cases ahead of us settle," says an articulate voice beside me. It's the junior counsel in the case, Collette Farren. "Here, push in here," she says, pointing at the spot of bench beside her.

"Oh, Hi Collette. I didn't see you there. Thanks," I say as I squash in beside her. I notice her eyes linger a little bit too long on my belly."Yes, Collette. I *am* pregnant," I say, vanity coming before prudence.

"I can see that," she says. "I wasn't sure if you'd been eating too many pies!" she laughs.

"Very funny!" I say, not at all amused though stifling a smile.

"Terrible situation in that Firm of yours," Collette says as diplomatic as ever. "I met Andrew once or twice. Awfully charming, wasn't he?" she says, under her breath. I simply nod, indicating my agreement. "A right snake in the grass though. He dated a friend of mine, you know, before he married his wife, Tanya. He led her a right merry dance I can tell you," Collette says, suggestively.

"Really?" I say, intrigued.

"Yes, she got pregnant and he made her have an abortion because he didn't want to marry her or he wasn't ready to get married or it didn't fit into his plan at the time." Collette whispers to me and I can smell coffee on her breath."Well, whatever his reason, the poor eejit hadn't the strength to stand up for herself. She was hopefully in love with him. He told her that if she didn't get an abortion he'd deny he was the father. You couldn't force a man to take a paternity test in those days you see. A woman's reputation was everything. And so my friend thought she'd no choice really. She was only seventeen," she concludes, a far away look in her eye.

"What happened to her? Did she meet someone else?" I ask hopefully.

"No. She lived on her own in a flat in Sandymount for years. She developed some sort of obsessive compulsive disorder. She was always washing her hands. I think she might have been anorexic as well. It's funny because she always maintained that Andrew was gay. He used to visit her now and then. I wouldn't be at all surprised if he was giving her a hand out over the years, probably from a guilt-induced conscience. She didn't work and I don't know where she got the money for the apartment. It was always in immaculate condition. She wouldn't hear a bad word about him. The poor thing would drive us all demented because of that but it was clear she still loved him all those years later. Puppy love, isn't that what they call it? I think they developed some kind of friendship in the end. She died a year ago from a massive heart attack and left her entire estate to the *Lord Leinster charity* I believe. Poor pet," Collette says, looking down at the brief on her lap.

What the f…?

"Number 12: George Mulvihill and Bridie Brennan," reads out

the Registrar.

"That's going on my Lord. Three days," says Luke Callanan, addressing the Judge.

"Thank you," says Judge Levine.

My mobile vibrates. It's the Engineer.

"Excuse me," I whisper to Collette, "I just want to take this call."

I walk out of the court and bump straight into the Engineer who has been expecting me. I listen to him, feigning concentration, as he takes me through his views on liability. My mind is elsewhere. The *Lord Leinster charity? Andrew gay?*

I can picture him now in my mind's eye as if he is standing in front of me. He is an arrogant man with a suave persona. There is ice underneath his veil of charm. I observe his pristine grooming, his tanned skin and gold cufflinks....*but gay?*

One of the senior counsel come out to talk to us. I can hear him and the Engineer talking but I'm not listening. I nod at appropriate intervals. After a few minutes I excuse myself and walk across the Round Hall, up the steps, past the Law Library and take a right into the Solicitor's writing room. It's the only place I'll get some peace and quiet. I put my head in my hands and take a few deep breaths. I need to get on with this case but I can't until I calm my nerves. I don't know what is going on but I've got to get to the bottom of it. *None of this makes any sense!* I stare at the coat stand lost in my own musings. Tanya must know, I think to myself. She must know what's going on. *And what a gay Lord Leinster he is....*what did she mean by that? I am at a loss to explain but it seems too much of a coincidence to ignore. The truth will come out in the end. It always does. In the meantime I have to get on with this case. I buy a bottle of water in the Law Society newsagent, take a few sips and gather my thoughts together.

"This report that I have prepared here is excellent on paper," says Jack Connolly, our expert Engineer, tapping it with his knuckle. My client is looking at him expectantly. "The difficulty I have is if I am cross-examined on the contents. Off the record I can safely tell you that this Defendant, who allegedly crashed into you, must have been doing no more than twenty five miles per hour at the time of the accident, which is well within the speed limit. She definitely wasn't speeding," Connolly states assuredly.

"Sure how can you tell that?" George says, disgruntled at this news.

"I can tell by the skid marks on the road and where the car was positioned following the impact," the Engineer replies. "Admittedly I wasn't at the scene of the accident but I have examined the locus with you and with the Defendant's Engineer present. I have also had access to the Garda Abstract in this case and all the statements. Look I'm down in court practically every day of the week doing these cases. Believe me I know what I am talking about," Connolly says.

"Well, what exactly are you saying?" my client says, not fully grasping the reality of Connolly's words.

"What I am saying?" Connolly says, sighing, "is that if I am asked under cross-examination if the Defendant was speeding then I would have to answer in the negative. I think there is an element of contributory negligence in this case. I am not saying that the impact was unavoidable, simply that this lady hardly braked at all in circumstances where the speed at which she was travelling didn't warrant it. That's all I am saying."

There is a heavy air in the consultation room.

"Well, if that's your professional opinion, Jack, then so be it," I say. "Many thanks for coming down here anyway. If you want to go and get a coffee or something I'll give you a shout when I've more news for you."

"I'm sorry I can't be more helpful, Helene," Jack adds as I walk him to the door, "but at least my report might spark an offer," he says with a conciliatory smile.

"Let's hope so Jack because they have an independent witness as well, one who will say that my client was inebriated at the time of the impact," I add, resignedly. Connolly doesn't appear to be too surprised by this revelation.

After Connolly has left I talk to my client for a little while and encourage him to consider any offer that is made by the other side.

"You will not lose this case, in my view, but there is a real risk that you will be penalised by the Judge for contributory negligence after he hears the evidence of your Engineer and this independent witness. If things went drastically wrong you could lose your case and then you run the risk of having High Court costs awarded against you. These could run into tens of thousands of euro. I just have to say it as it is, George. There are no guarantees here today, I'm afraid," I say, not relishing being the bearer of bad news but better he is forewarned than leave him open to a legal suit.

I walk back towards the Round Hall, hoping for an update from Luke Callanan or the other senior, who seems to busy to even make an appearance. Perhaps Collette, the junior counsel, might know something. I am still completely distracted by her story about Andrew, so much so that I don't even notice Murdoch until he is standing there in front of me.

"Helene! I was hoping I'd see you," Murdoch says, "Can we have a quick word?" he asks. We stand near the wall beside the information desk at the Round hall. "I happened to be talking to Collette Farren there," Murdoch says, softly. "I believe she is the junior counsel in the case you are in today?"

"That's right," I say, wondering where this conversation is going.

"Yeah, well, it's just she mentioned a propos nothing really, that you are, well, pregnant. Is that true?" he asks, his blue eyes staring at me.

"Eh, yes, it's true," I stutter, trying to meet his gaze but my eyes flicker away.

"Right," he says. "Who is the father?" he asks, still staring at me.

"What do you mean who is the father?" I hiss irately. "How dare you! Dan is the father, of course," I say, feeling my cheeks flush hotly. *She who doth protest too much.* "What's with the Spanish inquisition?" I say, indignantly.

"Well, how long are you gone?" Murdoch asks.

"Em, about four months or so I think," I say, desperately trying to appear non-chalant.

"You think?" he says.

"Oh don't do the barrister cross-examination thing we me, Murdoch! What are you trying to insinuate? Do you think you are the father or something? Hah!" I say, hassled.

"Well, am I?" he asks.

"Oh grow up, Murdoch!" I exclaim. "I really haven't the time for this nonsense," I say, storming off like a spoiled child.

Well, talk about making thinks obvious, I think to myself, as I walk aimlessly into the Round Hall. I find myself standing outside Court 3 with no reason to go in only I can feel Murdoch's eyes boring into my back. I walk up the steps and sit in the back of the court. The judge has a quick glance to see who is entering his kingdom, then resumes his listening stance as a Barrister regales him on some technical matter. I try to blend into the background, keeping my head down so as not to bring any unwarranted attention to myself. My eyes are moist, a flood of tears welling up behind them. *When did life become this complicated?*

I resign to stay here until my heartbeat calms down and Murdoch is safely out of the way. After a while I feel sufficiently calm to be able to leave the court. I detour to the ladies on my way back to my client.

"Ah Helene, perfect timing," the senior counsel says, as I arrive back into the consultation room. "We were just going to have a word with your client."

I sit down beside Luke Callanan. Collette is also present and smiles when I walk in.

"Now there has been a couple of developments. I can give you the bad news or the good news?" Callanan says, glancing at George.

"Give me the bad news first," he replies passively.

"It would appear that the other side have another independent witness. It wasn't included in the disclosure notice until the amended version was faxed over this morning. Helene, I believe a copy of it was faxed over to you about twenty minutes ago," Callanan adds casually. I glance at my mobile and see a number of missed calls from the office.

"He is a gentleman by the way of Johnny Butler? Apparently, he will allege in the witness box that you had been in his company since lunchtime on the day of the accident. He will also give evidence for the Defendant, that you both consumed a large quantity of alcohol over a period of nearly eight hours–"

"That is just sour grapes on Butler's part!" George interrupts, highly incensed by this news.

George's wife, Ita, shifts uncomfortably in her chair.

"That may well be, Mr. Mulvihill, but is it the truth?" Callanan asks plaintively. "And before you reply, I'll give you the good news. Bearing in mind our concerns in relation to liability in this case, all of which have been outlined to you in full, the other side have, nevertheless, made an offer of €375,000 plus High Court costs to dispose of this case. I am strongly urging you to accept this offer. I can tell you now that there isn't a cent more to be had, even a sweetner, so although I know the ultimate decision is yours, it is my strongest recommendation that you accept it," Callanan advises gravely.

"I'll take it," George says, unequivocally.

Ita nearly faints with relief.

"You've done the right thing," I say to my client, after counsel has left. "There were too many risks. The last thing you would have wanted was an order for costs against you. The settlement cheque should be here in six to eight weeks. Our solicitor/client fee is 10% plus VAT as you know. The other side will pay for the Barristers, the medical reports, Engineer, the actuary and the stand-by fees but if there is any shortfall you will need to make this up. I'll let you know anyway."

George and Ita shake my hand and leave. He has no idea how grateful I am that he has accepted this settlement, for his own sake as well as my own. I have the ghost of Andrew Peterson hanging over me and I will not rest until I get to the bottom of it. I know that as sure as night follows day Andrew will be on to me again. This time I want to be prepared.

204 | NEGLIGENT BEHAVIOUR

Chapter 24

"Ok, just to recap, there are a few ways we can proceed with this," I tell a pale-faced Caroline when we meet at my offices to discuss her imminent separation from James. "You can both attend mediation, we can go down the collaborative law route or you can issue Judicial Separation proceedings," I say, explaining Caroline's options as best I can. "The first two will result in a separation deed and if you can stick being in the same room as him, then I'd recommend either option. If there are going to be issues over custody or access to the children then I think Judicial Separation is the best route. It's up to you really," I say, gutted that my friend's marriage is over.

"I can't believe it's come to this," Caroline says, shaking her head. "The twins don't even know yet. We want to wait until we know what way we are proceeding with the legal separation first. I'm going to continue with counselling for myself anyway." She blows her nose into another tissue and tosses it into the wastepaper basket.

"You have the right idea, Helene, not believing in this marriage business. Sure look how I've ended up!" she says, in a defeatist manner.

If only she knew! "Oh, don't be fooled by appearances," I reassure her "We all have our problems, believe me," I say, sincerely. "How is everything at home now?" I ask, "Will James move out or what will you do about the living arrangements?"

Caroline just shrugs, bet by the unravelling of her relationship. "It's really tense to be honest. I'd love if he'd move on but I don't think he will. I just need to work out the finances first and see where we're at then," she says, sighing loudly. "Thanks for the advice, Helene. I really appreciate it. I'll think about everything and read the literature you've given me. Hopefully we'll be able to work this out as amicably as possible," Caroline says, looking at me for confirmation.

"Hopefully" I say.

I have enough experience to know that separations are highly emotive and anything can happen. "I don't usually act for friends, Caroline, but in this instance I'll do my best to help. I never really go to know James, to be honest, so I can't say I have any allegiance to him. It's you and the kids I'm concerned about but obviously he is their father so we don't want to affect that relationship either, if we can help it at all. Have a think about everything and give me a ring when you want to go ahead" I add, hugging her tight before she leaves. "Don't worry, we'll work it out" I tell her. "You'll get through it."

I sit at my desk staring into space when someone knocks on my door.

"Yes," I say instinctively. The door opens and Barnaby Walsh is standing there as if waiting for me to say something. I think he does actually speak but I don't hear him. "Sorry I missed that," I say, finally focusing on him.

"Don Glennon is ready to meet with you and Conor when you are ready," Walsh says, staring at me quizzically.

"Ok fine," I say, "I'll be there in a few minutes," I say, distractedly.

Just as Walsh leaves, my mobile rings. It's a blocked number. *It must be Andrew.* I don't answer it but put it back into my handbag and walk out of the door, leaving it ring on in silence.

"So, how are things panning out for you both?" Glennon says, fiddling his wedding ring as he speaks. "I'd imagine it must be just a matter of weeks now and we'll be able to close the door of this Firm once and for all," he says smiling, as if he is talking about what he'll have for lunch today. I glare at him. "Not that the Law Society would have wished that to happen," he adds hurriedly, as if to offer an antidote to the sting in his words or perhaps noticing the venom in my eyes.

"Either way, it all seems very strange that you guys allowed us in to finish off these files at all," Conor suddenly says, out of the blue. "I mean it just doesn't make sense. Why didn't you just ship off the rest of these files to another solicitor? You did that for most of them. You said yourself, at our last meeting, that you weren't even sure we were guilty of any negligence and we're *not* but if that was the case, why entrust us with this job? I mean, is there someone else who is putting pressure on the Law Society to clear up matters?" Conor asks, finally coming to the crux of the question. Glennon sits there with his mouth open. Walsh's cheeks redden like ripe apples. "Helene and I have discussed this at some length and whilst we are grateful for the opportunity to be back here practising as solicitors, we really don't understand why we were asked? Was there pressure from some other source?" Conor asks again.

Oh God I know he is eluding to the Minister and the letter we found in Walsh's papers. Next thing I know he'll drag in his actual name and then we'll be in real trouble! *Jesus, Conor, don't drag me into this even further!*

"Yes, well, I don't think it really matters what the reason was, I mean, does it Conor?" I say tersely, doing my best to fob off his remarks. "The main thing is that we are here to help and I believe that we are doing that to the best of our ability," I say as calmly as possible and giving Glennon my full attention. I don't want Glennon to know we suspect anything. I need more time.

He sits there, seemingly at a complete loss as to what to say. "We, the Law Society, are simply doing our best to put this matter to bed so-to-speak. No one is putting us under any pressure," he says, looking us in the eye. *He's lying.* "It's simply that we wish, eh, to be proactive in this particular instance and to be seen to be serving justice. That's all," Glennon concludes, standing up prematurely and resting his hands on the desk. He hesitates for a moment as if he is about to add something else but thinks better of it.

"I'll come back in two weeks again for an update. Many thanks for your continued assistance in this matter," he says abruptly. Glennon fixes his tie and walks out the door without so much as a sideways glance in our direction. Walsh follows him out like a chick following the mother hen.

"Thanks a bunch, Helene!" Conor says sarcastically. "We could have got to the bottom of that letter in there, if you'd only stuck up for me but oh no, you have to go and say the bloody opposite! What did you go and do that for?" he says, getting angrier by the minute. I think he is going to use the boardroom desk as a punch bag.

"I'm sorry, Conor. I just don't think you know what you are up against here. It's not as simple as that...look, just let's get on with our jobs. None of the rest of it is our business anyway," I say, flustered. *I shouldn't have said that.*

"What do you mean, 'it's not as simple as that'? What's the 'rest of it' that you're talking about? It's not like you, Helene, to run from the truth. Is it your hormones or what?" he says, going straight for my Achilles heel. He knows I won't tolerate sexist remarks.

"No, it's not my hormones!" I practically scream at him as I close the boardroom door. I can't see Walsh anywhere which is just as well given the gradual increase in the level of noise in the room. "Just take it from me that you're better off not probing any further with this, Conor. Believe me, I *know* what I am talking about!" I say, nearly exploding. Now I've completely lost the run of myself. *Oh God.* I'm losing control.

"You see, that's it there!" Conor says, pouncing on the cracks in my sentences. "That's exactly it! What do you mean, *you* know what you are talking about?" he says, "and that I am *better off* not probing any further with this?! What do you know that I don't know?" he asks me straight out as my mind scrambles to find a way out.

"I didn't mean that. I was just saying that *we are* better off not..." I say, stumbling over my words.

"No, you didn't say *we.* You said *I.*" he says, accusatorily. "I know you a long time, Helene. I know when you are lying to me. Now, what the hell is going on?"

I put my hands over my ears to block out the sound. *I can't take any more of this stress. I've nowhere to hide.* I feel the tears flooding down my face and splashing onto my shirt. I bawl like a baby, loud and snotty.

"Hey Helene. Hey, I'm sorry. Jeez, I didn't mean to come down hard on you. I'm just frustrated with this bullshit," Conor says, putting his arm over me. "You're right, we should just move on and forget the reasons we are here and..."

"Andrew's blackmailed me," I say, my voice taking me by surprise and making me shiver. "I took cash out of this office, about one million actually and gave it to his wife. It was in that box that I made you bring up from the safe. Otherwise he was going to tell Dan about…" I start crying even more. Conor wait patiently then prods further.

"About what?" he asks with a forced calmness. I can tell he is doing his utmost to subdue his natural impatience.

"About eh, a fling I had with a barrister. I don't really want to say his name to be honest, I am so embarrassed by my behaviour. It was a mistake…" I say, my breathing erratic from such a burst of emotion. My body heaves in and out with shock.

"The whole truth and nothing but the truth, Ms. McBain!" Conor says, mimicking the Registrar in a court scenario and holding out the notepad as if it's a bible. His sense of humour breaks the ice and I can't help but laugh nervously amidst the tears.

"His name is Murdoch Pierce. You wouldn't know him, I don't think. He doesn't do any work in your area. Anyway, none of that really matters. There are more important things we need to find out about," I say, looking at Conor. He sits down silently, prepared for the long haul. I tell him about everything in more detail. I tell him about Andrew's phone calls, my removal of the cash from the office at night and my subsequent visit to Tanya. I include my chance conversation with Collette and what she told me about Andrew.

"Maybe that's why we are back in here, or you at least," Conor says slowly, his mind working overtime. "I could have just answered my own question. Andrew obviously wanted *you* back in here so he could bribe you to get the money to Tanya. He used you because he could blackmail you but why does he want me back?" Conor says, pondering the question.

"Maybe you are just collateral damage," I reply. "Anyway, it's the Minister, Robert Singleton, who got us back in here, not Andrew…unless…"

"Unless what?" Conor asks.

"Unless they are connected in some way? I mean, they must be. How else could Andrew get us back in here if he didn't apply pressure on the Minister? But why would Singleton do what Andrew says and why would the Law Society do what Singleton says?" I ask, confusing myself further.

"Yes, but isn't it strange that Tanya and Collette both mentioned *the Lord Leinster charity*. I wonder is there a connection there between Andrew and Singleton? And I can't fathom this reference to Andrew being gay either. You said yourself that Tanya said something like 'and what a gay Lord Leinster he is'. We've got to get to the bottom of this, Helene, none of it makes any sense! That bastard Andrew! I can't believe you didn't tell me about this before now," Conor says, streaking his hand through his thinning hair. "Have you any idea where he is?" he asks somewhat suspiciously.

"No," I reply, thinking about the cuckoo clock. "I'm sorry, Conor. Really I am. I just didn't know what to do. I was like a rabbit caught in headlights! I didn't know where to turn. I should have trusted you, I know that now. I was weak. He just managed to manipulate me. I was so scared he would tell Dan about Murdoch. Dan would leave me if he knew," I say, crying again, any shred of dignity gone at this stage.

"Well, if that bastard rings again I'll tell him where he can ram his blackmail–"

"Conor, he *can't* know that you know anything," I interrupt. "We have *got* to outwit him. He rang me earlier but I ignored his call. He knows he has me now and will probably try and blackmail me to do something else for him. I'm already in massive trouble!"

"And so am I now," Conor says sombrely. "Now that I know, I am too. To all intents and purposes I should be going out to Barnaby–potato-head-Walsh out there and telling him all about your little transgressions on behalf of the fraudster fugitive, Andrew Peterson!" Conor says, lowering his voice at the end of the sentence. I look at him with despair. "Luckily for you, I won't," he says, gratuitously. "I want that good for nothing criminal, hung, drawn and quartered as much as the next man. Together we can bring him down, Helene. I know we can. There are two of us now. If we put our heads together we can work this out. There is something *major* going down here!" Conor says, pacing the room now and punching the air with his fist. "I can almost taste it. We're on the brink of blowing down the entire stack of cards. Just a few little questions to be answered first."

"A few?" I say, exasperated. "It's a minefield, Conor! We have no idea the depth and breath of what is going on here. Do you remember being in the commercial court the other day? Now BND bank is being investigated by the DPP. We need to find out for what? There is someone in there who has some connection with Andrew as well. I think he might have an accomplice in there. I mean, maybe this person helped Andrew get his hands on all the money through dubious loans?"

"Sure, he did that himself, through all the fraudulent undertakings he gave."

"I don't know. My instincts tell me there is something else going on but who knows? What do I know? I'm just a solicitor turned criminal!" I say, whining now, the tears cascading in pools of water on my sleeves.

"Feeling sorry for yourself isn't going to help," Conor scolds.

"Why would you help me, Conor? What have you got to gain?" I ask him, a moment of fleeting mistrust crossing my mind. "I'd never say I told you anything. You can walk out the door now and pretend that you didn't know anything. I don't want to drag you into this mess with me. It wouldn't be fair," I say, a large sigh extending from me.

"I'm not that altruistic, Helene" Conor says, speaking his truth as always. "For once I have an opportunity to help bring a man to justice. This is a man who has caused suffering to an inordinate amount of innocent people. You have suffered. He has caused me and my family untold grief. The staff in Peterson & Co have suffered, losing their jobs and tarnishing their reputations. Countless clients have lost their properties and are in huge debt because of his selfish, greedy actions." Conor appears unusually emotional and clears his throat with a terse cough before he continues. "I am not going to stand idly by and do nothing when this opportunity has now presented itself. I know this might sound strange, coming from me, Helene, but maybe I'm supposed to help. I do believe in fate, you know," he says, self-consciously and appearing almost embarrassed by his belief. I am bewildered by this revelation. My startled look must register a chord as Conor pulls back instantaneously and resumes his alpha male persona once more. "Now, on to practicalities. I'm going to investigate this dubious *Lord Leinster charity* a bit further and see what I can dig up there. I want you to keep me abreast of all and any contact with Andrew from now on or any other information that you hear at all about him. And I mean, *everything,* Helene," he says, tapping my shoulder briskly with a biro on his lap around the boardroom. It nearly makes me jump. "This is a time for action. We might have no choice but to suss out Tanya as well. We need to establish whose side she is on in all this. We can't be certain of that as yet. We have got to find out more information before we can even start going off pointing the finger. In the meantime, keep this conversation strictly between me and you, Helene," Conor says, finally halting his manic rambling around the boardroom. It's just as well because looking at him is making me dizzy. He pulls out a chair, swivels it around with the flick of his leg and straddles it like a cowboy taming a wild Appaloosa. "It's probably best we leave my wife and Dan out of this for the moment. They'll only worry. We'll just take this step by step and unearth what the hell has been going on in front of our noses once and for all," he says, wearily.

"I *am* sorry, Conor," I say, feeling an enormous sense of relief that I am no longer on my own. I nibble absentmindedly on the skin around my fingernails until I notice Conor's face which registers its disgust. I direct my hands back in my lap.

"I'm sorry I didn't tell you before this and I'm sorry that I've brought you into all of this *but…*" I stare at my hands on my lap. *I wish I could have a cigarette.*

"But what?" Conor asks

"But I *am* grateful that it is you who knows now. I appreciate your lack of judgement and your desire to help. I can't do it on my own," I say, afraid I might set off again on another journey of tears.

"We'll sort this out once and for all," Conor says, looking me straight in the eye. "Believe me."

And I do.

PART III

CHAPTER 25

"Jesus, the net is closing in on us!" Walter Goodings says hysterically. The palm of his hand sweats as he holds the receiver of the telephone. "You remember I told you that the Judge in the commercial court ordered that a file be sent to the DPP on *that* loan in the bank? Well, the DPP has now issued charges against me and they have confiscated my passport pending the arraignment!" Walter continues, his words tripping over one another in their haste to come out. "I know I'm going to be found out! I can't back up some of the loans at all. Whatever about the other underwriters in my department and the undertakings you gave, I had the authority to sanction the bigger loans in BND. I'm in deep shit here."

"Don't be ridiculous, Goody. You'll be fine. You just play dumb," says the voice sweetly on the other end of the line.

"I should have just left everything and come over to you last week," Walter says, pinching the skin on his forearm in quiet desperation. "I shouldn't have come back here after Easter. I can't face this on my own," Walter sobs uncontrollably into the phone. There is a red blotch on his forearm now. It's sore but he ignores the pain. He continues to pinch it frenetically. "This isn't the way things were supposed to work out for us, was it? The plan is that once we had a good few million, we'd move over where you are for good and I could finally set up my own art studio and get out of this hellhole of a job I'm in!"

"Hey, calm down, darling. That *will* happen, don't you worry," the voice says, relaxed.

"Tanya's sorted. She won't grass. She knows she could be landed in it too. Anyway, she is too watchful of her brood, spoilt brats that they are," the voice says spitefully.

Walter cringes inside when he hears this criticism. He continues to pinch the red spot on his forearm noticing with a smirk that it resembles the continent of Asia. He doesn't like innocent children being branded with any kind of evil sentiment. Walter had enough of that growing up, always in Dan's shadow. *Nearly never won the race.*

"Oh! Do leave the children out of it, at least!" Walter shrieks theatrically. "God knows they have enough on their plate with their father just disappearing into thin air!" he says, sniffling indignantly.

"That's why I love you, my darling. You *are* my conscience. At least one of us has one!" the voice says, laughing jollily. "I wish you were here so I can give you one of my *extra-special* hugs and make you feel all snug and satisfied again," the voice purrs sexily.

"I better not get implicated in all this. It'd break my parents' hearts," Walters says, still lapping up his lover's attention. "They'll be so proud when they see my studio and exhibitions and…oh yes, I can see it now…" he says in a faraway voice, day dreaming of a life not yet lived, a life just within reach.

"Our little emerald isle is going to pot as far as I can see," the voice says, realising any attempt at phone sex is now firmly out of the question. "The DPP won't be wasting his time pursuing you with any kind of vengeance. There are bigger fish to fry, out there. All the banks are on the verge of collapse anyway. Sure you'll be lucky to have a job at all in that bank in a few months. Not that you will need one anyway as you'll be safely ensconced with me over here," the voice says matter-of-factly, always managing to allay Walter's fears. Walter wipes his wet eyes with the back of his sleeve.

"Thanks, Cowboy," Walter says affectionately, "If they hadn't taken my bloody passport off me, I'd be with you by now. Hopefully, I can try and take them off the scent. They've no link between us anyway so that's something. I'm going to ask my solicitor to tell the court that I'm not a flight risk and to let me out on bail pending trial. I don't even know the full extent of the charges yet. I just know that they've enough evidence to take all our passports off us, pending the hearing. After your exodus, they are not taking any chances with the rest of us!"

"Don't you worry your head about anything, pet," the voice orders self-assuredly. "Don't forget we have our *Leinster* pal who can help us out with your passport if needs be…I mean, he is the

Minister for Justice after all!" the voice says, cackling loudly.

"Oh, you are a naughty boy!" Walter says, chiding his lover admiringly.

Andrew always makes him feel better about everything. He totally trusts him and knows that, for once he has found true love. They are made for each other. Soon he will be living a life beyond his wildest dreams and to share it with a man like Andrew is the icing on the cake. All the monies in the Leinster charity club that they set up have been siphoned off into their joint swiss bank account. There isn't a sheckle left in it, thank the Lord. At least that means there'll be no trace of the *other* connection. It'd be far too easy for someone to stumble across that. There's no need to mention it to Andrew. He wants to make him proud of his initiative. He'll just have to sit this DPP thing out. He won't get caught out and it'll be worth the wait...

Andrew rests his feet on his canary yellow poof and flicks through the Swiss newspaper absent-mindedly. He feels a sense of unease at this latest turn of events. How can he be sure Walter won't spill the beans on him? Andrew then chuckles to himself, as if answering his own question. He knows Walter *adores* him. Walter is handsome, young and foolish. Even better, he is utterly and gorgeously camp. They plan on moving to the Castro area in San Francisco once Andrew's surgery is complete. A smile creeps up Andrew's face when he thinks of San Fran: the golden gate bridge, *Salsalito* and the ululating stretches of street. He touches his cheek with an index finger. He winces at the acute, throbbing pain under the bandages. *Goddamn plastic surgeons.* Still, it beats being recognised, he says to himself. Only four more surgeries and he is done. It's the only way he can live totally free in this world and start a new life. A new face with millions in his Swiss bank account, he laughs. He sips some alpine spring water with elderflower from a crystal glass then rings the bell beside the leather recliner. He almost pulls the drip out of his wrist with the effort.

"Ah, Britta. Be a dear and put the glass back down for me while you are here. *Danke.* Now, can you get me some more of those strong painkillers please? My face is very tender today. I want to feel as little as possible at bandage-changing time. The pain is really quite unbearable," Andrew says, hoping to elicit some sympathy from his warden.

"Ov course," Britta says, in a concise Germanic tone. Andrew grimaces, gritting his teeth as she undertakes her nursing duties on her patient with clockwork precision.

When Britta has left, Andrew summons up the strength to make a phone call.

"Good afternoon, Bobby boy!" Andrew says, in a jovial manner.

"What do you want?" Robert Singleton replies curtly.

"My, we are a bit moody today, aren't we?" Andrew says, sarcastically. "I suppose it must be difficult being at the helm of that sinking ship of a government of not to mind steering the country through turbulent waters! Hah! Hah!" Andrew guffaws noisily then stops suddenly as his face screams in pain. He must remember not to laugh too much. "I just wanted to eh, ask you a simple favour, if you must know," he continues lackadaisically. "Nothing *too* onerous, mind. Just a little matter of quashing any charges made against my darling, Walter. Now, don't be jealous, Bobby boy, I know he was *yours* once but now he's all mine!" Andrew adds, throwing in a characteristic sting in the tail.

"You're welcome to him," Singleton mumbles.

"What was that you said, Bobby boy? You'll have to speak up a bit?"

"Please stop calling me *that*!" Singleton shouts. He wishes he could throw the phone out the back window of the car. His chauffeur glances in the rear mirror briefly but following a steely eyeball from the Minister, re-focuses his attention on the road.

"Now, now!" Andrew scolds. "Let's not forget our manners: Manners maketh the man, remember! I am sure your wifey honey might find her manners difficult to locate if she knew of your partiality for the stronger sex, *nicht*?" he says, reminding Singleton of his ammunition. There is silence on the other end of the phone."Oooh...and I wonder what your party and your *loyal* electorate would think of your penchant for delectable *younger* men, hmmm? "Andrew teases, the painkillers making his mouth feel dry but his mind high.

"Enough, Andrew. I'll see what I can do," Singleton says, gripping the handle of the door for support. No matter what way he looks, he cannot seem to find a way out. He has resigned himself to do as he is told and pray he will never be caught. I don't know how much longer I can live like this, he thinks to himself.

"Yes, you do that, Bobby boy," Andrew says patronisingly. "Walter always says you were a bit of a soft touch," he adds caustically. "Actually, *Grateful*, was the word I think he said." Andrew muses. Singleton shuts his eyes in tight torture."I expect it must be hard to get even a crumb of testosterone-filled loving these days. It's a pity you broke his heart now, isn't it? I guess you just didn't realise it at the time but you had it *so* easy then, didn't you?" Andrew adds as Singleton puts on his ray-bans with a shaky hand. He hopes his chauffeur won't see his tears. "I am sorry your foreign property portfolio isn't what it should be but you didn't *really* expect me to invest your ill-gotten cash properly, did you? I mean, where did you get that cash anyway, Bobby boy? Did a few developers bribe you over the years when you were a county councillor and a TD, huh? I'd say a few of them had their zoning applications dragged over the line for a bit of cash under the table, isn't that right, Mr. Singelton?" Andrew says, his words flowing now the drugs have taken affect.

Singleton holds the phone and let's Andrew talk on and on. He is used to it. He rues the day he ever met Andrew or Walter. The pair set him up, luring him in on the pretext of making millions and all of them heading off to San Fran to live out the life they always wanted. *They preyed on my vulnerability or my greed or both.* Besides, he'd been in love with Walter. He had always been useless at hiding it, wearing his heart on his sleeve all his life. But then he got cocky and wanted more thrills. He had tasted the love of a boy and he wanted more. The only problem was he liked the *younger* ones. He couldn't help it, he was just drawn to them. Singleton identified with them and felt protective of them.

He had never been cut out for politics, winning his father's seat in a by-election but not having the first clue of the sheer graft it actually involved. He wishes he could throw off the shackles of responsibility around him, leave his wife and set up a home with a lover, but alas, his sense of duty confounds him. Singleton knows his pride won't let him either.

He can't do it to himself or his family. Instead he labours under the threat of blackmail at any given moment of the day or night, now knowing what he'll be asked to do or even how he'll do it. *I'm weak*, he thinks.

Singleton carries his father's legacy on his shoulders. He must carry the name forward for his sons or his daughter. Laura is already showing a keen interest in it, becoming secretary of the youth branch in Dun Laoghaire and tirelessly campaigning for those lucky enough to get on the ticket. Singleton marvels at her innocence and her illusionary hero-worship of her father. Her mother blazes through the ladies-who-lunch charity circuit, waxed, botoxed and coiffed. Dressed in only the best designer couture, her shallow existence irks him as he realises he has married his mother's *doppelganger*.

His wife has never been interested in sex, subconsciously getting her kicks instead from the adoration of her flattering girlfriends who are only too thrilled to be socialising with the wife of a Minister no less. Who will fund her lifestyle, not to mention their children's private schooling and ski-trips if he takes off into the sunset?

Singleton watches the traffic go by and yearns for a simple existence. He takes out the debriefing for the next meeting, scanning his eyes over the contents. It's a waste of time. Singleton leaves his ray bans on as that mean red fury takes him over again. His anger gives him heart palpitations. Reaching into his pocket, Singleton takes out his pill box and pops another Valium into his mouth. Between those and the sleeping pills he could open a pharmacy.

"If you wouldn't mind organising that press release to go out on Tuesday," Don Glennon asks his assistant. He hands her a yellow file. "It's important it gets into the paper on Wednesday. That might take some of the heat off this other story about BND bank being investigated. We've had enough bad press about Andrew Peterson, we don't want to be adding fuel to the fire. We want to keep his name out of the media as much as we can. It's not doing any good for the solicitor's profession," he comments, genuinely flummoxed at the scale of damage that Mr. Peterson has left behind him.

"Yes, Mr. Glennon. I'll see to that straight away," his assistant says. *At least she's the conscientious type*, Glennon thinks. "Also, the Minister for Justice's office has confirmed your meeting with the Minister at midday. I understand he is on his way."

"Good," Glennon says, not looking at her but concentrating on what he wants to get across to Robert Singleton.

Glennon is beginning to think that his appointment as

Director-General of the Law Society may not actually be the poison chalice he originally thought. It would appear that a bill has been recently enacted which will allow the Minister appoint solicitors to the Supreme court bench. Glennon fancies himself quite nicely for this job. He's always been underestimated in his academic achievement and this will show his colleagues who look down their noses at him that there is more to Don Glennon than meets the eye. Some of them seem to think that running the Law Society isn't a real job at all, that he isn't really *practising* as a solicitor. The nerve of them! It takes a lot of guts and dedication to do this job, always in the eye of the media, constantly juggling the stresses of the public and his profession. Glennon believes he is adequately qualified to be elected to the bench. He has even written a law book on a particular tiresome area of contract law, contracts of guarantee. It's hard to believe but no publisher seems to think there is a market for it.

Luckily for Glennon, the Minister seems to be reasonably impressed with the job he is doing on getting matters attended to swiftly in Peterson & Co. Singleton seems very eager to have everything sorted out, like yesterday. I suppose, being a solicitor himself he wants to help his old profession, Glennon muses. He has no doubt that Singleton will push for his judicial appointment at the next opportunity. He has hinted, on more than one occasion, that Glennon will be *'looked after'*. I mean, he even wrote it in down in the letter he got saying that *he wouldn't forget* his honourable action. He has said nothing to his family yet but he has thrown in a few riddles for them to figure out, every now and then. Just a few teasers, like, *oh wait till I'm wearing my wig and gown* and that kind of thing. Glennon knows they all think he has gone a bit daft but he doesn't mind. They'll be overjoyed with a Judge in the family. Far from that they were reared, his wife would probably say, which wouldn't be far from the truth. Glennon is the only one from his family who went on to third level education, not to mind any professional training. He is proud of his achievements and this appointment will be the pinnacle of his career. Nothing is going to stop him in his tracks and he will do whatever it takes to ensure the Minister is kept happy. That Conor Carroll seemed a bit cheeky the other day, he must keep an eye on him. Glennon wouldn't have left neither Conor nor that snooty Helene back in the door of the Firm if he had his way but he is not the puppet master. What the Minister says, goes, even if he has to keep his *real* motivation to himself.

CHAPTER 26

"If this baby kicks me one more time, then it must be a boy. There's an entire football team in there I can tell you!" I say, as I observe Conor's eyes glaze over. "I really don't want to bore you, Conor but I'm exhausted all the time. I really just want to sort all this out before my health suffers. I can tell you have news for me, though?" I ask, half afraid of the reply.

"Hmmm. Yes, I do and it's very interesting. I just googled the *Lord Leinster charity* and surprise, surprise, nothing came up. The only information I could get was that it *is* a charity but it wouldn't even give me the names of the directors or the address of the charity or anything at all. "

"I guess that would have been *too* easy," I say, disappointed.

"Yes, but I didn't know that you don't have to actually *register* a charity in Ireland. There is no such thing. There isn't even a facility for them to do so. The Revenue Commissioners do give out CHY numbers which simply recognises that the organisation is a charity for the purposes of the tax laws. But this doesn't mean it's a 'registered charity' and it does not involve the Revenue Commissioners having any supervisory role."

"Does *The Lord Leinster charity* have a CHY number?" I ask, hopefully.

"I was just coming to that...yes, luckily for us they do. It's 11863. I went onto the Revenue site and looked up the list of bodies granted charitable tax exemption as on 22nd December 2009. It's under Section 207 of the Taxes Consolidation Act, 1997," Conor explains. "Not that that's of any relevance but not surprisingly *the Lord Leinster charity* lists its charity address as the same address as

Peterson & Co."

"Ok, no surprises there," I say, unimpressed. "I mean, Andrew probably knows I'd check out the name and the charity addresses anyway."

"Yes, of course," Conor concedes. "He is certainly no eejit but here's the thing," Conor says, keeping a beady eye on the door of my office. "My wife's sister works in the Revenue and she owes me a favour. Basically I didn't charge her and my brother-in-law for their conveyance. Thankfully, it was one of the houses Andrew didn't exploit, mainly because I had dealt with the paperwork. Anyway, I told her I needed some information on this charity for a client. I just thought it might be worth a shot..."

"And?" I say, getting impatient.

"Well, it looks like the charity also has another address in Ireland, like a branch address, which isn't documented online but it is retained in the annual return documents. It has to be by law," Conor adds.

"Right. Where?" I say, intrigued.

"It's an address in Sandymount: 38B Auburn Court," Conor says, looking at me, both of us thinking the same thing.

"Collette," both of us say together. "She mentioned that lady to me, the one who died at an address in Sandymount!" I say, excited. "Collette said that she left everything to the Lord Leinster charity!"

"Yes, but why have an address there now? What's Andrew hiding there?" Conor asks gravely. "The plot just keeps thickening, Helene. And there's more," Conor says, his voice almost a whisper. "Trudy was able to find out through another contact of hers in BND bank that only yesterday, the entire monies from the Irish account have been transferred to an international account number."

"Gosh," I say, gobsmacked.

"Trudy said that her contact in BND said there had been no activity on the account for a few months and that this transaction was done by electronic transfer in one day."

"Something urgent must be up," I say, not fully understanding what's going on.

"Yes, but the contact told Trudy that it seems it is someone from BND bank as in an *employee* of the Bank that ordered the transfer of funds and not an outside client. It was done *in-house*, it would appear," Conor says, mesmerised by the intrigue himself.

"That would tie in with Judge Smythson in the commercial

court sending that file off to the DPP to investigate someone action's in that bank?" I say, my mind trying to work out the puzzle before me.

"Ah yes, but that's not all," Conor says, fixing me with an intense gaze.

"What?" I ask, "Oh put me out of my agony for God's sake!" I exclaim tetchily.

"The amount was for exactly €48 million! The *same* amount that Judge Smythson was eluding to in the commercial court that day. Smythson *knows* that something is up with that money and that it shouldn't have been authorised as a payment out *at all*. In fact, I suspect, since he sent the file off to the DPP, that he knows there is fraud being committed in BND bank by someone and that the €48 million is no more a loan than the man in the moon."

"And the entire amount was transferred only yesterday into a foreign bank account. How convenient!" I say, clapping my hands with awe at the simplicity of it all.

"And that would make sense," Conor explains "since it was only yesterday that all the employees' passports were confiscated pending trial." He opens his briefcase and takes out a red folder."And look, here is a list of all the employees whose passports have been confiscated pending a full investigation. A Garda pal in Ringsend did me the honours," he adds, amused at his own creative dexterity.

"Nice to have friends in high places!" I tease, jabbing Conor in the arm as I take the A4 sheet of names from him.

I get such a fright that I have to read it again:

John Matthews
Eilis Baxter
Walter Goodings
Mark O'Reilly
Phillipa Fenton

"You look like you've just seen a ghost!" Conor says, "Are you alright?"

"Walter is Dan's brother, his younger brother," I say, feeling weak.

"Are you sure it's the same one?" Conor asks, diplomatically.

"Yeah," I reply, wishing it wasn't true. "He's an artist but he works as a freelance underwriter in various Banks. I know Dan mentioned to me that he had been working on and off with a bank but I didn't think that it was BND bank," I say, getting worried now. "Actually I don't think Dan said what Bank he was working for and I don't think I asked."

"It doesn't mean anything anyway," Conor says, helpfully. "It could easily be one of the other employees?"

"You don't understand Conor," I say, knowing the answer in my heart. "Walter is gay."

"Oh," Conor says quizzically. "What's the significance of that?"

"Well," I say, not entirely sure where I am going with this "there is what Collette said about Andrew being gay, there is Tanya's reference to a gay Lord Leinster and now Walter is thrown into the mix. This is just completely confusing, Conor!" I say, exasperated. "It's staring us in the face but we just can't seem to piece it all together."

"Does Walter know Andrew?" Conor asks.

"I don't know and I don't know how I'd find that out," Helene says, her brow creasing at the thought of confronting Walter. Conor mulls this over for a moment.

"I think I do," Conor replies. "I'm convinced that this Lord Leinster charity has an international address, probably where this foreign bank account is. I am *sure* that's where Andrew is hiding out. He won't stay far from his monies, I bet. We have a lead remember. We have this address in Sandymount. I think we need to check out this gaff," Conor says, enthusiastically.

"God, Conor," I say, feeling scared, "we could be getting in way over our heads here! Andrew has been on twice already as you know. How he expects me to get more cash to Tanya is beyond me. He seems to have cash hidden here there and everywhere! He said he'd call me tomorrow with firm instructions but I don't know if I can do this again…"

"Helene, Andrew will continue to blackmail you: for the rest of your life if we don't get to him first!" Conor says, wagging his nail-bitten finger at me. "We can't just let him continue hurting people, propagating misery and deceit everywhere he goes. We've got to stop him and put an end to his evil! Besides, you're already in deep trouble, as am I now, but at least if we can catch the bastard, the Gardai might go easier on us," Conor says, rationalising the lesser of two evils. Conor's courage and resolve amaze me. He knows the difference between right and wrong and refuses to stand idly by.

"We will find Andrew, Helene, if it's the last thing I do!" Conor warns. "Let me know if he rings again. Just keep him sweet. In the meantime I'll check out a few other things and we'll check out this Sandymount place tomorrow. We better keep Barnaby Walsh off our backs for the moment," Conor says, strategising our plan of action.

"I just can't believe that Walter could be involved in this scam," I say to Conor before he leaves, "but something has just occurred to me." I feel a shiver down my spine.

"What?" Conor asks, turning around.

"Dan said that Walter has been very up and down recently. I mean, even more than normal. He said Wally is always talking about 'breaking free' and heading off for a new life somewhere with his 'true love'. When Dan prodded him a bit more on this 'true love', Walter got defensive and said that Dan didn't know the meaning of sacrifice and pure, unconditional love. Dan and I laughed at this, because, to be honest, Walter is always falling in love. But then Dan told me Wally said something else...something about the fact that he'll prove them all wrong in the not too distant future and how his life is going to turnaround in the blink of an eye and that we'd all be looking at him in utter admiration for a change. He told Dan that 'foreign shores' beckoned and a 'windfall' awaited him. As I said, Dan and I found this highly amusing at the time but now...well, now, it seems just a bit coincidental that he happens to be on the list of suspects."

"I see," Conor says, "it does sound a bit coincidental but let's not jump to any conclusions yet. I'll come back to you later, ok? Barnaby is on the hunt out there and by the way, not a word to Dan yet. We've nothing proven anyway."

"Ok. You have my word," I say. I owe Conor that much.

It would break Dan's heart, not to mention their parents if Walter is involved. The more I think of it, the more I can't dismiss the fact that Andrew and Walter might be connected...*No, could it be?* It makes me sick when I think of a possible romantic link between them? *Surely not!* Could that be the truth? Was Andrew living in one of those so-called "Lavender relationships" where the person enters into a fake relationship in order to keep at bay any rumours that they might be anything less than heterosexual?

I mean, the legal profession may not be perceived as the most liberal profession but there's no reason why Andrew can't be openly gay and remain the managing partner of his Firm? There are a good few Solicitors and Barristers who are publicly gay and at the top of their field. And why shouldn't they be? What's the big deal?

More importantly, apart from his wife and children, why would Andrew be so keen on keeping his sexuality under wraps? Was he afraid to lose business by coming out or was it simply that he didn't want to be the source of other people's salacious gossip? Maybe I'm jumping to conclusions, I think to myself, but something makes sense about Andrew and Walter. I can feel it in my gut. *And wait!* something else. Ah! That makes sense! I think to myself. Otherwise how on earth would Andrew *always* seem to know my mobile number? Because *Walter* gave them to him! I copy all my family, including Walter and Dan's parents with my new mobile details each time I replace an old model. It just seems *too* coincidental...

"Hey Dan," I say, "How are things?" I ask, trying to sound casual.

"To what do I owe this pleasure?" Dan asks, knowing me far too well.

"What do you mean, hon?" I ask, innocently. "I'm just wondering how your day is going and...well, I was wondering if you wanted to ask your Mum and Dad and eh, Wally, of course, over to Sunday lunch?"

"You are definitely getting broody or nesty, should I say, these days! I suppose at eight months pregnant, that's bound to happen," Dan chuckles. "Yeah, that's great, sure I've been trying to get them over for weeks but you've been too tired...Wally isn't the best of form, though, I have to admit."

"Oh?" I ask, expectantly.

"Yeah, there's some fiasco going down at work. I don't know exactly what as he won't give us the details yet anyway. I'm a bit worried about him to tell you the truth. He's been moaning again about leaving this 'blasted' country of ours, as he put it. Sure I told him he's not long back from Switzerland and that he..."

"Walter was in Switzerland? When?"

"What's got you so interested in Wally all of a sudden, Helene McBain?" Dan asks, clearly amused. "He usually drives you around the twist! Don't mention the war, anyway. No seriously, he let that slip to me one day when he had a few too many gins as usual. He doesn't want anyone to know he was over there a few weeks ago for some reason. I've a feeling there was a gay pride festival on or maybe he even has a lover boy over there, I don't know, but he was at pains for me not to breathe a word. Sure I don't even think he remembered telling me the next day. He was going on about how much he needed a holiday the next morning, but I kept schtum. I didn't want to embarrass him. The whole bottle of Bombay Sapphire was empty so that'll tell you just how ossified he was!"

"He likes his gin," I say, forcing myself not to bombard Dan with more questions.

"He certainly does. Anyway, be a dear and don't mention it on Sunday, will you? He'll only kill me and I don't want to embarrass him. I think he is going through a hard enough time as it is. He seems like, well, *lovesick* or something," Dan says, naively.

Is he now? "Hopefully we'll manage to cheer him up," I say, not meaning a word of it.

"See you later darling," Dan says, "don't work too hard."

"I won't," I say, again not meaning a word of it. I make a mental note to stock up on gin for Sunday lunchtime.

For a couple of hours I am in consultations with clients. Reluctantly, I have to wait to impart my news on Walter's recent trip to Conor. Finally, I buzz Conor on his mobile instead of the in-house intercom system. I'm so paranoid that the phones could be tapped. I fill him in on my conversation with Dan. This mention of Switzerland has my antennae up.

"Why is that interesting?" Conor says.

"Because I'm wondering is that where Andrew is?" I ask

"But you're *assuming* a link between him and Walter? We can't prove that yet."

"I know," I say, "but my instincts tell me otherwise. I bet you €48 million euro on it!"

"We can't go on instincts alone, Helene," Conor warns. "Anyway, listen up. I've more news for you...just let me make sure the door is shut properly," Conor says. I hear him walk over to the door and double check it. The last thing we need is Barnaby Walsh suspecting anything. "This garda pal of mine has just given me some fascinating information on Robert Singleton. He has dug up some dirt on him alright. I don't know why we didn't do this earlier when we nabbed the letter of Walsh. I knew something wasn't right."

"What is it?" I say, desperate to know.

"It turns out our Minister for Justice is *gay* as well"

"Ah, here! you're joking," I gasp.

"Nope. I'm not. Apparently it's well known in the Dail but the other members turn a blind eye. I believe only last year an opposition member of the Seanad tried to go public with it he was bought off: A brown envelope and all that."

"God," I say

"Anyway, the majority view is that he is a good husband and father so his own personal business is his own, if you get my drift?"

"Right," I say, wondering where Conor is going with this.

"Except two months ago he was stopped coming out of a property with a much younger male. The Gardai questioned him one Thursday evening about ten o'clock. Apparently the boy looked about fourteen."

"Oh Gross, Conor!" I say, not sure if I want to hear anymore

"The boy told the Gardai he was eighteen and the Beangarda and the other Garda decided not to persist with their line of enquiry. I mean, their behaviour looked normal enough on the outside but the Beangarda had enough experience to be suspicious. The upshot of it all is that they were coming out of *38B Auburn Court, Sandymount.*"

"OmiGod! There's a link to Andrew!" I say, shocked "And Singelton and this boy were definitely coming out of there?" I ask, completely perplexed.

"Yes," Conor replies "so I'm thinking that's the unofficial registered address of *the Lord Leinster* charity, right?"

"Yes?" I say

"And Singleton is a member of *Leinster* house…"

"And *what a gay Lord Leinster he* is!" we say in unison. There is a momentary silence as we let this information sink in.

"So that is a reference to Singleton! He's the Lord Leinster! God. That's ingenious," I say, mesmerised. "I wonder does Tanya know that?" I ask.

"That's what we are going to find out. We are going to bring this house of cards to its knees!" Conor says, with a determination the like of which I've never seen.

"That's what I'm scared of," I say.

Chapter 27

"I'll have the money to you by next week," Andrew says, through gritted teeth. His jaw is in acute pain. It is a gargantuan task just to speak.

"As usual you bulldoze your way into the conversation before I even had a chance to say anything. I am shutting Sandymount down. Robert rang me and told me he was quizzed by the Gardai not too long ago coming out of there. I bet you he didn't tell you that, did he?" Tanya asks, tapping her fingers on the marble fireplace. "He was seen leaving with one of those unfortunate wren boys, or whatever your call them these days. If Lord Leinster, as you put it, was arrested, God knows what could have happened!" she says, staring at the reflection of herself in the drawing room mirror. *I've aged.* "The Media would go to town on it! I gave Robert a piece of my mind I can tell you for being indiscreet. I set up a perfectly smooth operation for you all. That fool of a woman left you that immaculate property and you and the others use it as a male escort parlour. It's sickening really. If it wasn't for the sleeping tablets I'm on I wouldn't sleep a wink thinking about it," Tanya says, lifting her eyebrow to pluck an errant hair from under its arch. *More grey hairs.* Tanya is terrified that her involvement will lead the police to her. She is ready to land Andrew in it as soon as she has the cash. "The only reason that I haven't shopped you in, Andrew, is because I need that money. The only way I could do that was by helping you run that disgusting service for sick men. I need the other two million so I can get the hell out of here for good," Tanya says, hoping she doesn't have to cut her losses too early. "You left your children high and dry and I'm damned if I am going to let you ruin their innocent lives! Another two million and I'll be set up in a reasonable enough manner in Canada. The first million will hardly buy me a decent property and a foot in the door with the *right* type of society. Our children deserve the best, despite what you might think."

"And how do I know you won't shop me in it after I have given you the last of the cash?" Andrew asks, feeling smug she knows nothing of his ongoing plastic surgery.

"Because I know you," Tanya says, wondering what took her this long. "Admittedly, I *didn't* before and I was *so* naïve but I know you now and thank the heavens for that! You'll be mid transit to whatever destination you have in mind at the exact time the cash arrives. I've no doubt about that. You'll cover your tracks. There'll be no trace of you. My parents would turn in their grave if they knew you have lived a lie all these years. You and the wonderful Minister for Justice, as gay as Christmas! To think that if it wasn't for the fact that your dumbass boyfriend Walter spilt the beans to me after I'd be none the wiser! He just couldn't help himself, could he? There I was, minding my own business and he blurts it all out. A few drinks and he'd tell anyone anything! I can't believe I thought he was just one of the wren boys, an aspiring actor or something earning a bit of cash on the side, but your boyfriend?!" Tanya exclaims as if re-living the moment habitually.

Andrew rolls his eyes. He has heard this story in different versions over and over.

"I was going to tell you where I was once I got settled. The Gardai would have been sniffing around you, I didn't want them to get the scent..."Andrew protests, a trace of guilt in his voice.

"Whatever, I don't believe a word of it. Me? I can survive but to leave your children fatherless is one thing but to leave them penniless is another. Anyway, when is the next cash deposit being made?" Tanya asks, smiling as she recalls that unfortunate Helene McBain struggle with the cash. It's even sweeter that Andrew doesn't realise she knows exactly who the courier is. Who knows? Helene may yet become the ally she needs to bring Andrew to justice. But not yet, not until she has all the cash she needs. "So your darling Walter is organising to get the cash to me?" Tanya asks. *I know its Helene.* She was so easily recognisable poor pet, Tanya thinks to herself. *I wonder what dirt Andrew has on her.*

"Yes. It'll be the full amount this time. Just one more week, that's all I need," Andrew says, having no intention whatsoever of giving her any money. He needs Tanya out of his hair. *In for a penny, in for a pound.*

"I loved our honeymoon in Switzerland," she says, "I knew you'd be hiding out there, just a wild guess but there you go, I was right about one thing anyway! And all that *sex*. You were always a bit kinky though, weren't you, Andy baby? The missionary position didn't totally titillate you. Now I know why. You must have been bored out of your mind. It's a miracle I didn't get AIDS when I think about it. You must surely have sampled the male flesh by that stage, huh?" she asks.

Andrew seethes in silence.

"That gorgeous Swiss waiter took a bit of a shine to me, you know," Tanya continues. "I regret that. I regret that I didn't suck his cock instead of yours or maybe I should have asked him to do it for me?" Tanya says, finding this hilariously funny and laughing uproariously for what seemed to Andrew like an eternity. He hated her laugh and she knows he hated her using foul language. Tanya had served her purpose but now he wanted her gone. He had no intention of giving her any more money. He pressed the buzzer for Britta. He needed painkillers and a hitman.

Glennon is not happy. He wipes his brow and steadies his half-moon glasses over the bump on his nose. It seems that Singleton has exited Glennon's plan for the future. Singleton was arrested yesterday for attempting to pervert the course of justice. Glennon is completely surprised by these revelations. What was Singleton doing trying to help this employee of BND bank? What for? *There goes my judicial appointment. Damn.*

He reads the newspaper headline: MINISTER ARRESTED IN PASSPORT SCANDAL KILLS HIMSELF.

It would seem that Singleton made covert submissions to get his employee's passport back to him. They haven't named the employee in the papers yet but Glennon knows it's only a matter of time. The reporter says that Singleton was kept for a twelve hour period and then charged with various offences including fraud and attempting to pervert the course of justice. It is understood that Singleton left a note in his cell outlining the extent of his misdemeanours. No further details are given. For the life of him

Glennon can't fathom what Singleton was up to? He idolised the Minister and thought him the epitome of principled living. The Taoiseach is quoted as saying that Singleton's death is a 'tragic loss' and extends his sympathy to his family. When asked about any other offences the Taoiseach simply replied that 'justice would have to run its course'. To Glennon this wasn't giving very much away. To be frank he didn't really care, he just knew that any hopes for a judicial appointment anytime soon would be slim now. It'd take a lot of brown-nosing up to Singleton's successor to be in with even half a chance. He didn't really have the energy anymore. It was just bad luck.

"Barnaby. You've seen the news I presume?"

"Yes, very tragic. A terrible shock," Walsh replies.

"Yes, terrible alright. *Terrible for me.* Let's wrap up this business in Peterson & Co by close of business tomorrow, Barnaby. Whatever files are still 'work in progress' can be sent out to locum solicitors or to the panel on our books. We've done enough now for the public to be satisfied that justice has been seen to be done."

"Tomorrow? With all due respect, Don, there are still quite a few files to get through. I have to say Conor and Helene seem to be doing a great job in here. I have to hand it to them really, particularly with the limited resources available to them and..."

"Tomorrow, Barnaby, ok?" Glennon says firmly wiping the sweat off his brow again. He is not prepared to waste anymore time on that Firm now that there is no need. He folds the newspaper and throws it into the green recycling basket beside his desk.

"Jesus Christ," Walter says out loud. He reads the headline mesmerised. He can't believe the Lord Leinster himself is dead! And all because he was trying to get my passport back, he thinks to himself. His man Andrew will hit the roof if he knows about this. This wasn't in the plan at all. Maybe he shouldn't tell him yet, Andrew will only worry. There is no Tanya to think about though, she might get alarmed, particularly as Robert seems to have left a suicide note. God knows what that says! At least Singleton doesn't know about Walter's relationship with Andrew. On the other hand he better tell Andrew, even though he is out of reach. He is going to find out one way or the other. Walter just doesn't want him worrying unnecessarily, especially since he is recovering from this third operation. Andrew jokes with Walter that he'll look like Brad Pitt by the time the surgery is complete. Walter doesn't tell Andrew that he doesn't even like that kind of look. He doesn't want to hurt his feelings. He prefers him the way he is but it's too late for that now. He doesn't really mind anyway. As long as Andrew is happy, that's the main thing. Besides, freedom is much more valuable than beauty.

Walter *is* worried about the BND investigation but he is trying to push it to the back of his mind. He hoped the DPP won't be able to prove that he had anything to do with the €48 million loan approval. Of course, it's not really a loan as it'll never be paid back. Hah! It's sitting cosy in the Lord Leinster account in Switzerland. Thank God Robert didn't know anything about that account. Then they would have been in *big* trouble. Walter prides himself on being excellent at forgery. Most people's signatures are easy to copy. A bit like art really, he thinks. And he is so very artistic. That is his real *metier* of choice after all. Walter just has a natural flair for that kind of thing. It'll be difficult for the DPP to prove that he forged not one but two signatures of the top underwriters in BND. It'll be hard for those underwriters to prove they *didn't* sign off on the "loan" as the signatures on the documents are perfectly in keeping with their normal signatures. How the DPP will have any evidence to prove it was Walter and not another employee who forged the signatures, if indeed they can prove the forgeries at all, is beyond him. Walter is that confident in his skill. He practiced for hours at home with tracing paper, going over the two names again and again. When he finally signed the names he didn't even need the tracing paper anymore. He knew each curve, stroke and line of every letter. He knew exactly at what point the letter broke through the line on the page. He studied the force of the pen on the page. Does the signatory bear heavily on the page when he signs his name or does he brush it lightly, just so?

He scrutinised the characters of the two men as if to feel their personality in their signature. It took weeks of research and preparation before he was ready to sign. When it came to the crunch it only took a matter of seconds to sign both their names but all that work was necessary for the perfect delivery. His mobile, with the theme tune to *Priscilla, Queen of the Desert* stirs him out of his reverie abruptly.

"Hi big boy, I was just about to call you myself," Walter says, wondering how he will broach the news of Singleton's death.

"I see Singleton has left us already," Andrew says.

"Oh," Walter says, unsubtly registering his surprise that Andrew knows.

"I do get the news over here, you know my darling. I certainly will not be grieving for our old friend Lord Leinster, it's more that he could have got us out of a bit of a bind. There is still the persistent problem of your passport to sort out. The main thing is that they don't link you to me, otherwise the suspicions of the Gardai might be aroused. I need to recuperate here for a while and I need to get you over here in case Singleton's death triggers an uncontrollable chain of events."

"I know," Walter says subdued, noticing that Andrew doesn't appear to know that Robert left a note behind. He is too afraid to tell him about it. "I can't stand being here any longer Andy, I just want to be with you. Dan and Helene have invited me over for Sunday lunch. I don't know if I can bear it!"

"Hang on in there, pet. Nothing else matters but that. I'm talking to some contacts over here and I'll be doing my utmost to sort out a fake passport for you. You might need to disguise yourself accordingly but leave it with me for the moment. Time is of the essence now, my love, I've got to get you over here before the police come looking for you. It's only a matter of time."

"I know," Walter says again with a lump in this throat. "I don't want all of this to have been in vain."

"Tanya might just have to disappear too, darling," Andrew says ominously.

Noooo! I don't want blood on my hands! Walter holds his breath."Is that really necessary?" he asks, disillusioned. Walter knows that Andrew hates Tanya as she reminds him of the lie he lived for far too long. He was always under the misapprehension that he was under her thumb. Sure look what he has done to her now?

"Don't you worry about anything, my love. I'll take care of it all. You just sit tight,"Andrew says, under the illusion he is placating Walter somewhat in the process.

After Andrew hangs up Walter curses him. *Why can't he just leave Tanya out of it?* She is the mother of his children for God's sake. If she does decide to tell where Andrew is he'll be long gone by that time. Andrew is smarter than her. What will happen to the children with no father and no mother? Yeah, he could blame Tanya for getting the truth out of him about his relationship with Andrew. But still he thought it was ok then because Andrew did leave her high and dry. To tell the truth he feels completely conflicted. He loves Andrew but he doesn't want Tanya or their children to suffer because of that. He is not *that* bad. It's amazing really that she guessed where Andrew was hiding, although for the wrong reasons. He had always told her that if he was going to do a runner he'd go back there. It was just an off the cuff comment, eleven years earlier but she'd remembered it. But Andrew didn't go to Switzerland out of some romantic posterity because Tanya and himself honeymooned there or for the breathtaking views over the lakes of Geneva, it was because Montreux city has the best plastic surgery sanatorium in Europe. Walter just can't believe this simple plan has embroiled him even further into criminality. He knows Andrew doesn't trust Tanya but seriously, this is going a step too far! This is at turn he didn't want to take. He wants no part of murder. That's not who he is, is he? A bit of harmless forgery from a bank with millions to spare is a world apart from killing someone! Not that he would be doing it but he does *know* about it. *All that is necessary for evil to triumph is that good men do nothing.* Walter shudders at the thought. His conscience is making itself known.

He knows Andrew will find someone to kill her. Does that make him equally guilty if he doesn't prevent it? Oh God, those poor little children. Still he does love Andrew massively. He has never felt this way about anyone. They may not be taking the most conventional route to be together but as Andrew says, sometimes you have to grab an opportunity. We only have one life, after all, and why shouldn't they enjoy the abundance the universe has to offer? Especially if they are not hurting anyone in the process...*oh but they are! They are!*

Walter doesn't hear the first knock on the door as his ears ring from the thoughts in his head. The second knock is louder forcing him to turn around swiftly. He looks at the door. *Who can that be?*

Walter walks to the door, regretting he never got a peephole installed.

"Who is it?" he asks, resting his right hand on the door.

"Is that Walter Goodings?" a stern voice replies.

"Yes, who is it?" Walter's voice trembles slightly.

"We have a warrant to search the premises," another voice

replies.

Walter weighs up his options momentarily. There is nowhere to hide. Anyway, they are not arresting him. He opens the door.

"Walter Goodings," says a clean-shaven uniformed Garda, accompanied by what appears to be a cute plain clothed detective. "We are arresting you on suspicion of fraud under Section 10 of the Criminal Justice (Theft and fraud Offences) Act 2001. You have the right to remain silent. Anything you say can and will be used against you in a court of law. You have the right..."

Walter's mouth opens wide involuntarily.

CHAPTER 28

"Helene, there is a *Murdoch Pierce* downstairs? He said he was passing and wanted a brief word with you about a case you are working on together," Walsh says, as I feel Conor's eyes burning into my face. I turn scarlet. "But before you depart can I just mention that I have received orders from the Law Society, from Don Glennon himself, that eh, well, that we must close the doors of this Firm by close of business tomorrow. I'm terribly sorry for any inconvenience but I'm afraid it's out of my hands."

"What?" Conor says, surprised "but sure we haven't finished working on the files yet!"

"Yes, I appreciate that," Walsh says, studying his slip-on shoes, "they will be taken care of by other solicitors. I'm afraid there are more pressing issues of concern right now."

"Yeah, like the Minister's death, you mean!" Conor shouts. Walsh says nothing, his face the picture of defeat as he slips out of the office.

"Calm down, Conor!" I snap at him, "What difference does it make now? Apart from the fact that I'm nearly nine months pregnant, it'll give us more time to investigate what's been going on. You'll get another job!" I say, hoping he can see this for himself. "There is no talk of our practising certificates being taken from us. We'll be ok; You'll be ok!" I tell him, my voice softening now.

"I should have kept taking those sleeping tablets I was on. They made life so much easier to cope with. I'm not sleeping a wink these days with all this going on," Conor says, clearly stressed by recent events.

I hear my phone ring and remember Murdoch is waiting for me

downstairs.

"I've to answer that Conor. I'll pop into you later once I've talked to Murdoch." Conor walks out of the door with tears in his eyes.

"Hi Dan," I say, not expecting his call.

"Fuck, Helene. Wally is after being arrested and it doesn't look good," Dan says, in a panicked voice. "Two members of the Garda Bureau of Fraud Investigation arrived at his home and arrested him. He was charged with a number of offences in Ringsend Garda Station, including forgery of all things, I mean, can you believe that?" he asks.

"No," I reply. *Of course I can believe it!*

"Apparently he can get up to ten years in prison! Mum and Dad are beside themselves," Dan says breathlessly. "Walter says the Office of the Director of Corporate Enforcement (ODCE) is also involved and trawling through thousands of pages of financial documents and computer records. No one else but Wally has been arrested. He says he is innocent, Helene, and I do believe him."

"Does he have a solicitor?" I ask, my knuckles white from gripping the phone.

"Not yet but..."

"I'll be there in an hour. I insist," I say pragmatically. "I know him better than any other solicitor. I'll help him," I tell Dan. *This is my chance to get to the bottom of this.*

"Helene, you are so good to offer but we need an expert in criminal law not family law! I was going to ask you for a recommendation," Dan protests.

"A solicitor is a solicitor," I dictate, not believing a word of it. "I'll be there in an hour. Can you let Ringsend station know please?"

As I hang up I can hear Dan still speaking on the other end of the line. There is no way I am letting this opportunity pass me by, I think. Walter is my link to Andrew.

I am taken aback at how handsome Murdoch looks as I walk out of the escalator. I am that distracted that I don't think to put on my long black maternity jacket over my dress. As a result my bump protrudes enormously. I waddle like a duck. As self-conscious as I am, there is nothing I can do about it. I feign a smile.

"Hi Helene," Murdoch stands to greet me, as chivalrous as always. He pulls out a chair for me in the expansive reception.

"Have you time for a coffee?" he asks hopefully.

"No, I'm afraid I don't," I say. He sits down in a chair beside me. Something about Murdoch and his kindnesses blow me away. I babble incoherently about Walter's arrest, not withholding my suspicions about his relationship with Andrew. Something compels me to tell him everything.

"Bloody hell," Murdoch says when I'm finished. "I can help you, particularly if it is going to assist in capturing that ego," he offers magnanimously, "if you want?"

"Oh Murdoch, I don't know what to say!" I reply, grateful for his assistance. *How can I refuse his help*? I know that whatever Walter says to Murdoch will be kept confidential; it *is* a fiduciary relationship after all.

"But can you help me in return?" he asks

"With what?" I ask, the obvious meaning eluding me entirely. Slowly I register what he is asking me. "I don't know," I reply.

"What do you mean?" he asks

"I don't know if you are the father of this baby, Murdoch," I say, putting my hand protectively on my belly. I spell it out. "That's the honest answer. I don't know. It could be you or it could be Dan." *I'm tired of lies*

"I see," he says, pensively. Murdoch knows there is such a thing as a paternity test if he has any suspicions. He can force me to have my baby undertake this test after it is born. He knows that I know that too but neither of us mention it. He is far too much of a gentleman. "So that's the end of my fantasy, I guess," he says forlornly.

"What do you mean?" I ask.

"You know I've been in love with you for a long time, Helene. I just wish it was reciprocated," Murdoch says, cupping my left elbow in his palm, his eyes locking with mine.

"I am attracted to you, Murdoch. I think I always will be but..."

"But what?" he says, his eyes pleading.

"But I love Dan," I blurt out, realising that I have always loved him. "I've waited too long for a love like his. I know you have recently separated from your wife but you *are* still married with kids for God's sake. It's all too complicated!" I say, extracting my arm from his grip. "What we shared *was* special, Murdoch. I know that," I say, feeling emotional. "Still it doesn't make it right. I'm at peace with myself now. I'm not looking for love anywhere else. I want to live the dream: me, Dan and our baby."

"A proper little family," Murdoch says and I detect a twinge of sarcasm.

"Well, you've had that chance Murdoch. I haven't yet so let me try and give it a go and if…"

"If what?" he says, hopefully.

"If this baby *is* yours well then I'm not going to stand between it and it's father, even if that means sacrificing my own relationship," I say, feeling completely overwhelmed with the truth of this statement. *I mean every word. I will be no part of any more deception.* "But I'll be honest and admit that I am hoping beyond hope that this baby is Dan's so please can we just wait and see," I implore, as Murdoch hands me a Kleenex.

"Of course, Helene," he says. "And thanks" he adds. He leans across and puts his arm around me. He pulls away when he feels me recoil. "Let's go" he says suddenly.

"Ok, but what will I say to Dan? He'll be there too."

"I'm a barrister am I not?" Murdoch replies convincingly.

"Yes, yes you are," I say, unconvinced. "Wait until I grab Conor though. He will want to come too. He knows everything. We have to leave this office by tomorrow anyway so he'll be happy for an excuse to leave. Conor has been through hell and back too," I explain, ringing him on my mobile. "I spoke to Andrew again this morning, Murdoch. He thinks I am going along with his plans. If he knew that I was talking to you or that Conor knows he would tell Dan immediately," I say, not looking at Murdoch directly. "Please don't ever tell Dan about us," I say cautiously, "unless we *have* to. Please promise. He doesn't deserve it," I say, hoping not to have to beg.

I know Murdoch has nothing to lose, now that his marriage is over.

"I promise," he says and I believe him.

We get to the police station and it's like all hell has broken loose. Walter has already been taken to jail, since he has already been charged. Taking him to the police station seems to have been an exercise in bureaucracy rather than actually serving any valid purpose, other than formally putting the charges to him.

"Dan, I'm in Ringsend police station and the Garda on duty is telling me that Walter has already been taken to Mountjoy. Is that right?" I ask as Conor and Murdoch check each other out. They both stand with their arms crossed defensively in front of them and lean against the station's graffitied walls.

"Yes and its highly unlikely he'll get out on bail, even if I or Mum and Dad went as bailsmen. The word on the ground is that he is too much of a flight risk. I don't know how they can be so sure but the evidence against him appears pretty compelling by all accounts. I'm only going on what one of the Gardai is telling me off the record."

"Right," I say. "I'll just..."

"Don't you even think of going to that prison, Helene McBain!" Dan scolds authoritatively. "That is no place for a pregnant woman. You could pick up all sorts of germs!"

"Oh for God's sake, Dan. I'm perfectly capable of looking after myself!" I chastise him. I notice that Conor and Murdoch must be feeling uncomfortable as they exchange a furtive glance in each other's direction. I lower my voice. "Well, I am going whether you like it or not. I have to talk to him," I say, hanging up on the man I love. He should know better than tell me what to do. I make my own decisions. "I'm going to Mountjoy if either of you want to accompany me?" I ask, not really caring one way or the other at this stage. It's turning into one of those days.

"Do you really need the two of us?" Conor says with a raised eyebrow, indicating that Murdoch is superfluous to Walter's needs. Murdoch glares at him.

"Do you know what?" I announce. "I actually think I will go on my own. If I need either of you, I'll holler," I say.

"Ah now, we can't let you go on your own!" they both protest in unison but I'm having none of it. "Listen, I think I will be better handling Wally on my own. If he is ambushed he may not talk. This is the best chance we have," I say, hopping into a taxi outside the station and waving goodbye to the two hapless figures on the pavement. I'm going to crack Walter, I say to myself. *Nothing is going to stop me now.*

"I would like to see Walter Goodings," I say to the middle-aged lady at the visitor's desk.

"Pris number?" she asks robotically.

"I don't know" I reply "but I believe he is expecting me."

"Just a minute" she says. Her face reminds me of a cabbage patch doll. "Pris number 982; What's your name?"

"Helene. Helene McBain," I am relieved Dan told Mountjoy I'd be here. I guess he thought better of trying to stop me.

"Follow me please," cabbage patch says as she escorts me to the visiting area.

"Wait!" I say, slightly put out. "I'm here in my capacity as a solicitor, to advise the prisoner, not as a visitor."

"Oh" the curmudgeonly face replies as she looks me up and down. "I see." I note that she surveys my bump with suspicion but after inflicting me with a basic body search she announces "Come this way."

We both shuffle down at least two or three long corridors at a snail's pace. Finally I find myself outside Walter's cell.

"You have an hour," she wheezes, opening the door with her key.

Walter hardly looks up when I walk into the cell. He looks wretched.

"Hi," I say, in a friendly manner. *Don't tell me I'll have to sit on the bed beside him. No, there is a chair.* I sit. There is an awkward silence. Wally's gangly legs hang over the side of the bed as if he is wearing an ill-fitting suit. He rests his head on his hand and stares vacantly at the floor. It's as if his exotic camp character has been snuffed out by the oppressive surroundings. He doesn't fit in here. *He won't last a day: too gay.* "So," I say, my voice sounding louder than normal in the artificial quiet. "You might not realise this Wally but I know a lot more about you than you think," I say, praying to Archangel Uriel to help me find the right words to speak. Walter doesn't budge. "But before I say anything, is there anything you want to tell me?" I ask, softly. "We can do this the hard way or the easy way. It's your choice," I tell him. No response. "So are you going to tell me about this Lord Leinster club then, if that's the way you want to play it?" I add, nonchalantly as if I have all the time in the world.

I note a faint flicker of recognition as Walter's eyelashes move involuntarily. He blinks a few times in rapid succession. *I've hit a nerve.*

"Just so you know, Wally, Dan knows nothing; Nothing at all about your relationship with Andrew," I bluff, taking a massive stab in the dark. "At least not yet anyway."

Walter's head suddenly jerks up and he stares frantically at me as if were a ghost. I meet his gaze without foundering. The adrenalin courses through my veins giving me a much needed boost.

"I don't know what you are talking about," Walter says, fidgeting with the tassels at the end of his red silk scarf. He looks away but his voice doesn't carry and the last few words do not even qualify as a whisper.

"I am aware of the club you set up with Andrew and a certain newly deceased Minister, Robert Singleton, may he rest in peace," I add. Beads of perspiration appear on Walter's chiselled features. *He knows his ship is sinking.* Out of the blue there is a knock on the cell door and Dan is standing there, evidently not amused. I stand up and walk out onto the corridor, closing the cell door behind me.

"Why did they let you in?" I seethe at Dan. "It's his legal counsel only. I was making progress in there!"

"That barrister you dined with Murdoch Pierce and a work colleague of yours, Conor something or other, are sitting in the waiting room out there in case they are needed by you! What on earth is going on here, Helene? You're like a dog with a bone. We don't need extra legal representatives. We need an expert criminal solicitor. Normally, you'd be the first to say so yourself!" Dan says, gesticulating wildly. Now it's my turn to hang my head.

"Dan, I think it's time we had a chat," I say. "I need to give you a bit more information on Andrew Peterson and more importantly on your brother; he just might be able to lead us to Andrew, secure his extradition back to Ireland and net himself a deal with the Gardai in the process," I say, relieved to finally tell him everything, except of course about Murdoch. *I'm not that much of a fool.*

Dan looks at me askance. "Never a dull moment," he quips under his breath.

"Please don't say anything until I'm finished Dan as we don't have much time. If my instincts are correct and Andrew gets wind of Walter's arrest he'll set sail to another horizon immediately and we'll never catch him. Just hear me out, please," I beg him.

I take off my shoes outside the cell door and start at the very beginning. My back aches from the weight of the baby inside me but I have to plough on. I tune out the pain and concentrate on the task at hand. I do not even have the gumption to track Dan's reaction as I tell him about Andrew's blackmail of me. This is the only part where I *don't* tell the whole truth. It is not a case of Dan never finding out the truth eventually, especially if the baby isn't his, it's that time is crucial now and there is no point overloading him. It has to be on a need to know basis.

"But what was he blackmailing you with?" Dan asks.

"Well I signed a few client account cheques apparently," I reply, thinking on the spot.

"You were a partner of the Firm and a signatory, so what's so wrong with that?" Dan retorts.

"Yes, well, Andrew alleged there weren't enough monies in the client account when I signed them. In other words what I did was illegal. Look, I panicked Dan! Stupidly or now we can get into that again. For now let me go through the rest of it," I say, wearily.

Dan is satisfied somewhat with this response as I elaborate further on the extent of Andrew's bribery, fraud and extortion. I tell him about Robert Singleton, the apartment in Sandymount, the Lord Leinster club and eventually my suspicions about Walter and the €48 million euro. I explain my theory to Dan who simply listens, nodding occasionally.

CHAPTER 29

"Please say something," I moan after I have finished my lengthy synopsis.

Dan stands with his right hand outstretched against the wall, leaning on it with his full body weight. I get the impression he is counting to ten.

"We have a lot to talk about, Helene. I can't believe all of this has been happening under my nose. I'm beginning to wonder if I know you at all?" he says, with a lump in his throat. I mouth *I'm sorry* to him. He doesn't react, just flicks a bit of fluff of his jacket.

"Can you even tell me why Murdoch Pierce and that Conor guy know before me? If that is in fact the case, which I presume it is?"

"Yes but that's only because I didn't want to worry you," I reply, completely deflated.

"But if there is even the *slightest* of chances that you are right and I mean the *slightest* chance, then I'll let you do what you have to do in there," Dan agrees reluctantly. "At the end of the day it's my brother and you that I care about, not Andrew fucking Peterson but if we can catch him and my brother can cut a deal with the Gardai, then it might just be worth having a go," Dan adds, his fists clenched tight as if he is about to enter a boxing ring.

"Thanks Dan," I say, embarrassed by the extent of my cover up.

"Helene," Dan grabs me lightly by the arm as I turn to go back into the cell. "I hope for your own sake you *are* right," he cautions. "You're already in enough trouble."

I don't try and analyse whether this is an ambiguous comment or not but just slip on my shoes, nod and totter back into the cell. I glance at my watch: half an hour left. The clock is ticking. Walter hasn't moved since I left. The only difference is that it's obvious he has been crying. *Sweet Lord above, please help me with this!*

"So, where were we?" I ask, not expecting an answer but simply gathering my thoughts.

"You were trying to tell me that I know Andrew Peterson. How absolutely absurd!" Walter responds, a mean red anger rising up in him. *Too defensive!* He uncrosses his legs and crosses them again.

"Walter, you have been giving Andrew my mobile phone numbers, haven't you? Did you get pleasure out of the fact that your beloved boyfriend was blackmailing me?" I say, spitefully. Walter doesn't answer. He just bites his lip as if he wants to say something but knows that it won't do him any good. "Do you know what he was blackmailing me about?! Do you know what he made me do to keep his silence?!" I yell at him, contemptuously. If Walter does know, I may as well tell Dan myself because Walter will tell him. Of that I am sure. He can't hold a secret for love nor money and that's what I'm banking on. In the meantime my heart thuds hard inside my ribcage. I put my hand over my left breast as if to still the life force beneath. My wrath has taken me by force and I am not ready for it. I worry for my unborn child. "Look, Wally," I say, winded. "It's in your interests to talk to me here. In twenty minutes I'll have to go and you'll be in the capable hands of your criminal lawyer who may turn out to be the best criminal solicitor in the world, but he will still *not* know what *I* know! If you're smart Walter, you can cut a deal here. Tell us where Andrew is and you'll get a lesser sentence. Don't let Andrew bring you down with him. Don't take the wrap for his greed. He's over in Switzerland having a whale of a time while you are left here to rot," I say, throwing caution to the wind and hoping beyond hope I've hit the jackpot.

"Switzerland?" Walter says weakly with a trace of *sehnsucht* in his voice.

"Yes," I reply. "That's where the money is, isn't it? All forty eight million of it. Sure you were there only weeks back," I continue, completely winging it now, "I bet you wish you had stayed over there the last time and never come home but I guess you had to. I mean, obviously, the money was *much* more important to Andrew than you were," I say, letting the words hang in the air like a bad smell. Walter darts a poison glance in my direction. *He's hurting.*

"What a pity. I mean how much is in that account now Wally? A hundred million I'd surmise at this stage," I start to laugh heartily.

"What's so funny?" Walter asks, his familiarity with me trapping him into a false comfort. He can't help himself.

"It's just the irony of it all really. There you are with millions, and I mean, *millions* not thousands in the bank but you're stuck here in a cell in Mountjoy with no hope of ever enjoying the fruits of it. Not for at least a decade anyway. Such a shame really," I sigh theatrically. "Ah well I'm sure Andrew will find another lover somewhere to help him spend it," I say, blasé.

"No, he won't!" Walter stands up abruptly and roars at me, waving his arms madly, his histrionics almost comedic. "Andy loves me!" he shrieks, clutching at his scarf and practically flaying his neck in the process.

I watch his face crumple as the reality of what he has said sinks in slowly. He bawls like a wounded hyena. He sits back down on the prison bed and let's out his rage in big sploshy tears. I let him, offering no encouragement, no sympathy, or disdain.

"At least we've made some progress," I tell him after a while. "And for what it's worth I don't believe you knew Andrew was blackmailing me, did you? I just don't think you are that callous or even, with all due respect, that smart."

"He said that..." Walter stumbles over his words. "He said that he might need a family law solicitor if he was ever caught, in case Tanya wanted to formalise their separation. I believed him," Walter says, sniffing self-pityingly.

I nearly laugh out loud at his stupidity and that my hunch paid off but manage to keep myself in check. The main thing is that Walter *doesn't* know (at least not yet) why Andrew blackmailed me. Remarkably he doesn't even ask. *Phew.*

"Robert Singleton was supposed to help him get your passport back to you, wasn't he? Except that eventually he got caught too. Who did he try to bribe, I wonder? His plan obviously backfired. What a courageous whistleblower that person was! Little does he know the domino effect of his actions. The precarious stack of cards is falling down because for once someone did something moral. Everyone gets caught in the end, you know, Wally. It's just a matter of time. So you might as well help yourself out here. Andrew will be half way to Sri Lanka when he hears of your arrest. We all know what a blabbermouth you are. He won't risk it," I conclude, wearily. *Five minutes.*

"Andrew loves me," Walter sobs. "I know he does."

"Well, where is he then?" I ask.

"He doesn't know I am here," Walter says.

"Doesn't he?" I say. The intrigue wafts around him. "Didn't I say he has my mobile number? He happened to ring me on the way over and I told him where I was going, not that I was a hundred per cent sure that you were lovers but just on the off chance. Believe me, Wally," I stress, eyeballing him, "he knows full well where you are and he has *no* intention of helping you out." I lie convincingly, patting his arm in consolation.

"I don't believe you. You're lying. What did he say then?" Walter asks innocently, like the big child that he is.

"Oh something about jetting off to America or something," I spoof, praying to Jesus Mary and Joseph that I've picked the right spot. With that Walter melts into a pool of snot and scarf, blubbering like an upset baby. "Where is he?" I ask, ignoring the meltdown in front of me. *Keep your wits about you.*

"He rescued me from that shithole of a place in Sandymount..." Walter sobs, ignoring me in turn.

"Yeah, 38B Auburn Court," I reply. "I think your pal the Minister used to be a client there too, wasn't he?"

"How do you know that?" Walter asks, looking agog at me.

"It's too long a story, Wally. But let me guess your story, you were working there as an upmarket male escort to earn extra cash on the side. Let's see, Andrew was one of your clients and you fell in love, am I right?" I ask sanctimoniously. "And now Wally is up the swanny."

"There's no need to be smart, Helene," he says, wounded. *He's right, get a grip.*

"My apologies, Wally. That was an unfortunate pun," I say, stifling a nervous laugh.

"It just started off as a dream really," Walter explains lyrically. "Andy was married in name only. Can you not imagine how difficult it must be to live a lie every day of your life? At least I was openly gay but Andrew couldn't do it. He visited me every month, then every week and then every day. We fell in love and he showered me with presents. The age gap didn't bother me at all. He was more mature and much more streetwise to boot. He taught me so much," he continues wistfully. "One day, Tanya, his wife, found the address in Sandymount with my name on it. She had been going through his belongings meticulously since he left on foot of the warrant for his arrest. Eventually she arrived one day into Auburn court and confronted me about him. We had been dating for two years at that stage. I was no longer working as an escort but as self-appointed manager of the place. Andrew used the Sandymount address under the auspices of *The Lord Leinster* charity to siphon money out from the law Firm. It was a good cover. She thought he was seeing another woman. I was hopelessly in love and jealous of her role in his life. We went for a drink and she succeeded in getting the truth out of me. Andrew had left the country at this stage and she hadn't a penny to rub together. Of course I had to tell Andrew who was none too pleased but in order to prevent him doing something stupid, she agreed not to tell if she could help out with the business side of things in Sandymount. That's where she met Robert. We were all involved and we made a lot of money out of it. I always knew Tanya's motivation was only to help their children. Tanya is a proud woman. She wasn't about to let her kids grow up in poverty. I don't blame her for blackmailing Andrew, even though I'd never say that to him," Walter concludes, getting emotional all over again.

"But tell me, how did Robert Singleton get involved in the first place?" I ask, trying to tie up the loose ends in my mind.

"He was a client of Andrew's, in the office I mean. They had originally met in a gay bar in the city centre, both on the prowl looking for someone to satisfy an urge that their wives never would or even could. Anyway, they both met other men that night but ended up back at the same party talking business and property development. Robert had an extensive property portfolio already but Andrew promised him he could triple it in a matter of months. Robert identified with Andrew: they were both married, both successful but both gay. Andrew knew that younger men were Robert's Achilles heel so Andrew supplied them on demand in Sandymount. It was Robert's laundered money, of course, that set up Auburn court in the first instance under the guise of the aptly-named *Lord Leinster charity*. Robert foolishly believed that his monies were safely invested in foreign properties under *Peterson holdings*. It was only when Robert wanted to see the fruits of his investments that Andrew started to blackmail him."

"I presume you mean he'd out him as gay and possibly ruin his political career?" I suggest.

"Yes, but he didn't really need to blackmail him, did he?" Walter ponders, more asking himself the question than me. "I mean, he could have just cut off all ties at that point?" Walter says, perplexed.

"I guess he felt that having the Minister for Justice in the palm of his hand was a useful tool. How ironic that he turned out to be the one who ultimately brought you all down," I say, not realising the extent of the truth of this statement.

"The Gardai have told me that he explains everything about me and Andrew and the Lord Leinster charity in the suicide note. They wouldn't let me see it but I believe them. "

Walter adds, shrugging his shoulders in resignation.

"And what about the lady who left him the property in Sandymount? What role did she play, other than her estate providing a perfect foil for a male escort agency and money laundering?" I say, sarcastically.

"He just borrowed her identity. What do you mean?" I ask confused.

"I mean he is now living as *Mr. Lesley Marant*. It's one of those names, isn't it? An androgynous name, if you like. I suppose you could say my adeptness at forgery helped change all her identification from female to male. Singleton helped out with the new passport.

"I see," I say, the pieces of the puzzle slotting in nicely.

"But how could you be part of this Wally? It's just not you at all," I say, genuinely bewildered. "You can be completely melodramatic but you're not a bad person. How could you have been this easily led?" I say, tactically putting the blame firmly at Andrew's feet as Walter stares at his own.

"I hated being around you and Dan, knowing everything that was going on and all the suffering Andrew has caused..." Walter breaks off, weeping hysterically.

"Please tell me where he is, Wally. You'll only both serve the same amount of time when Andrew is caught anyway, especially if Singleton has mentioned the link with you in his suicide note. I mean, who knows you could both end up in Mountjoy? Then you'd be together," I say, pouncing on his weak spot. I'm gambling on that romantic softy at the core of him.

"Please tell me, Walter," I glance at my watch. *One minute.*

Walter sighs in surrender as if it was his last breath. His body shakes as his heart and his head fight out their last battle.

"He's..."

"Go on," I urge him gently.

"He's in a plastic surgery clinic on the lakes of Geneva, in the city of Montreux," Walter says, bashfully. "He is in the process of getting a face lift under the name of Mr. Lesley Marant."

There is a knock on the door which helps lift my jaw off the floor.

"Thank you," I say as the cabbage patch lady barks at me that our time is up. I give her a nod and she closes the door briefly.

"But before you go, Helene," Wally grabs me with an air of desperation. "I need you to know why I am telling you because it's not for myself," he explains with some reticence then pauses, as if the words themselves elude him. The tears stream down his face in a never-ending cascading waterfall. He smoothes out the iron crease on his trousers and pulls his scarf closer around him.

"Yes," I say, impatiently, as I memorise the name of the clinic over and over in my mind.

"He is going to kill Tanya. He may already have." Walter looks at me full of pain and I know he is telling the truth.

"Oh God, Wally. Oh God" I whisper, the shock robbing my voice.

254 | NEGLIGENT BEHAVIOUR

EPILOGUE

"Montreux city plastic surgery clinic – near the lakes of Geneva, Switzerland – that's where Andrew is," I announce as if reading a telegram. Dan, Murdoch and Conor simply stare at me.

"She's in shock," Murdoch says, concerned. Conor just chews his fingernails.

"I'm, I'm not in shock," I say, pushing the words forcefully out of my mouth. "Please Dan ring that Garda in Ringsend now! Get them to contact Interpol and have Andrew arrested. He is undergoing a face lift as we speak!" I say, enunciating my words slowly as if to pull the reins on my mind which is quickly running away with itself.

Dan looks at me aghast. "What? A face lift?"

"Dan, please!" I beg him, "this will help Walter in the wrong run. Trust me on this one. Andrew is getting a face lift under the name of *Mr. Lesley Marant*. That's his alias. Will you remember that name?" I squeeze Dan's arm.

"Ouch!" Dan grimaces. "Take it easy, Helene. This is a lot for me to take in. I'll ring them now, ok? I just want to talk to Walter first–"

"Dan, trust me please," I beg him, cutting him off. "There is no time. Ring Ringsend first, I bet one of the fraud squad will still be there. Then talk to Wally. You can be proud of him, Dan, he has done the right thing in the end."

"Alright, Helene. Only for you," Dan says, kissing the top of my head.

"Thanks Dan," I say, hugging him tight. "And can you meet me in Tanya Peterson's house in Mount Merrion in thirty minutes," I order. "You were at a drinks party there before, you know where it is."

"What?" he says, searching my face, "What is going on now?" he asks, worried again.

"Please Dan, trust me," I plead with him. I can't tell him why I'm going to her house because otherwise he'd never let me go. I grab a banana out of my handbag. I feel faint and need an energy boost fast.

"We'll take my car," Murdoch says, confused but at least thinking on his feet. "I'll bring it up the front. You two wait here."

I eat my banana as Conor congratulates me on Walter's interrogation.

"It's not over yet. Get in and I'll explain," I tell him, pointing at Murdoch's banged up jeep. He opens the door for Conor and helps me into the front passenger seat, brushing old newspapers onto the floor in his haste.

"This car stinks of dog!" Conor moans as he sits in the back like a petulant child.

"Well, I'm a country man at heart" Murdoch laughs, "You should be grateful you have none sitting on your lap or lying at your feet. Then you'd really be stinking!"

"Will you two stop jibing at each other!" I chide. "I haven't even told you why we are going to see Tanya Peterson."

"To tell her that her husband is about to be caught, I presume?" Murdoch says absent mindedly.

"Not quite, although that is part of the reason. No, Walter has just told me that Andrew has hired a hitman to kill Tanya," I reply.

"Jesus Christ!" Murdoch cries out loudly. "And what the hell are we doing on our way there? This is a matter for the Gardai, Helene." Murdoch says, turning his head to look at me. *We have no choice but to warn her in person.*

"Murdoch, please keep your eye on the road," Conor shouts from the back.

"We need to warn Tanya," I say, "who else is going to tell her? We have no phone number for her. I'll go on my own if you are both too scared," I say, pointedly.

"We're not cowards, Helene," Murdoch replies agitated, "It's simply that I don't think it necessary to put any of us in danger..."

"I doubt there is any imminent danger, Murdoch. Let's just see how we get on when we get there," I say, curtly.

"So how did you get Walter to spill the beans?" Conor asks, enthralled. "That was no easy task, I'd imagine."

"It wasn't that difficult, Conor," I say, frankly. "I knew I could get the truth out of him by playing to his weaknesses. His conscience got the better of him really. I think he probably realised that he could be up for a murder charge as well if he didn't forewarn us about Andrew's intentions to kill his wife."

"But why would he want to kill her?" Murdoch asks, baffled.

"God knows, Murdoch. Walter didn't elaborate on that point. He probably doesn't trust her or just feels like it. You wouldn't know with Andrew. Anyway, wait until I tell you the rest of it."

I am nearly finished recounting the entire details of my conversation/interrogation with Walter when we arrive at our destination.

"Just pull up over on that kerb, Murdoch," I direct him. The Jeep glides up on the curb effortlessly. I look at my watch. Nearly forty minutes has passed since we left Mountjoy. There is no sign of Dan as yet.

"Wow! What a story!" Murdoch says, "Unbelievable."

"Wait till they catch that bastard!" Conor echoes all our thoughts.

"Listen, just let me call Dan and establish where he is before we go in. He should have been here ages ago."

As it transpires Dan got delayed talking to the Gardai but is on his way. He says he'll be here in a matter of minutes.

The three of us get out of the jeep and walk towards Tanya Peterson's house. I have a vague sense of foreboding. My body is tired and I rub my belly instinctively. We ring the doorbell and wait.

I hear quick, organised steps. The front door opens wide and Tanya smiles.

"I've just heard. Andrew has been captured," she says, addressing me directly, not appearing to notice the two men by my side. "I'm assuming that's why you are here?" she asks, practically. Conor responds with some inane chatter about her husband. Meanwhile I am transfixed. I watch mesmerised as a shadow appears over Tanya's left shoulder in the distance. *I hear a click then the noise of a cuckoo clock or am I imagining it?* This shadow is light-footed and agile like a panther. He is hunched down by the back of the stairs, a momentary flash of steel the only give away. I hear a group of children singing "the wheels on the bus go round and round" somewhere downstairs on the right. I see him clearer now the sun is off my face. *He can see us!* I hear a swift shuffle. *Where is he gone?! Jesus!*

"OmiGod, Tanya!" I shout, hobbling up the step and clumsily pulling her towards me. I am wrapping my body around her protectively. Suddenly I am dragged backwards by the scruff of the neck. I fall limply on my side. It hurts. *There is a shot! OmiGod! And another shot!* There is blood all over me, red blood. *Am I bleeding*? I see Dan's face. I try and speak but nothing comes out. My baby moves. I feel a rush of warm water between my legs. Blood and water. I hear Tanya's screams. I see Murdoch's body lying motionless beside me. Blood streams from his open mouth, trickling down onto the steps. His eyes are that of a trout on an icy bed.

Murdoch, Murdoch, I shout but no words leave my mouth.

"You saved my life," Tanya tells me, holding my hand and wiping my brow. "I'll save yours," she whispers in my ear.

I stare at Murdoch. Someone holds his wrist, checks his pulse then pushes down his eyelids with their fingers.

"The Ambulance is on the way, Helene. Your waters have broken. Hang on in there, my love. You're going to have our baby!" Dan says, holding my head, his shadow blocking my view.

THE END

CPSIA information can be obtained at www.ICGtesting.com
Printed in the USA
BVOW021501261211
279178BV00012B/112/P